PRAISE FOR *WONDER*:

'It makes ordinary things extraordinary . . .
Reminiscent of *To Kill a Mockingbird*.
It has the power to move hearts and change minds'
Guardian

'A gem of a story. Moving and heart-warming.
This book made me laugh, made me angry,
made me cry' *Malorie Blackman*

'Destined to go the way of Mark Haddon's
The Curious Incident of the Dog in the Night-Time
and then some . . . Dark, funny, touching'
The Times

'It wreaks emotional havoc' *Independent*

'Tremendously moving . . . An uplifting,
hopeful and important book' *The Bookseller*

'A children's book that's making grown men cry'
Observer

www.randomhousechildrens.co.uk

Auggie & Me

three wonder stories

R. J. Palacio

CORGI BOOKS

AUGGIE & ME
A CORGI BOOK 978 0 552 57477 8

First published in Great Britain by Corgi,
an imprint of Random House Children's Publishers UK
A Penguin Random House Company

Penguin
Random House
UK

This edition published 2015

THE JULIAN CHAPTER first published by RHCP Digital,
an imprint of Random House Children's Publishers UK
A Penguin Random House Company
RHCP Digital edition published 2014

PLUTO first published by RHCP Digital,
an imprint of Random House Children's Publishers UK
A Penguin Random House Company
RHCP Digital edition published 2015

SHINGALING first published by RHCP Digital,
an imprint of Random House Children's Publishers UK
A Penguin Random House Company
RHCP Digital edition published 2015

12

Text copyright © R. J. Palacio, 2014, 2015
Cover and interior illustrations © Tad Carpenter, 2014, 2015

Typeset in Goudy

RANDOM HOUSE CHILDREN'S PUBLISHERS UK
61–63 Uxbridge Road, London W5 5SA

www.randomhousechildrens.co.uk
www.totallyrandombooks.co.uk
www.randomhouse.co.uk

Addresses for companies within The Random House Group Limited
can be found at: www.randomhouse.co.uk/offices.htm

THE RANDOM HOUSE GROUP Limited Reg. No. 954009

A CIP catalogue record for this book is available from the British Library.

Printed in Great Britain by Clays Ltd, Elcograf S.p.A.

Penguin Random House is committed to a sustainable future for our business, our readers
and our planet. This book is made from Forest Stewardship Council® certified paper.

CONTENTS

Introduction

"Is there going to be a sequel to *Wonder*?" someone in the audience asks.

"No, I'm sorry," I answer, a little embarrassed. "I don't think it's the kind of book that really lends itself to a sequel. I like to think that fans of *Wonder* will imagine for themselves what will happen next to Auggie Pullman and all the other people in his world."

That exchange, or something like it, has happened at just about every book signing, speaking engagement, or reading I've done since *Wonder* came out on February 14, 2012. It's probably the question I get asked the most, aside from "Will there be a movie of *Wonder*?" and "What inspired you to write *Wonder*?"

Yet here I am, writing an introduction to a book that is, for all intents and purposes, a companion to *Wonder*. So how exactly did that happen?

To answer that question, I have to discuss *Wonder* just a little bit. If you've bought this book or been given it as a gift, there's a good chance you've read *Wonder* already, so I don't need to tell you too much about it. Suffice it to say that *Wonder* is the story of a ten-year-old boy named Auggie Pullman, who was born with a craniofacial difference, as he navigates the ups and downs of being the new kid at Beecher Prep middle school. We see this journey through his eyes and the eyes of several characters whose lives happen to intersect with his over the course of that pivotal year, and whose insights enhance the reader's understanding of Auggie's passage to self-acceptance. We don't hear from any characters whose stories don't directly expand upon Auggie's story within the time frame of that fifth-grade year, or whose understanding of Auggie is too limited to shed light upon his character. *Wonder* is Auggie's story, after all, from beginning to end. And I was very strict with myself about telling his story in a simple and linear way. If a character didn't propel the narrative forward— or told a story that ran parallel to, or before or after, the events in *Wonder*—then he or she didn't get a voice in the book.

That's not to say that some of these other characters didn't have interesting stories to tell, however—stories that might have explained their own motivations a bit even if those revelations didn't directly affect Auggie.

Which is exactly where this book comes in.

To be clear: *Auggie & Me* is not a sequel. It doesn't pick up where *Wonder* left off. It doesn't continue to tell the story of Auggie Pullman navigating middle school. In fact, Auggie is only a minor character in these stories.

What this book is, precisely, is an expansion of Auggie's world. The three stories in *Auggie & Me—The Julian Chapter, Pluto,* and *Shingaling,* all originally published as short ebooks—are told from the perspective of Julian, Christopher, and Charlotte, respectively. They are three completely different narratives, telling the stories of characters who only occasionally, if at all, appear in each other's stories. They all do have one thing in common, though, which is Auggie Pullman. His presence in their lives serves as a catalyst by which they're each transformed in subtle and not-so-subtle ways.

Auggie & Me is also not a sequel in a traditional sense because there's no continuation of Auggie's story, other than a brief fast-forward in Julian's chapter to the summer after fifth grade, which provides a nice coda to the Julian/Auggie story line. But other than that, readers don't find out what happens to Auggie Pullman in the sixth grade, or in high school, or beyond. I can guarantee that *that* book, the de facto sequel, will never be written. And that's a good thing, folks. One of the most beautiful by-products of writing *Wonder* is the amazing fan fiction it has generated. Teachers are using it in classrooms, asking students to get into character and write their own chapters on Auggie, or Summer, or Jack. I've read stories devoted to Via, Justin, and Miranda. Chapters written from Amos's point of view, and Miles's and Henry's. I've even read one child's very poignant short chapter from Daisy's point of view!

But perhaps the most touching story-writing I've read has been about Auggie, with whom readers seem to have a passionate sense of involvement. I've had kids tell me they know for sure that Auggie will grow up to be an astronaut. Or a teacher. Or a veterinarian. They tell me these things with great—almost empirical—authority, by the way. No dillydallying. No guesswork. So who am I to disagree with them? And why would I write a sequel that would limit all those options? Auggie, as far as I'm concerned, has a bright and amazing future full of infinite possibilities, each one as lofty as the one before.

I am truly blessed that readers of *Wonder* feel close enough to him to envision for themselves how his life will go. I know they understand that just because I chose to end *Wonder* on a happy day in Auggie's life, it doesn't guarantee him a happy life. He will surely face more than his fair share of challenges as he grows older, with new ups and downs, new friends, other Julians and Jacks and, of course, Summers. Readers will hopefully intuit from how Auggie has handled himself over the course of his first year at Beecher Prep, with all its accompanying trials and tribulations, that he has what he needs inside of him to triumph over whatever life hurls his way, withstand the challenges as they come, stare down the starers (or laugh them away). There with him always, through good times and bad, will be his amazing family—Isabel and Nate and Via. "The only thing I know that truly heals people is unconditional love," wrote Elisabeth Kübler-Ross, which may be why Auggie will never succumb to any wounds inflicted by the careless words of passersby or the choices of his friends. Those he has, too—friends both known and unseen—who will stand up for him when it counts the most.

In the end, readers of *Wonder* know that the book has never really been about what happens to Auggie Pullman. It's about how Auggie Pullman happens to the world.

Which brings me back to this book—or, more accurately, the three stories contained in *Auggie & Me*.

When it was first suggested to me that I write these short ebooks, these *Wonder* stories, I jumped at the chance—most specifically on behalf of Julian, who had become a much-loathed persona among *Wonder* fans. "Keep calm and don't be a Julian" is even something you can Google now, as people have taken it upon themselves to make their own cautionary posters.

And I completely get why Julian is so disliked. Until now, we've only seen him through the eyes of Auggie,

Jack, Summer, and Justin. He's rude. He's mean. His stares, his nicknames for Auggie, his efforts to manipulate his classmates to turn against Jack are tantamount to bullying. But what's at the root of all this rage against Auggie? What's up with Julian, and why is he such a jerk?

Even as I was writing *Wonder*, I knew that Julian had a story to tell. I also knew that his story of bullying, or why he bullies, was of little consequence to Auggie and had no impact on the story line, and therefore didn't belong in *Wonder*. It's not for the victims of bullying to find compassion for their tormentors, after all. But I loved the idea of exploring Julian's character in a short book of his own—not to exonerate his actions, since his actions in *Wonder* are reprehensible and indefensible, but to try to understand him better. It's important to remember that Julian is still just a little kid. He has acted badly, yes, but that doesn't necessarily mean he's a "bad kid." Our mistakes don't define us. The hard part is coming to terms with our mistakes. Will Julian redeem himself? Can he? Does he want to? These are the questions I ask and answer in *The Julian Chapter*, even as I shed some light on why Julian behaves toward Auggie the way he does.

The second short book in *Auggie & Me* is *Pluto*. Told from the point of view of Auggie's oldest friend, Christopher, who moved away several years before the events of *Wonder* take place, *Pluto* is a unique look into

Auggie's life before Beecher Prep. Christopher was there with Auggie through his early hardships and heart-breaks—the horrific surgeries, the day Nate Pullman brought Daisy home for the first time, the old neighborhood friends who seem to vanish from Auggie's life. Now that he's older, Christopher struggles with the challenges of staying friends with Auggie—the stares, the awkward reactions of new friends. It's tempting to walk away from a friendship when it becomes difficult, even under the best of circumstances—and Auggie's not the only one who is testing Christopher's loyalty. Will he hang on or let go?

The third short book is *Shingaling*, told from the point of view of Charlotte, the only girl chosen by Mr. Tushman to be one of Auggie's welcome buddies. Throughout *Wonder*, Charlotte maintains a friendly, if somewhat distant, relationship with Auggie. She waves hello when she sees him. She never sides with the kids who are mean to him. She tries to help Jack, even if it's in secret so no one else knows. She's a nice girl—no doubt about that. But she never goes out of her way to be more than nice. *Shingaling* delves into the life of Charlotte Cody during fifth grade at Beecher Prep, and readers learn there was a lot of other stuff going on that year about which Auggie Pullman didn't know: dance performances, mean girls, old allegiances, and new cliques. Maya, Ximena, Savanna, and especially Summer feature prominently in *Shingaling*, which, like *Pluto* and

The Julian Chapter, explores the life of an ordinary kid who is touched by extraordinary circumstances.

Whether it's about Auggie and Julian, or Auggie and Christopher, or Auggie and Charlotte, the three stories in *Auggie & Me* examine the complexities of friendship, loyalty, and compassion, and—most especially—explore the enduring effects of kindness. Much has been written about middle school and the preteen years, and how it's a time in kids' lives when they are almost expected to be unkind to one another as they navigate their way through new social situations on their own, often without parental oversight. But I've seen a different side to kids—a tendency toward nobility, a yearning to do right. I believe in children and their limitless capacity to care and to love and to want to save the world. I have no doubt that they will lead us to a place of greater tolerance and acceptance for all the birds in the universe. For all the underdogs and misfits. And for Auggie and me.

—RJP

The *Julian* Chapter

Be kind, for everyone you meet is fighting a hard battle.

–Ian Maclaren

Before

Perhaps I have created the stars and the sun

and this enormous house, but I no longer remember.

—Jorge Luis Borges, "The House of Asterion"

• • •

Fear can't hurt you any more than a dream.

—William Golding, *Lord of the Flies*

Ordinary

Okay, okay, okay.

I know, I know, I know.

I haven't been nice to August Pullman!

Big deal. It's not the end of the world, people! Let's stop with the drama, okay? There's a whole big world out there, and not everyone is nice to everyone else. That's just the way it is. So, can you please get over it? I think it's time to move on and get on with your life, don't you?

Jeez!

I don't get it. I really don't. One minute, I'm like, the most popular kid in the fifth grade. And the next minute, I'm like, I don't know. Whatever. This bites. This whole year bites! I wish Auggie Pullman had never come to Beecher Prep in the first place! I wish he had kept his creepy little face hidden away like in *The Phantom of the Opera* or something. Put a mask on, Auggie! Get your face out of my face, please. Everything would be a lot easier if you would just disappear.

At least for me. I'm not saying it's a picnic for him, either, by the way. I know it can't be easy for him to look in the mirror every day, or walk down the street. But that's not my problem. My problem is that everything's different since he's been coming to my school. The kids are different. I'm different. And it sucks big-time.

I wish everything was the way it used to be in the fourth grade. We had so, so, so much fun back then. We would play tackle-tag in the yard, and not to brag, but everyone always wanted a piece of me, you know? I'm just sayin'. Everyone always wanted to be my partner when we'd do social studies projects. And everyone always laughed when I said something funny.

At lunchtime, I'd always sit with my peeps, and we were like, it. We were totally *it*. Henry. Miles. Amos. Jack. We were it! It was so cool. We had all these secret jokes. Little hand signals for stuff.

I don't know why that had to change. I don't know why everyone got so stupid about stuff.

Actually, I do know why: it was because of Auggie Pullman. The moment he showed up, that's when things stopped being the way they used to be. Everything was totally ordinary. And now things are messed up. And it's because of him.

And Mr. Tushman. In fact, it's kind of totally Mr. Tushman's fault.

The Call

I remember Mom made a big deal about the call we got from Mr. Tushman. At dinner that night, she went on and on about what a big honor it was. The middle-school director had called us at home to ask if I could be a welcome buddy to some new kid in school. Wow! Big news! Mom acted like I won an Oscar or something. She said it showed her that the school really did recognize who the "special" kids were, which she thought was awesome. Mom had never met Mr. Tushman before, because he was the middle-school director and I was still in the lower school, but she couldn't stop raving about how nice he'd been on the phone.

Mom's always been kind of a bigwig at school. She's on this board of trustees thing, which I don't even know what it is but apparently it's a big deal. She's always volunteering for stuff, too. Like, she's always been the class mom for every grade I've been in at Beecher. Always. She does a lot for the school.

So, the day I was supposed to be a welcome buddy,

she dropped me off in front of the middle school. She wanted to take me inside, but I was like, "Mom, it's middle school!" She took the hint and drove off before I went inside.

Charlotte Cody and Jack Will were already in the front lobby, and we said hello to each other. Jack and I did our peeps' handshake and we said hello to the security guard. Then we went up to Mr. Tushman's office. It was so weird being in the school when there was no one there!

"Dude, we could totally skateboard in here and no one would know!" I said to Jack, running and gliding on the smooth floor of the hallway after the security guard couldn't see us anymore.

"Ha, yeah," said Jack, but I noticed that the closer we got to Mr. Tushman's office, the quieter Jack got. In fact, he kind of looked like he was going to blow chunks.

As we got near the top of the stairs, he stopped.

"I don't want to do this!" he said.

I stopped next to him. Charlotte had already gotten to the top landing.

"Come on!" she said.

"You're not the boss!" I answered.

She shook her head and rolled her eyes at me. I laughed and nudged Jack with my elbow. We loved egging Charlotte Cody on. She was always such a Goody Two-shoes!

"This is so messed up," said Jack, rubbing his hand over his face.

"What is?" I asked.

"Do you know who this new kid is?" he asked. I shook my head.

"You know who he is, right?" Jack said to Charlotte, looking up at her.

Charlotte walked down the stairs toward us. "I think so," she said. She made a face, like she had just tasted something bad.

Jack shook his head and then smacked it three times with his palm.

"I'm such an idiot for saying yes to this!" he said, his teeth clenched.

"Wait, who is it?" I said. I pushed Jack's shoulder so he'd look at me.

"It's that kid called August," he said to me. "You know, the kid with the face?"

I had no idea who he was talking about.

"Are you kidding me?" said Jack. "You never seen that kid before? He lives in this neighborhood! He hangs out in the playground sometimes. You have to have seen him. Everyone has!"

"He doesn't live in this neighborhood," answered Charlotte.

"Yes he does!" Jack answered impatiently.

"No, *Julian* doesn't live in this neighborhood," she answered, just as impatiently.

"What does that have to do with anything?" I said.

"Whatever!" Jack interrupted. "It doesn't matter. Trust me, dude, you've never seen anything like this before."

"Please don't be mean, Jack," Charlotte said. "It's not nice."

"I'm not being mean!" said Jack. "I'm just being truthful."

"What, exactly, does he look like?" I asked.

Jack didn't answer. He just stood there, shaking his head. I looked at Charlotte, who frowned.

"You'll see," she said. "Let's just go already, okay?" She turned around and went up the stairs and disappeared down the hall to Mr. Tushman's office.

"Let's just go already, okay?" I said to Jack, imitating Charlotte perfectly. I thought this would totally make him laugh, but it didn't.

"Jack, dude, come on!" I said.

I pretended to give him a hard slap in the face. This actually did make him laugh a bit, and he threw a slow-motion punch back at me. This led to a quick game of "spleen," which is where we try to jab each other in the rib cage.

"Guys, let's go!" Charlotte commanded from the top of the stairs. She had come back to get us.

"Guys, let's go!" I whispered to Jack, and this time he did kind of laugh.

But as soon as we rounded the corner of the hallway

and got to Mr. Tushman's office, we all got pretty serious.

When we went inside, Mrs. Garcia told us to wait in Nurse Molly's office, which was a small room to the side of Mr. Tushman's office. We didn't say anything to each other while we waited. I resisted the temptation to make a balloon out of the latex gloves that were in a box by the exam table, though I know it would have made everyone laugh.

Mr. Tushman

Mr. Tushman came into the office. He was tall, kind of thin, with messy gray hair.

"Hey, guys," he said, smiling. "I'm Mr. Tushman. You must be Charlotte." He shook Charlotte's hand. "And you are . . . ?" He looked at me.

"Julian," I said.

"Julian," he repeated, smiling. He shook my hand.

"And you're Jack Will," he said to Jack, and shook his hand, too.

He sat down on the chair next to Nurse Molly's desk. "First of all, I just want to thank you guys so much for coming here today. I know it's a hot day and you probably have other stuff you want to do. How's the summer been treating you? Okay?"

We all kind of nodded, looking at each other.

"How's the summer been for you?" I asked him.

"Oh, so nice of you to ask, Julian!" he answered. "It's been a great summer, thank you. Though I am seriously looking forward to the fall. I hate this hot weather."

He pulled his shirt. "I'm so ready for the winter."

All three of us were bobbing our heads up and down like doofballs at this point. I don't know why grown-ups ever bother chitchatting with kids. It just makes us feel weird. I mean, I personally am pretty okay talking to adults—maybe because I travel a lot and I've talked to a lot of adults before—but most kids really don't like talking to grown-ups. That's just the way it is. Like, if I see the parent of some friend of mine and we're not actually in school, I try to avoid eye contact so I don't have to talk to them. It's too weird. It's also really weird when you bump into a teacher outside of school. Like, one time I saw my third-grade teacher at a restaurant with her boyfriend, and I was like, ewww! I don't want to see my teacher hanging out with her boyfriend, you know?

Anyway, so there we were, me, Charlotte, and Jack, nodding away like total bobbleheads as Mr. Tushman went on and on about the summer. But finally— finally!—he got to the point.

"So, guys," he said, kind of slapping his hands against his thighs. "It's really nice of you to give up your afternoon to do this. In a few minutes, I'm going to introduce you to the boy who's coming to my office, and I just wanted to give you a heads-up about him beforehand. I mean, I told your moms a little bit about him—did they talk to you?"

Charlotte and Jack both nodded, but I shook my head.

"My mom just said he'd had a bunch of surgeries," I said.

"Well, yes," answered Mr. Tushman. "But did she explain about his face?"

I have to say, this is the point when I started thinking, *Okay, what the heck am I doing here?*

"I mean, I don't know," I said, scratching my head. I tried to think back to what Mom had told me. I hadn't really paid attention. I think most of the time she was going on and on about what an honor it was that I'd been chosen: she really didn't emphasize that there was something wrong with the kid. "She said that you said the kid had a lot of scars and stuff. Like he'd been in a fire."

"I didn't quite say that," said Mr. Tushman, raising his eyebrows. "What I told your mom is that this boy has a severe craniofacial difference—"

"Oh, right right right!" I interrupted, because now I remembered. "She did use that word. She said it was like a cleft lip or something."

Mr. Tushman scrunched up his face.

"Well," he said, lifting his shoulders and tilting his head left and right, "it's a little more than that." He got up and patted my shoulder. "I'm sorry if I didn't make that clear to your mom. In any case, I don't mean to make this awkward for you. In fact, it's exactly because I don't want it to be awkward that I'm talking to you right now. I just wanted to give you a heads-up that this boy definitely looks very different from other children. And that's not a secret. He knows he looks different. He was born that way. He gets that. He's a great kid. Very smart. Very nice. He's never gone to a regular school before because he was homeschooled, you know, because of all his surgeries. So that's why I just want you guys to show him around a bit, get to know him, be his welcome buddies. You can totally ask him questions, if you want. Talk to him normally. He's really just a normal kid with a face that . . . you know, is not so normal." He looked at us and took a deep breath. "Oh boy, I think I've just made you all more nervous, haven't I?"

We shook our heads. He rubbed his forehead.

"You know," he said, "one of the things you learn when you get old like me is that sometimes, a new situation will come along, and you'll have no idea what to do. There's no rule book that tells you how to act in every given situation in life, you know? So what I always say is that it's always better to err on the side of kindness. That's the secret. If you don't know what to do, just be kind. You can't go wrong. Which is why I asked you three to help me out here, because I'd heard from your lower-school teachers that you're all really nice kids."

We didn't know what to say to this, so we all just kind of smiled like goobers.

"Just treat him like you would treat any kid you've just met," he said. "That's all I'm trying to say. Okay, guys?"

14

We nodded at the same time now, too. Bobbling heads.

"You guys rock," he said. "So, relax, wait here a bit, and Mrs. Garcia will come and get you in a few minutes." He opened the door. "And, guys, really, thanks again for doing this. It's good karma to do good. It's a mitzvah, you know?"

With that, he smiled, winked at us, and left the room.

All three of us exhaled at the same time. We looked at each other, our eyes kind of wide.

"Okay," Jack said, "I don't know what the heck karma is and I don't know what the heck mitzvah is!"

This made us all laugh a little, though it was kind of a nervous type of laugh.

First Look

I'm not going to go into detail about the rest of what happened that day. I'm just going to point out that, for the first time in his life, Jack had not exaggerated. In fact, he had done the opposite. Is there a word that means the opposite of exaggerated? "Unexaggerated"? I don't know. But Jack had totally not exaggerated about this kid's face.

The first look I got of August, well, it made me want to cover my eyes and run away screaming. Bam. I know that sounds mean, and I'm sorry about that. But it's the truth. And anyone who says that that's not *their* first reaction when seeing Auggie Pullman isn't being honest. Seriously.

I totally would have walked out the door after I saw him, but I knew I would get in trouble if I did. So I just kept looking at Mr. Tushman, and I tried to listen to what he was saying, but all I heard was yak yak yak yak yak because my ears were burning. In my head, I was like, *Dude! Dude! Dude! Dude! Dude! Dude! Dude! Dude! Dude! Dude!*

Dude! Dude! Dude! Dude! Dude!

I think I said that word a thousand times to myself. I don't know why.

At some point, he introduced us to Auggie. Ahh! I think I actually shook his hand. Triple ahh! I wanted to zoom out of there so fast and wash my hand. But before I knew what was happening, we were headed out the door, down the hallway, and up the stairs.

Dude! Dude! Dude! Dude! Dude! Dude! Dude! Dude!

I caught Jack's eye as we were going up the stairs to homeroom. I opened my eyes really wide at him and mouthed the words, "No way!"

Jack mouthed back, "I told you!"

Scared

When I was about five, I remember watching an episode of *SpongeBob* one night, and a commercial came on TV that totally freaked me out. It was a few days before Halloween. A lot of commercials came on during that time of year that were kind of scary, but this one was for a new teen thriller I'd never heard about before. Suddenly, while I was watching the commercial, a close-up of a zombie's face popped up on the screen. Well, it totally and completely terrified me. I mean, terrified me like the kind of terrified where you actually run out of the room screaming with your arms in the air. TERRRRR-IFFF-FIED!

After that, I was so scared of seeing that zombie face again, I stopped watching any TV until Halloween was over and the movie was no longer playing in theaters. Seriously, I stopped watching TV completely—that's how scared I was!

Not too long after that, I was on a playdate with some kid whose name I don't even remember. And this kid was really into Harry Potter, so we started watching one of the Harry Potter movies (I'd never seen any of them before). Well, when I saw Voldemort's face for the first time, the same thing happened that had happened when the Halloween commercial came on. I started screaming hysterically, wailing like a total baby. It was so bad, the kid's mother couldn't calm me down, and she had to call my mother to come pick me up. My mom got really annoyed at the kid's mom for letting me watch the movie, so they ended up getting into an argument and—long story short—I never had another playdate there again. But anyway, between the Halloween zombie commercial and Voldemort's noseless face, I was kind of a mess.

Then, unfortunately, my dad took me to the movies at around that same time. Again, I was only about five. Maybe six by now. It shouldn't have been an issue: the movie we went to see was rated G, totally fine, not scary at all. But one of the trailers that came on was for *Scary Fairy*, a movie about demon fairies. I know—fairies are so lame!—and when I look back I can't believe I was so scared of this stuff, but I freaked out at this trailer. My dad had to take me out of the theater because—yet again!—I couldn't stop crying. It was so embarrassing! I mean, being scared of fairies? What's next? Flying ponies? Cabbage Patch dolls? Snowflakes? It was crazy! But there I was, shaking and screaming as I left the movie theater, hiding my face in my dad's coat. I'm sure there were three-year-olds in the audience who were looking at me like I was the biggest loser!

That's the thing about being scared, though. You can't control it. When you're scared, you're scared. And when you're scared, everything seems scarier than it ordinarily would be—even things that aren't. Everything that scares you kind of mushes together to become this big, terrifying feeling. It's like you're covered in this blanket of fear, and this blanket is made out of broken glass and dog poop and oozy pus and bloody zombie zits.

I started having awful nightmares. Every night, I'd wake up screaming. It got to a point where I was afraid to go to sleep because I didn't want to have another nightmare, so then I started sleeping in my parents' bed. I wish I could say this was just for a couple of nights, but it went like this for six weeks. I wouldn't let them turn off the lights. I had a panic attack every time I started drifting off to sleep. I mean, my palms would literally start to sweat and my heart would start to race, and I'd start to cry and scream before going to bed.

My parents took me to see a "feelings" doctor, which I only later realized was a child psychologist. Dr. Patel helped me a little bit. She said what I was experiencing were "night terrors," and it did help me to talk about them with her. But I think what really got me over the nightmares were the Discovery Channel nature videos my mom brought home for me one day. Woo-hoo for those nature videos! Every night, we'd pop one of them into the DVD player and I'd fall asleep to the sound of some guy with an English accent talking about meerkats or koalas or jellyfish.

Eventually, I did get over the nightmares, though. Everything went back to normal. But every once in a while, I'd have what Mom would call a "minor setback." Like, for instance, although I love *Star Wars* now, the very first time I saw *Star Wars: Episode II*, which was at a birthday sleepover when I was eight, I had to text my mom to come get me at two a.m. because I couldn't fall asleep: every time I'd close my eyes, Darth Sidious's face would pop into my head. It took about three weeks of nature videos to get over that setback (and I stopped going to sleepovers for about a year after that, too). Then, when I was nine, I saw *Lord of the Rings: The Two Towers* for the first time, and the same thing happened to me again, though this time it only took me about a week to get over Gollum.

By the time I turned ten, though, all those nightmares had pretty much gone away. Even the fear of having a nightmare was gone by then, too. Like, if I was at Henry's house and he would say, "Hey, let's watch a scary movie," my first reaction wasn't to think, *No, I might have a nightmare!* (which is what it used to be). My first reaction would be like, *Yeah, cool! Where's the popcorn?* I finally started being able to see all kinds of movies again. I even started getting into zombie apocalypse stuff, and none of it ever bothered me. That nightmare stuff was all behind me.

Or at least I thought it was.

But then, the night after I met Auggie Pullman, I started having nightmares again. I couldn't believe it. Not just passing bad dreams, but the full-blown, heart-pounding, wake-up-screaming kind of nightmares I used to have when I was a little kid. Only, I wasn't a little kid anymore.

I was in the fifth grade! Eleven years old! This wasn't supposed to be happening to me anymore!

But there I was again—watching nature videos to help me fall asleep.

Class Picture

I tried to describe what Auggie looked like to my mom, but she didn't get it until the school pictures arrived in the mail. Up until then, she'd never really seen him. She'd been away on a business trip during the Thanksgiving Sharing Festival, so she didn't see him then. On Egyptian Museum day, Auggie's face had been covered with mummy gauze. And there hadn't been any after-school concerts yet. So, the first time Mom saw Auggie and *finally* started understanding my nightmare situation was when she opened that large envelope with my class picture in it.

It was actually kind of funny. I can tell you exactly how she reacted because I was watching her as she opened it. First, she excitedly slit open the top of the envelope with a letter opener. Then, she pulled out my individual portrait. She put her hand on her chest.

"Awww, Julian, you look so handsome!" she said. "I'm so glad you wore that tie Grandmère sent you."

I was eating some ice cream at the kitchen table, and just smiled and nodded at her.

Then I watched her take the class picture out of the envelope. In lower school, every class would get its own picture taken with its own teacher, but in middle school, it's just one group picture of the entire fifth grade. So sixty kids standing in front of the entrance to the school. Fifteen kids in each row. Four rows. I was in the back row, in between Amos and Henry.

Mom was looking at the photo with a smile on her face.

"Oh, there you are!" she said when she spotted me.

She continued looking at the picture with a smile on her face.

"Oh my, look at how big Miles got!" said Mom. "And is that Henry? He looks like he's getting a mustache! And who is—"

And then she stopped talking. The smile on her face stayed frozen for a second or two, and then her face slowly transformed into a state of shock.

She put the photo down and stared blankly in front of her. Then she looked at the photo again.

Then she looked at me. She wasn't smiling.

"This is the kid you've been talking about?" she asked me. Her voice had completely changed from the way it sounded moments before.

"I told you," I answered.

She looked at the picture again. "This isn't just a cleft palate."

"No one ever said it *was* a cleft palate," I said to her. "Mr. Tushman never said that."

"Yes he did. On the phone that time."

"No, Mom," I answered her. "What he said was 'facial issues,' and you just assumed that he meant cleft palate. But he never actually said 'cleft palate.' "

"I could swear he said the boy had a cleft palate," she answered, "but this is so much worse than that." She really looked stunned. She couldn't stop staring at the photo. "What does he have, exactly? Is he developmentally delayed? He looks like he might be."

"I don't think so," I said, shrugging.

"Does he talk okay?"

"He kind of mumbles," I answered. "He's hard to understand sometimes."

Mom put the picture down on the table and sat down. She started tapping her fingers on the table.

"I'm trying to think of who his mother is," she said, shaking her head. "There are so many new parents in the school, I can't think of who it might be. Is she blond?"

"No, she has dark hair," I answered. "I see her at drop-off sometimes."

"Does she look . . . like the son?"

"Oh no, not at all," I said. I sat down next to her and picked up the picture, squinting at it so my eyes wouldn't see it too clearly. Auggie was in the front row, all the way on the left. "I told you, Mom. You didn't believe me, but I told you."

"It's not that I didn't believe you," she answered defensively. "I'm just kind of . . . surprised. I didn't realize it was this severe. Oh, I think I know who she is, his mom. Is she very pretty, kind of exotic, has dark wavy hair?"

"What?" I said, shrugging. "I don't know. She's a mom."

"I think I know who she is," answered Mom, nodding to herself. "I saw her on parents' night. Her husband's handsome, too."

"I have no idea," I said, shaking my head.

"Oh, those poor people!" She put her hand over her heart.

"Now you get why I've been having nightmares again?" I asked her.

She ran her hands through my hair.

"But are you still having nightmares?" she asked.

"Yes. Not every night like I did for the first month of school, but yeah!" I said, throwing the picture down on the tabletop. "Why did he have to come to Beecher Prep, anyway?"

I looked at Mom, who didn't know what to say. She started putting the picture back into the envelope.

"Don't even think of putting that in my school album, by the way," I said loudly. "You should just burn it or something."

"Julian," she said.

Then, out of the blue, I started crying.

"Oh, my darling!" said Mom, kind of surprised. She hugged me.

"I can't help it, Mom," I said through my tears. "I hate that I have to see him every day!"

That night, I had the same nightmare I've been having since the start of school. I'm walking down the main hallway, and all the kids are in front of their lockers, staring at me, whispering about me as I walk past them. I keep walking up the stairwell until I get to the bathroom, and then I look in the mirror. When I see myself, though, it's not me I'm seeing. It's Auggie. And then I scream.

Photoshop

The next morning, I overheard Mom and Dad talking as they were getting ready for work. I was getting dressed for school.

"They should have done more to prepare the kids," Mom said to Dad. "The school should have sent home a letter or something, I don't know."

"Come on," answered Dad. "Saying what? What can they possibly say? There's a homely kid in your class? Come on."

"It's much more than that."

"Let's not make too big a deal about it, Melissa."

"You haven't seen him, Jules," said Mom. "It's quite severe. Parents should have been told. I should have been told! Especially with Julian's anxiety issues."

"Anxiety issues?" I yelled from my room. I ran into their bedroom. "You think I have anxiety issues?"

"No, Julian," said Dad. "No one's saying that."

"Mom just said that!" I answered, pointing at Mom.

"I just heard her say 'anxiety issues.' What, so you guys think I have mental problems?"

"No!" they both said.

"Just because I get nightmares?"

"No!" they yelled.

"It's not my fault he goes to my school!" I cried. "It's not my fault his face freaks me out!"

"Of course it's not, darling," said Mom. "No one is saying that. All I meant is that because of your history of nightmares, the school should have alerted me. Then at least I would have known better about the nightmares you're having. I would have known what triggered them."

I sat down on the edge of their bed. Dad had the class picture in his hands and had obviously just been looking at it.

"I hope you're planning on burning that," I said. And I wasn't joking.

"No, darling," said Mom, sitting on the other side of me. "We don't need to burn anything. Look what I've done."

She picked up a different photo from the nightstand and handed it to me to look at. At first, I thought it was just another copy of the class picture, because it was exactly the same size as the class picture Dad had in his hands, and everything in it was exactly the same. I started to look away in disgust, but Mom pointed to a place on the photo—the place where Auggie used to be! He was nowhere in the photo.

I couldn't believe it! There was no trace of him!

I looked up at Mom, who was beaming.

"The magic of Photoshop!" she said happily, clapping her hands. "Now you can look at this picture and not have to have your memory of fifth grade tarnished," she said.

"That's so cool!" I said. "How did you do that?"

"I've gotten pretty good at Photoshop," she answered. "Remember last year, how I made all the skies blue in the Hawaii pictures?"

"You would never have known it rained every day," answered Dad, shaking his head.

"Laugh if you want," said Mom. "But now, when I look at those pictures, I don't have to be reminded of the bad weather that almost ruined our trip. I can remember it for the beautiful vacation that it was! Which is exactly how I want you to remember your fifth-grade year at Beecher Prep. Okay, Julian? Good memories. Not ugly ones."

"Thanks, Mom!" I said, hugging her tightly.

I didn't say it, of course, but even though she changed the skies to light blue on the photos, all I ever really remembered about our Hawaii trip was how cold and wet it was when we were there—despite the magic of Photoshop.

Mean

Look, I didn't start out being mean. I mean, I'm not a mean kid! Sure, sometimes I make jokes, but they're not mean jokes. They're just teasing jokes. People have to lighten up a little! Okay, maybe sometimes my jokes are a little mean, but I only make those jokes behind someone's back. I never say stuff to anyone's face that will actually hurt someone. I'm not a bully like that! I'm not a hater, dudes!

Attention, people! Stop being so sensitive!

Some people totally got the whole Photoshop thing, and some didn't. Henry and Miles thought it was so cool and wanted my mom to email their moms the photo. Amos thought it was "weird." Charlotte completely disapproved. I don't know what Jack thought, because he had gone over to the dark side by now. It's like he totally abandoned his peeps this year and only hangs out with Auggie now. Which bugged me, because that meant I couldn't hang out with him anymore. No way was I going to catch the "plague" from that freak.

That was the name of the game I invented. The Plague. It was simple. If you touched Auggie, and you didn't wash off the contamination, you died. Everyone in the whole grade played. Except Jack.

And Summer.

So here's the strange thing. I've known Summer since we were in third grade, and I never really paid any attention to her, but this year Henry started liking Savanna and they were like, "going out." Now, by "going out" I don't mean like high-school stuff, which would be kind of gross barf disgusting. All it means when you're "going out" is that you hang out together and meet each other at the lockers and sometimes go to the ice-cream shop on Amesfort Avenue after school. So, first Henry started going out with Savanna, and then Miles started going out with Ximena. And I was like, "Yo, what about me?" And then Amos said, "I'm going to ask Summer out," and I was like, "No way, I'm asking her out!" So that's when I started kind of liking Summer.

But it totally bit that Summer, like Jack, was on Team Auggie. It meant I couldn't hang out with her at all. I couldn't even say "Wassup" to her because the freak might think I was talking to him or something. So I told Henry to have Savanna invite Summer to the Halloween party at her house. I figured I could hang out with her and maybe even ask her to go out with me. That didn't work, though, because she ended up leaving the party early. And ever since then, she's been spending all her time with the freak.

Okay, okay. I know it's not nice to call him "the freak," but like I said before, people have to start being a little less sensitive around here! It's only a joke, everyone! Don't take me so seriously! I'm not being mean. I'm just being funny.

And that's all I was doing, being totally funny, the day that Jack Will punched me. I had been totally joking! Fooling around.

I didn't see it coming at *all*!

The way I remember it, we were just goofing together, and all of a sudden, he whacks me in the mouth for no reason! Boom!

And I was like, *Owwwww! You crazy jerkface! You punched me? You actually punched me?*

And the next thing I know, I'm in Nurse Molly's office, holding one of my teeth in my hand, and Mr. Tushman is there, and I hear him on the phone with my mom saying they're taking me to the hospital. I could hear my mom screaming on the other end of the line. Then Ms. Rubin, the dean, is leading me into the back of an ambulance and we're on the way to a hospital! Crazy stuff!

When we were riding in the ambulance, Ms. Rubin asked me if I knew why Jack hit me. I was like, *Duh, because he's totally insane!* Not that I could talk much, because my lips were swollen and there was blood all over my mouth.

Ms. Rubin stayed with me in the hospital until Mom showed up. Mom was more than a little hysterical, as you can imagine. She was crying kind of dramatically every time she saw my face. It was, I have to admit, a little embarrassing.

Then Dad showed up.

"Who did this?" was the first thing he said, shouting at Ms. Rubin.

"Jack Will," answered Ms. Rubin calmly. "He's with Mr. Tushman now."

"Jack Will?" cried Mom in shock. "We know the Wills! How could that happen?"

"There will be a thorough investigation," answered Ms. Rubin. "Right now, what's most important is that Julian's going to be fine . . ."

"Fine?" yelled Mom. "Look at his face! Do you think that's fine? I don't think that's fine. This is outrageous. What kind of school is this? I thought kids didn't punch each other at a school like Beecher Prep. I thought that's why we pay forty thousand dollars a year, so that our kids don't get hurt."

"Mrs. Albans," said Ms. Rubin, "I know you're upset . . ."

"I'm assuming the kid will get expelled, right?" said Dad.

"Dad!" I yelled.

"We will definitely deal with this matter in the appropriate way, I promise," answered Ms. Rubin, trying to keep her voice calm. "And now, if you don't mind, I think I'll leave you guys alone for a bit. The doctor will be back and you can check in with him, but he said that nothing was broken. Julian's fine. He lost a lower first molar, but that was on its way out anyway. He's going to give him some pain medication and you should keep icing it. Let's talk more in the morning."

It was only then that I realized that poor Ms. Rubin's blouse and skirt were completely covered in my blood. Boy, mouths do bleed a lot!

Later that night, when I could finally talk again without it hurting, Mom and Dad wanted to know every detail of what had happened, starting with what Jack and I had been talking about right before he hit me.

"Jack wath upthet becauth he wath paired up with the deformed kid," I answered. "I told him he could thwitch partnerth if he wanted to. And then he punched me!"

Mom shook her head. That was it for her. She was literally madder than I'd ever seen her before (and I've seen my mom pretty mad before, believe me!).

"This is what happens, Jules!" she said to Dad, crossing her arms and nodding quickly. "This is what happens when you make little kids deal with issues they're not equipped to deal with! They're just too young to be exposed to this kind of stuff! That Tushman is an *idiot*!"

And she said a whole bunch of other things, too, but

those are kind of too inapro-pro (if you know what I mean) for me to repeat.

"But, Dad, I don't want Jack to get ecthpelled from thkool," I said later on in the night. He was putting more ice on my mouth because the painkiller they had given me at the hospital was wearing off.

"That's not up to us," he answered. "But I wouldn't trouble myself about it if I were you. Whatever happens, Jack will get what he deserves for this."

I have to admit, I started feeling kind of bad for Jack. I mean, sure, he was a total dipstick for punching me, and I wanted him to get in trouble—but I really didn't want him to get kicked out of school or anything.

But Mom, I could tell, was on one of her missions now (as Dad would say). She gets like that sometimes, when she gets so outraged about something that there's just no stopping her. She was like that a few years ago when a kid got hit by a car a couple of blocks away from Beecher Prep, and she had like a million people sign a petition to have a traffic light installed. That was a super-mom moment. She was also like that last month when our favorite restaurant changed its menu and they no longer made my favorite dish the way I liked it. That was another super-mom moment because after she talked to the new owner, they agreed to special-order the dish—just for me! But Mom also gets like that for not-so-nice stuff, like when a waiter messes up a food order. That's a not-so-super-mom moment because, well, you know, it can get kind of weird when your mom starts talking to a waiter like he's five years old. *Awkward!* Also, like Dad says, you don't want to get a waiter mad at you, you know? They have your food in *their* hands—duh!

So, I wasn't totally clear on how I felt when I realized that my mom was declaring war on Mr. Tushman, Auggie Pullman, and all of Beecher Prep. Was it going to be a super-mom moment or a not-so-super-mom moment? Like, would it end up with Auggie going to a different school—yay!—or with Mr. Tushman blowing his nose in my cafeteria food—ugh!

Party

It took about two weeks for the swelling to go completely down. Because of that, we ended up not going to Paris over winter break. Mom didn't want our relatives to see me looking like I'd been in a "prize fight." She also wouldn't take any pictures of me over the holidays because she said she didn't want to remember me looking like that. For our annual Christmas card, we used one of the rejects from last year's photo shoot.

Even though I wasn't having a lot of nightmares anymore, the fact that I had started having nightmares again really worried Mom. I could tell she was totally stressed out about it. Then, the day before our Christmas party, she found out from one of the other moms that Auggie had not been through the same kind of admissions screening that the rest of us had been. See, every kid who applies to Beecher Prep is supposed to be interviewed and take a test at the school—but some kind of exception had been made for Auggie. He didn't come to the school for the interview and he got to take the admissions test at home. Mom thought that was really unfair!

"This kid should not have gotten into the school," I heard her telling a group of other moms at the party. "Beecher Prep is just not set up to handle situations like this! We're not an inclusion school! We don't have the psychologists needed to deal with how it affects the other kids. Poor Julian had nightmares for a whole month!"

Ugh, Mom! I hate your telling people about my nightmares!

"Henry was upset as well," Henry's mom said, and the other moms nodded.

"They didn't even prepare us beforehand!" Mom went on. "That's what gets me the most. If they're not going to provide additional psychological support, at least warn the parents ahead of time!"

"Absolutely!" said Miles's mom, and the other moms nodded again.

"Obviously, Jack Will could have used some therapy," Mom said, rolling her eyes.

"I was surprised they didn't expel him," said Henry's mom.

"Oh, they would have!" answered Mom, "but we asked them not to. We've known the Will family since kindergarten. They're good people. We don't blame Jack, really. I think he just cracked under the pressure of having to be this kid's caretaker. That's what happens when you put little kids into these kinds of situations. I honestly don't know what Tushman was thinking!"

"I'm sorry, I just have to step in here," said another mom (I think it was Charlotte's mom because she had the same bright blond hair and big blue eyes). "It's not like there's anything wrong with this kid, Melissa. He's a great kid, who just happens to look different, but . . ."

"Oh, I know!" Mom answered, and she put her hand over her heart. "Oh, Brigit, no one's saying he's not a great kid, believe me. I'm sure he is. And I hear the parents are lovely people. That's not the issue. To me, ultimately, the simple fact of the matter is that Tushman didn't follow protocol. He flagrantly disregarded the applications process by not having the boy come to Beecher Prep for the interview—or take the test like every one of our kids did. He broke the rules. And rules are rules. That's it." Mom made a sad face at Brigit. "Oh dear, Brigit. I can see you totally disapprove!"

"No, Melissa, not at all," Charlotte's mom said, shaking her head. "It's a tough situation all around. Look, the fact is, your son got punched in the face. You have every right to feel angry and demand some answers."

"Thank you." Mom nodded and crossed her arms. "I just think the whole thing's been handled terribly, that's all. And I blame Tushman. Completely."

"Absolutely," said Henry's mom.

"He's got to go," agreed Miles's mom.

I looked at Mom, surrounded by nodding moms, and I thought, *Okay, so maybe this is going to turn out to be one of those really super-mom moments.* Maybe everything she was doing would make it so that Auggie ended up going to a different school, and then things could go back to the way it used to be at Beecher Prep. That would be so awesome!

But a part of me was thinking, *Maybe this is going to turn into a not-so-super-mom moment.* I mean, some of the stuff she was saying sounded kind of . . . I don't know. Kind of harsh, I guess. It's like when she gets mad at a waiter. You end up feeling sorry for the waiter. The thing is, I know she's on this anti-Tushman mission because of me. If I hadn't started getting nightmares again, and if Jack hadn't punched me, none of this would be happening. She wouldn't be making a big deal about Auggie, or Tushman, and she'd be concentrating all her time and energy on good stuff, like raising money for the school and volunteering at the homeless shelter. Mom does good stuff like that all the time!

So I don't know. On the one hand, I'm happy she's trying to help me. And on the other hand, I would love for her to stop.

Team Julian

The thing that annoyed me the most when we got back from winter break was that Jack had gone back to being friends with Auggie again. They had had some kind of fight after Halloween, which is why Jack and I started being bros again. But after winter break was over, they were best buds again.

It was so lame!

I told everyone we needed to really ice Jack out, for his own good. He had to choose, once and for all, whether he wanted to be on Team Auggie or Team Julian and the Rest of the World. So we started completely ignoring Jack: not talking to him, not answering his questions. It was like he didn't exist.

That'll show him!

And that's when I started leaving my little notes. One day, someone had left some Post-it notes on one of the benches in the yard, which is what gave me the idea. I wrote in this really psycho-killer handwriting:

Nobody likes you anymore!

I slipped it into the slits in Jack's locker when no one was looking. I watched him out of the corner of my eye when he found it. He turned around and saw Henry opening his locker nearby.

"Did Julian write this?" he asked.

But Henry was one of my peeps, you know? He just iced Jack out, pretended like no one was even talking to him. Jack crumpled the Post-it and flicked it into his locker and banged the door shut.

After Jack left, I went over to Henry.

"Hollah!" I said, giving him the devil's sign, which made Henry laugh.

Over the next couple of days, I left a few more notes in Jack's locker. And then I started leaving some in Auggie's locker.

They were not—I repeat, not—a big deal. They were mostly stupid stuff. I didn't think anyone would ever take them seriously. I mean, they were actually kind of funny!

Well, kind of. At least, some of them were.

> *You stink, big cheese!*
> *Freak!*
> *Get out of our school, orc!*

No one but Henry and Miles knew that I was writing these notes. And they were sworn to secrecy.

Dr. Jansen's Office

I don't know how the heck Mr. Tushman found out about them. I don't think Jack or Auggie would have been dumb enough to rat on me, because they had started leaving me notes in my locker, too. I mean, how stupid would you have to be to rat someone out about something that you were doing, too?

So, here's what happened. A few days before the Fifth-Grade Nature Retreat, which I was totally looking forward to, Mom got a phone call from Dr. Jansen, the headmaster of Beecher Prep. He said he wanted to discuss something with her and Dad, and asked for a meeting.

Mom assumed it probably had to do with Mr. Tushman, that maybe he was getting fired. So she was actually kind of excited about the meeting!

They showed up for the appointment at ten a.m., and they were waiting in Dr. Jansen's office when, all of a sudden, they see me walking into the office, too. Ms. Rubin had taken me out of class, asked me to follow her, and brought me there: I had no idea what was up. I'd never even been to the headmaster's office before, so when I saw Mom and Dad there, I looked as confused as they looked.

"What's going on?" Mom said to Ms. Rubin. Before Ms. Rubin could say anything, Mr. Tushman and Dr. Jansen came into the office.

Everyone shook hands and they were all smiles as they greeted one another. Ms. Rubin said she had to go back to class but that she would call Mom and Dad later to check in. This surprised Mom. I could tell she started thinking that maybe this wasn't about Mr. Tushman getting fired, after all.

Then Dr. Jansen asked us to sit on the sofa opposite his desk. Mr. Tushman sat down in a chair next to us, and Dr. Jansen sat behind his desk.

"Well, thank you so much for coming, Melissa and Jules," Dr. Jansen said to my parents. It was strange hearing him call them by their first names. I knew they all knew each other from being on the board, but it sounded weird. "I know how busy you are. And I'm sure you're wondering what this is all about."

"Well, yes . . ." said Mom, but her voice drifted off. Dad coughed into his hand.

"The reason we asked you here today is because, unfortunately," Dr. Jansen continued, "we have a serious matter on our hands, and we'd like to figure out the best way to resolve it. Julian, do you have any inkling of what I might be talking about?" He looked at me.

I opened my eyes wide.

"Me?" I snapped my head back and made a face. "No."

Dr. Jansen smiled and sighed at me at the same time. He took off his glasses.

"You understand," he said, looking at me, "we take bullying very seriously at Beecher Prep. There's zero tolerance for any kind of bullying. We feel that every single one of our students deserves the right to learn in a caring and respectful atmosphere—"

"Excuse me, but can someone tell me what's going on here?" Mom interrupted, looking at Dr. Jansen impatiently. "We obviously know the mission statement at Beecher Prep, Hal: we practically wrote it! Let's cut to the chase—what's going on?"

Evidence

Dr. Jansen looked at Mr. Tushman. "Why don't you explain, Larry?" he said.

Mr. Tushman handed an envelope to Mom and Dad. Mom opened it and pulled out the last three Post-it notes I had left in Auggie's locker. I knew immediately that's what they were because these were actually pink Post-its and not yellow ones like all the others had been.

So, I thought: *Ah-ha! So it was Auggie who told Mr. Tushman about the Post-it notes! What a turd!!*

Mom read through the notes quickly, raised her eyebrows, and passed them to Dad. He read them and looked at me.

"You wrote these, Julian?" he said, holding the notes out for me.

I swallowed. I looked at him kind of blankly. He handed me the notes, and I just stared at them.

"Um . . . well," I answered. "Yeah, I guess. But, Dad, they were writing notes, too!"

"Who was writing notes?" asked Dad.

"Jack and Auggie," I answered. "They were writing notes to me, too! It wasn't just me!"

"But you started the note writing, didn't you?" asked Mr. Tushman.

"Excuse me," Mom interjected angrily. "Let's not forget that it was Jack Will who punched Julian in the mouth, not the other way around. Obviously, there's going to be residual anger—"

"How many of these notes did you write, Julian?" Dad interrupted, tapping on the Post-its I was holding.

"I don't know," I said. It was hard for me to get the words out. "Like, six or something. But the other ones weren't this . . . you know, bad. These notes are worse than the other ones I wrote. The other ones weren't so . . ." My voice kind of drifted off as I reread what I'd written on the three notes:

Yo, Darth Hideous. You're so ugly you should wear a mask every day!

And:

I h8 u, Freak!

And the last one:

I bet your mother wishes you'd never been born. You should do everybody a favor—and die.

Of course, looking at them now, they seemed a lot worse than when I wrote them. But I was mad then— super mad. I had just gotten one of their notes and . . .

"Wait!" I said, and I reached into my pocket. I found

the last Post-it that Auggie and Jack had left for me in my locker, just yesterday. It was kind of crumpled up now, but I held it out to Mr. Tushman to read. "Look! They wrote mean stuff to me, too!"

Mr. Tushman took the Post-it, read it quickly, and handed it to my parents. My mom read it and then looked at the floor. My dad read it and shook his head, puzzled.

He handed me the Post-it and I reread it.

Julian, you're so hot! Summer doesn't like you, but I want to have your babies! Smell my armpits! Love, Beulah.

"Who the heck is Beulah?" asked Dad.

"Never mind," I answered. "I can't explain." I handed the Post-it back to Mr. Tushman, who gave it to Dr. Jansen to read. I noticed he actually tried to hide a smile.

"Julian," said Mr. Tushman, "the three notes you wrote don't compare at all to this note in content."

"I don't think it's for anyone else to judge the semantics of a note," said Mom. "It doesn't matter whether you think one note is worse than the other— it's how the person reading the note reads it. The fact is, Julian's had a little crush on this Summer girl all year long, and it probably hurt his feelings—"

"Mom!" I yelled, and I covered my face with my hands. "That's so embarrassing!"

"All I'm saying is that a note can be hurtful to a child—whether *you* see it or not," Mom said to Mr. Tushman.

"Are you kidding me?" answered Mr. Tushman, shaking his head. He sounded angrier than I had ever heard him before. "Are you telling me you don't find the Post-its your son wrote completely horrifying? Because I do!"

"I'm not defending the notes!" answered Mom. "I'm just reminding you that it was a two-way street. You have to realize that Julian was obviously writing those notes as a reaction to something."

"Look," said Dr. Jansen, holding his hand out in front of him like a crossing guard. "There's no doubt there's some history here."

"Those notes hurt my feelings!" I said, and I didn't mind that I sounded like I was going to cry.

"I don't doubt that their notes hurt your feelings, Julian," Dr. Jansen answered. "And you were trying to hurt their feelings. That's the problem with stuff like this—everyone keeps trying to top one another, and then things escalate out of control."

"Exactly!" said Mom, and it almost sounded like she screamed it.

"But the fact is," Dr. Jansen continued, holding up his finger, "there is a line, Julian. There is a line. And your notes crossed that line. They're completely unacceptable. If Auggie had read these notes, how do you think he'd feel?"

He was looking at me so intensely that I felt like disappearing under the sofa.

"You mean he hasn't read them?" I asked.

"No," answered Dr. Jansen. "Thank goodness someone reported the notes to Mr. Tushman yesterday, and he opened Auggie's locker and intercepted them before Auggie ever saw them." I nodded and lowered my head. I have to admit—I was glad Auggie hadn't read them. I guess I knew what Dr. Jansen meant about "crossing the line." But then I thought, *So if it wasn't Auggie who ratted me out, who was it?*

We were all quiet for a minute or two. It was awkward beyond belief.

The Verdict

"Okay," said Dad finally, rubbing his palm over his face. "Obviously, we understand the seriousness of the situation now, and we will . . . do something about it."

I don't think I'd ever seen Dad look so uncomfortable. I'm sorry, Dad!

"Well, we have some recommendations," answered Dr. Jansen. "Obviously, we want to help everyone involved . . ."

"Thank you for understanding," said Mom, getting her pocketbook ready as if she were getting up.

"But there are consequences!" said Mr. Tushman, looking at Mom.

"Excuse me?" she shot back at him.

"As I said in the beginning," Dr. Jansen interjected, "the school has a very strict anti-bullying policy."

"Yeah, we saw how strict it was when you *didn't* expel Jack Will for punching Julian in the mouth," Mom answered quickly. Yeah, take that, Mr. Tushman!

"Oh, come on! That was completely different," Mr. Tushman answered dismissively.

"Oh?" answered Mom. "Punching someone in the face isn't bullying to you?"

"Okay, okay," said Dad, raising his hand to keep Mr. Tushman from answering. "Let's just cut to the chase, okay? What exactly are your recommendations, Hal?"

Dr. Jansen looked at him.

"Julian is being suspended for two weeks," he said.

"What?" yelled Mom, looking at Dad. But Dad didn't look back.

"In addition," said Dr. Jansen, "we're recommending counseling. Nurse Molly has the names of several therapists who we think Julian should see—"

"This is outrageous," interrupted Mom, steaming.

"Wait," I said. "You mean, I can't go to school?"

"Not for two weeks," answered Mr. Tushman. "Starting immediately."

"But what about the trip to the nature retreat?" I asked.

"You can't go," he answered coldly.

"No!" I said, and now I really was about to cry. "I want to go to the nature retreat!"

"I'm sorry, Julian," Dr. Jansen said gently.

"This is absolutely ridiculous," said Mom, looking at Dr. Jansen. "Don't you think you're overreacting a little? That kid didn't even read the notes!"

"That's not the point!" answered Mr. Tushman.

"I'll tell you what I think!" said Mom. "This is because you admitted a kid into the school who shouldn't have been admitted into the school in the first place. And you broke the rules to do it. And now you're just taking this out on my kid because I'm the one who had the guts to call you on it!"

"Melissa," said Dr. Jansen, trying to calm her down.

"These children are too young to deal with things like this . . . facial deformities, disfigurement," Mom continued, talking to Dr. Jansen. "You must see that! Julian's had nightmares because of that boy. Did you know that? Julian has anxiety issues."

"Mom!" I said, clenching my teeth.

"The board should have been consulted about whether Beecher Prep was the right place for a child like that," Mom continued. "That's all I'm saying! We're just not set up for it. There are other schools that are, but we're not!"

"You can choose to believe that if you want," answered Mr. Tushman, not looking at her.

Mom rolled her eyes.

"This is a witch hunt," she muttered quietly, looking out the window. She was fuming.

I had no idea what she was talking about. Witches? What witches?

"Okay, Hal, you said you had some recommendations," Dad said to Dr. Jansen. He sounded gruff. "Is that it? Two-week suspension and counseling?"

"We'd also like for Julian to write a letter of apology to August Pullman," said Mr. Tushman.

"Apology for what exactly?" answered Mom. "He wrote some stupid notes. Surely he's not the only kid in the world who's ever written a stupid note."

"It's more than a stupid note!" answered Mr. Tushman. "It's a pattern of behavior." He started counting on his fingers. "It's the making faces behind the kid's back. It's the 'game' he initiated, where if someone touches Auggie he has to wash his hands . . ."

I couldn't believe Mr. Tushman even knew about the Plague game! How do teachers know so much?

"It's social isolation," Mr. Tushman continued. "It's creating a hostile atmosphere."

"And you know for a fact that it's Julian who initiated all this?" asked Dad. "Social isolation? Hostile atmosphere? Are you saying that Julian was the only kid who wasn't nice to this boy? Or are you suspending every kid who stuck his tongue out at this kid?"

Good one, Dad! Score one for the Albanses!

"Doesn't it trouble you at all that Julian doesn't seem to be showing the least bit of remorse?" said Mr. Tushman, squinting at Dad.

"Okay, let's just stop right here," Dad said quietly, pointing his finger in Mr. Tushman's face.

"Please, everyone," said Dr. Jansen. "Let's calm down a bit. Obviously, this is difficult."

"After all we've done for this school," Mom answered,

shaking her head. "After all the money and the time we've put into this school, you would think we'd get just a little bit of consideration." She put her thumb and her index finger together. "Just a little."

Dad nodded. He was still looking angrily at Mr. Tushman, but then he looked at Dr. Jansen. "Melissa's right," he said. "I think we deserved a little better than this, Hal. A friendly warning would have been nice. Instead, you call us in here like children . . ." He stood up. "We deserved better."

"I'm sorry you feel that way," said Dr. Jansen, standing up as well.

"The board of trustees will hear about this," said Mom. She got up, too.

"I'm sure they will," answered Dr. Jansen, crossing his arms and nodding.

Mr. Tushman was the only adult still sitting down.

"The point of the suspension isn't punitive," he said quietly. "We're trying to help Julian, too. He can't fully understand the ramifications of his actions if you keep trying to justify them away. We want him to feel some empathy—"

"You know, I've heard just about enough!" said Mom, holding her palm in front of Mr. Tushman's face. "I don't need parenting advice. Not from someone who doesn't have kids of his own. You don't know what it's like to see your kid having a panic attack every time he shuts his eyes to go to sleep, okay? You don't know what it's like."

56

Her voice cracked a bit, like she was going to cry. She looked at Dr. Jansen. "This affected Julian deeply, Hal. I'm sorry if that's not politically correct to say, but it's the truth, and I'm just trying to do what I think is best for my son! That's all. Do you understand?"

"Yes, Melissa," Dr. Jansen answered softly.

Mom nodded. Her chin quivered. "Are we done here? Can we go now?"

"Sure," he answered.

"Come on, Julian," she said, and she walked out of the office.

I stood up. I admit, I wasn't exactly sure what was going on.

"Wait, is that it?" I asked. "But what about my things? All my stuff's in my locker."

"Ms. Rubin will get your things ready and she'll get them to you later this week," answered Dr. Jansen. He looked at Dad. "I'm really sorry it came to this, Jules." He held out his hand for a handshake.

Dad looked at his hand but didn't shake it. He looked at Dr. Jansen.

"Here's the only thing I want from you, Hal," he said quietly. "I want that this—all of this—be kept confidential. Is that clear? It doesn't go beyond this room. I don't want Julian turned into some kind of anti-bullying poster boy by the school. No one is to know he's been suspended. We'll make up some excuse about why he's not in school, and that's it. Are we clear, Hal? I don't want him made into an example. I'm not going to stand by while this school drags my family's reputation through the mud."

Oh, by the way, in case I hadn't mentioned it before: Dad's a lawyer.

Dr. Jansen and Mr. Tushman exchanged looks.

"We are not looking to make an example of any of our students," Dr. Jansen answered. "This suspension really is about a reasonable response to unreasonable behavior."

"Give me a break," answered Dad, looking at his watch. "It's a massive overreaction."

Dr. Jansen looked at Dad, and then he looked at me.

"Julian," he said, looking me right in the eye. "Can I ask you something point-blank?"

I looked at Dad, who nodded. I shrugged.

"Do you feel at all remorseful for what you've done?" Dr. Jansen asked me.

I thought about it a second. I could tell all the grown-ups were watching me, waiting for me to answer something magical that would make this whole situation better.

"Yes," I said quietly. "I'm really sorry I wrote those last notes."

Dr. Jansen nodded. "Is there anything else you feel remorse for?" he asked.

I looked at Dad again. I'm not an idiot. I knew what

he was dying for me to say. I just wasn't going to say it. So I looked down and shrugged.

"Can I ask you this, then?" said Dr. Jansen. "Will you consider writing Auggie a letter of apology?"

I shrugged again. "How many words does it have to be?" was all I could think to say.

I knew the moment I said it that I probably shouldn't have. Dr. Jansen looked at my dad, who just looked down.

"Julian," said Dad. "Go find Mom. Wait for me by the reception area. I'll be out in a second."

Just as I closed the door on my way out, Dad started whispering something to Dr. Jansen and Mr. Tushman. It was a hushed, angry whisper.

When I got to the reception area, I found Mom sitting on a a chair with her sunglasses on. I sat down next to her. She rubbed my back but she didn't say anything. I think she had been crying.

I looked at the clock: 10:20 a.m. Right about now, Ms. Rubin was probably going over the results of yesterday's quiz in science class. As I looked around the lobby, I had a blip of a memory— that day before school started, when me, Jack Will, and Charlotte had met up here before meeting our "welcome buddy" for the first time. I remember how nervous Jack had been that day, and how I didn't even know who Auggie was.

So much had happened since then.

Out of School

Dad didn't say anything when he met us in the lobby. We just walked out the doors without saying goodbye— even to the security guard at the reception desk. It was weird leaving the school when everyone was still inside. I wondered what Miles and Henry would think when I didn't come back to class. I hated that I was going to miss PE that afternoon.

My parents were quiet the whole way back to the house. We live on the Upper West Side, which is about a half-hour drive from Beecher Prep, but it felt like it took forever to get home.

"I can't believe I got suspended," I said, just as we pulled into the parking garage in our building.

"It's not your fault, honey," answered Mom. "They have it in for us."

"Melissa!" Dad yelled, which surprised Mom a bit. "Yes, of course it's his fault. This whole situation is his fault! Julian, what the heck were you thinking, writing notes like that?"

"He was goaded into writing them!" answered Mom.

We had pulled to a stop inside the garage. The parking-garage attendant was waiting for us to get out of the car, but we didn't get out.

Dad turned around and looked at me. "I'm not saying I think the school handled this right," he said. "Two weeks' suspension is ridiculous. But, Julian, you should know better!"

"I know!" I said. "It was a mistake, Dad!"

"We all make mistakes," said Mom.

Dad turned back around. He looked at Mom. "Jansen's right, Melissa. If you keep trying to justify his actions—"

"That's not what I'm doing, Jules."

Dad didn't answer right away. Then he said, "I told Jansen that we're pulling Julian out of Beecher Prep next year."

Mom was literally speechless. It took a second for what he said to hit me. "You *what?*" I said.

"Jules," Mom said slowly.

"I told Jansen that we'll finish out this year at Beecher Prep," Dad continued calmly. "But next year, Julian's going to a different school."

"I can't believe this!" I cried. "I love Beecher Prep, Dad! I have friends! Mom!"

"I'm not sending you back to that school, Julian," Dad said firmly. "No way am I spending another dime on that school. There are plenty of other great private schools in New York City."

"Mom!" I said.

Mom wiped her hand across her face. She shook her head. "Don't you think we should have talked about this first?" she said to Dad.

"You don't agree?" he countered.

She rubbed her forehead with her fingers.

"No, I do agree," she said softly, nodding.

"Mom!" I screamed.

She turned around in her seat. "Honey, I think Daddy's right."

"I can't believe this!" I yelled, punching the car seat.

"They have it in for us now," she continued. "Because we complained about the situation with that boy . . ."

"But that was your fault!" I said through clenched teeth. "I didn't tell you to try and get Auggie thrown out of the school. I didn't want you to get Tushman fired. That was you!"

"And I'm sorry about that, sweetheart," she said meekly.

"Julian!" said Dad. "Your mom did everything she did to try and protect you. It's not her fault you wrote those notes, is it?"

"No, but if she hadn't made such a big stink about everything . . ." I started to say.

"Julian, do you hear yourself?" said Dad. "Now you're blaming your mom. Before you were blaming the other boys for writing those notes. I'm starting to wonder if what they were saying is right! Don't you feel any remorse for what you've done?"

"Of course he does!" said Mom.

"Melissa, let him answer for himself!" Dad said loudly.

"No, okay?" I yelled. "I'm not sorry! I know everybody thinks I should be all, *I'm sorry for being mean to Auggie, I'm sorry I talked smack about him, I'm sorry I dissed him.* But I'm not. So sue me."

Before Dad could respond, the garage attendant knocked on the car window. Another car had pulled into the garage and they needed us to get out.

Spring

I didn't tell anyone about the suspension. When Henry texted me a few days later asking why I wasn't in school, I told him I had strep throat. That's what we told everyone.

It turns out, two weeks' suspension isn't so bad, by the way. I spent most of my time at home watching *SpongeBob* reruns and playing *Knights of the Old Republic*. I was still supposed to keep up on my schoolwork, though, so it's not like I totally got to goof off. Ms. Rubin dropped by the apartment one afternoon with all my locker stuff: my textbooks, my loose-leaf book, and all the assignments I would need to make up. And there was a lot!

Everything went really well with social studies and English, but I had so much trouble doing the math homework that Mom got me a math tutor.

Despite all the time off, I really was excited about going back. Or at least I thought I was. The night before my first day back, I had one of my nightmares again.

Only this time, it wasn't me who looked like Auggie—it was everyone else!

I should have taken that as a premonition. When I got back to school, as soon as I arrived, I could tell something was up. Something was different. The first thing I noticed is that no one was really excited about seeing me again. I mean, people said hello and asked me how I was feeling, but no one was like, "Dude, I missed you!"

I would have thought Miles and Henry would be like that, but they weren't. In fact, at lunchtime, they didn't even sit at our usual table. They sat with Amos. So I had to take my tray and find a place to squeeze in at Amos's table, which was kind of humiliating. Then I overheard the three of them talking about hanging out at the playground after school and shooting hoops, but no one asked me to come!

The thing that was weirdest of all, though, was that everyone was being really nice to Auggie. Like, ridiculously nice. It was like I had entered the portal to a different dimension, an alternate universe in which Auggie and I had changed places. Suddenly, he was the popular one, and I was the outsider.

Right after last period, I pulled Henry over to talk to him.

"Yo, dude, why is everyone being so nice to the freak all of a sudden?" I asked.

"Oh, um," said Henry, looking around kind of

nervously. "Yeah, well, people don't really call him that anymore."

And then he told me all about the stuff that had gone down at the nature retreat. Basically, what had happened was that Auggie and Jack got picked on by some seventh-grade bullies from another school. Henry, Miles, and Amos had rescued them, got into a fight with the bullies—like with real punches flying—and then they all escaped through a corn maze. It sounded really exciting, and as he was telling me, I got mad all over again that Mr. Tushman had made me miss it.

"Oh man," I said excitedly. "I wish I'd been there! I totally would have creamed those jerks."

"Wait, which jerks?"

"The seventh graders!"

"Really?" He looked puzzled, though Henry always looked a little puzzled. "Because, I don't know, Julian. I kind of think that if you had been there, we might not have rescued them at all. You probably would have been cheering for the seventh graders!"

I looked at him like he was an idiot. "No I wouldn't," I said.

"Seriously?" he said, giving me a look.

"No!" I said.

"Okay!" he answered, shrugging.

"Yo, Henry, are you coming?" Amos called out from down the hallway.

"Look, I gotta go," said Henry.

"Wait," I said.

"Gotta go."

"Want to hang out tomorrow after school?"

"Not sure," he answered, backing away. "Text me tonight and we'll see."

As I watched him jog away, I had this terrible feeling in the pit of my stomach. Did he really think I was that awful that I would have been rooting for some seventh graders while they beat Auggie up? Is that what other people think? That I would have been that much of a dirtwad?

Look, I'm the first one to say I don't like Auggie Pullman, but I would never want to see him get beat up or anything! I mean, come on! I'm not a psycho. It really annoyed me that that's what people thought about me.

I texted Henry later on: "Yo, btw, I would never have just stood by and let those creeps beat Auggie and Jack up!"

But he never texted me back.

Mr. Tushman

That last month in school was awful. It's not like anyone was out-and-out mean to me, but I felt iced out by Amos and Henry and Miles. I just didn't feel popular anymore. No one really ever laughed at my jokes. No one wanted to hang out with me. I felt like I could disappear from the school and nobody would miss me. Meanwhile, Auggie was walking down the hallways like some cool dude, getting high-fived by all the jocks in the upper grades.

Whatever.

Mr. Tushman called me into his office one day.

"How's it going, Julian?" he asked me.

"Fine."

"Did you ever write that apology letter I asked you to write?"

"My dad says I'm leaving the school, so I don't have to write anything," I answered.

"Oh," he said, nodding. "I guess I was hoping you'd want to write it on your own."

"Why?" I said back. "Everyone thinks I'm this big dirtbag now anyway. What the heck is writing a letter going to accomplish?"

"Julian—"

"Look, I know everyone thinks I'm this unfeeling kid who doesn't feel 'remorse'!" I said, using air quotes.

"Julian," said Mr. Tushman. "No one—"

Suddenly, I felt like I was about to cry, so I just interrupted him. "I'm really late for class and I don't want to get in trouble, so can I please go?"

Mr. Tushman looked sad. He nodded. Then I left his office without looking back.

A few days later, we received an official notice from the school telling us that they had withdrawn their invitation to re-enroll in the fall.

I didn't think it mattered, since Dad had told them we weren't going back anyway. But we still hadn't heard from the other schools I had applied to, and if I didn't get into any of them, we had planned on my going back to Beecher Prep. But now that was impossible.

Mom and Dad were furious at the school. Like, *crazy* mad. Mostly because they had already paid the tuition for the next year in advance. And the school wasn't planning on returning the money. See, that's the thing with private schools: they can kick you out for any reason.

Luckily, a few days later, we did find out that I'd gotten into my first-choice private school, not far from where I lived. I'd have to wear a uniform, but that was okay. Better than having to go to Beecher Prep every day!

Needless to say, we skipped the graduation ceremony at the end of the year.

After

"That is only tears such as men use," said Bagheera.

"Now I know thou art a man, and a man's cub no longer.

The jungle is shut indeed to thee henceforward.

Let them fall, Mowgli. They are only tears."

—Rudyard Kipling, *The Jungle Book*

. . .

Oh, the wind, the wind is blowing,

through the graves the wind is blowing,

freedom soon will come;

then we'll come from the shadows.

—Leonard Cohen, "The Partisan"

Summer Vacation

My parents and I went to Paris in June. The original plan was that we would return to New York in July, since I was supposed to go to rock-and-roll camp with Henry and Miles. But after everything that happened, I didn't want to do that anymore. My parents decided to let me stay with my grandmother for the rest of the summer.

Usually, I hated staying with Grandmère, but I was okay about it this time. I knew that after my parents went home, I could spend the entire day in my PJs playing *Halo*, and Grandmère wouldn't care in the least. I could pretty much do whatever I wanted.

Grandmère wasn't exactly the typical "grandma" type. No baking cookies for Grandmère. No knitting sweaters. She was, as Dad always said, something of a "character." Even though she was in her eighties, she dressed like a fashion model. Super glamorous. Lots of makeup and perfume. High heels. She never woke up until two in the afternoon, and then she'd take at least two hours to get dressed. Once she was up, she would take me out shopping or to a museum or a fancy restaurant. She wasn't into doing kid stuff, if you know what I mean. She'd never sit through a PG movie with me, for instance, so I ended up seeing a lot of movies that were totally age-inappropriate. Mom, I knew, would go completely ballistic if she got wind of some of the movies Grandmère took me to see. But Grandmère was French, and was always saying my parents were too "American" anyway.

Grandmère also didn't talk to me like I was a little kid. Even when I was younger, she never used baby words or talked to me the way grown-ups usually talk to little kids. She used regular words to describe everything. Like, if I would say, "*Je veux faire pipi*," meaning "I want to make pee-pee," she would say, "You need to urinate? Go to the lavatory."

And she cursed sometimes, too. Boy, she could curse! And if I didn't know what a curse word meant, all I had to do was ask her and she would explain it to me—in detail. I can't even tell you some of the words she explained to me!

Anyway, I was glad to be away from NYC for the whole summer. I was hoping that I would get all those kids out of my head. Auggie. Jack. Summer. Henry. Miles. All of them. If I never saw any of those kids again, seriously, I would be the happiest kid in Paris.

Mr. Browne

The only thing I was a little bummed about is that I never got to say goodbye to any of my teachers at Beecher Prep. I really liked some of them. Mr. Browne, my English teacher, was probably my favorite teacher of all time. He had always been really nice to me. I loved writing, and he was really complimentary about it. And I never got to tell him I wasn't coming back to Beecher Prep.

At the beginning of the year, Mr. Browne had told all of us that he wanted us to send him one of our own precepts over the summer. So, one afternoon, while Grandmère was sleeping, I started thinking about sending him a precept from Paris. I went to one of the tourist shops down the block and bought a postcard of a gargoyle, one of those at the top of Notre-Dame. The first thing I thought when I saw it was that it reminded me of Auggie. And then I thought, *Ugh! Why am I still thinking about him? Why do I still see his face wherever I go? I can't wait to start over!*

And that's when it hit me: my precept. I wrote it down really quickly.

Sometimes it's good to start over.

There. Perfect. I loved it. I got Mr. Browne's address from his teacher page on the Beecher Prep website, and dropped it in the mail that same day.

But then, after I sent it, I realized he wasn't going to understand what it meant. Not really. He didn't have the whole background story about why I was so happy to be leaving Beecher Prep and starting over somewhere new. So, I decided to write him an email to tell him everything that had happened last year. I mean, not *everything*. Dad had specifically told me not to ever tell anyone at the school about the mean stuff I did to Auggie—for legal reasons. But I wanted Mr. Browne to know enough so that he would understand my precept. I also wanted him to know that I thought he was a great teacher. Mom had told everyone that I wasn't going back to Beecher Prep because we were unhappy with the academics—and the teachers. I felt kind of bad about that because I didn't want Mr. Browne to ever think I was unhappy with him.

So, anyway, I decided to send Mr. Browne an email.

To: tbrowne@beecherschool.edu
Fr: julianalbans@ezmail.com
Re: My precept

Hi, Mr. Browne! I just sent you my precept in the mail:

75

"Sometimes it's good to start over." It's on a postcard of a gargoyle. I wrote this precept because I'm going to a new school in September. I ended up hating Beecher Prep. I didn't like the students. But I DID like the teachers. I thought your class was great. So don't take my not going back personally.

I don't know if you know the whole long story, but basically the reason I'm not going back to Beecher Prep is . . . well, not to name names, but there was one student I really didn't get along with. Actually, it was two students. (You can probably guess who they are because one of them punched me in the mouth.) Anyway, these kids were not my favorite people in the world. We started writing mean notes to each other. I repeat: each other. It was a 2-way street! But I'm the one who got in trouble for it! Just me! It was so unfair! The truth is, Mr. Tushman had it in for me because my mom was trying to get him fired. Anyway, long story short: I got suspended for two weeks for writing the notes! (No one knows this, though. It's a secret so please don't tell anyone.) The school said it had a "zero tolerance" policy against bullying. But I don't think what I did was bullying! My parents got so mad at the school! They decided to enroll me in a different school next year. So, yeah, that's the story.

I really wish that that "student" had never come to Beecher Prep! My whole year would have been so much better! I hated having to be in his classes. He gave me nightmares. I would still be going to Beecher

76

Prep if he hadn't been there. It's a bummer.

I really liked your class, though. You were a great teacher. I wanted you to know that.

I thought it was good that I hadn't named "names." But I figured he'd know who I was talking about. I really didn't expect to hear back from him, but the very next day, when I checked my in-box, there was an email from Mr. Browne. I was so excited!

To: julianalbans@ezmail.com
Fr: tbrowne@beecherschool.edu
Re: re: My precept

Hi, Julian. Thanks so much for your email! I'm looking forward to getting the gargoyle postcard. I was sorry to hear you wouldn't be coming back to Beecher Prep. I always thought you were a great student and a gifted writer.

By the way, I love your precept. I agree, sometimes it's good to start over. A fresh start gives us the chance to reflect on the past, weigh the things we've done, and apply what we've learned from those things to the future. If we don't examine the past, we don't learn from it.

As for the "kids" you didn't like, I do think I know who you're talking about. I'm sorry the year didn't turn out to be a happy one for you, but I hope you take a little time to ask yourself why. Things that happen to us, even the bad stuff, can often teach us a little bit about ourselves. Do you ever wonder why you had such a hard time with these two students? Was it, perhaps, their friendship that bothered you? Were you troubled by Auggie's physical appearance? You mentioned that you started having nightmares. Did you ever consider that maybe you were just a little afraid of Auggie, Julian? Sometimes fear can make even the nicest kids say and do things they wouldn't ordinarily say or do. Perhaps you should explore these feelings further?

   In any case, I wish you the best of luck in your new school, Julian. You're a good kid. A natural leader. Just remember to use your leadership for good, huh? Don't forget: always choose kind!

I don't know why, but I was so, so, *so* happy to get that email from Mr. Browne! I knew he would be understanding! I was so tired of everyone thinking I was this demon-child, you know? It was obvious that Mr. Browne knew I wasn't. I reread his email like, ten times. I was smiling from ear to ear.

"So?" Grandmère asked me. She had just woken up and was having her breakfast: a croissant and *café au lait* delivered from downstairs. "I haven't seen you this happy all summer long. What is it that you are reading, *mon cher?*"

"Oh, I got an email from one of my teachers," I answered. "Mr. Browne."

"From your old school?" she asked. "I thought they

were all bad, those teachers. I thought it was 'good riddance' to all of them!" Grandmère had a thick French accent that was hard to understand sometimes.

"What?"

"Good riddance!" she repeated. "Never mind. I thought the teachers were all stupid." The way she pronounced "stupid" was funny: like stew-peed!

"Not all. Not Mr. Browne," I answered.

"So, what did he write to make you so happy?"

"Oh, nothing much," I said. "It's just . . . I thought everyone hated me, but now I know Mr. Browne doesn't."

Grandmère looked at me.

"Why would everyone hate you, Julian?" she asked. "You are such a good boy."

"I don't know," I answered.

"Read me the email," she said.

"No, Grandmère . . ." I started to say.

"Read," she commanded, pointing her finger at the screen.

So I read Mr. Browne's letter aloud to her. Now, Grandmère knew a little bit about what had happened at Beecher Prep, but I don't think she knew the whole story. I mean, I think Mom and Dad told her the version of the story they told everyone else, with maybe a few more details. Grandmère knew there were a couple of kids who had made my life miserable, for instance, but she didn't know the specifics. She knew I'd gotten punched in the mouth, but she didn't know why. If anything, Grandmère probably assumed I had gotten bullied, and that's why I was leaving the school.

So, there were parts of Mr. Browne's email she really didn't understand.

"What does he mean," she said, squinting as she tried to read off my screen. "Auggie's 'physical appearance'? *Qu'est-ce que c'est?*"

"One of the kids that I didn't like, Auggie, he had like this awful . . . facial deformity," I answered. "It was really bad. He looked like a gargoyle!"

"Julian!" she said. "That is not very nice."

"Sorry."

"And this boy, he was not *sympathique?*" she asked innocently. "He was not nice to you? Was he a bully?"

I thought about that. "No, he wasn't a bully."

"So, why did you not like him?"

I shrugged. "I don't know. He just got on my nerves."

"What do you mean, you don't know?" she answered quickly. "Your parents told me you were leaving school because of some bullies, no? You got punched in the face? No?"

"Well, yeah, I got punched, but not by the deformed kid. By his friend."

"Ah! So his friend was the bully!"

"No, not exactly," I said. "I can't say they were bullies, Grandmère. I mean, it wasn't like that. We just didn't get along, that's all. We hated each other. It's kind of hard to explain, you kind of had to be there. Here, let me show you what he looked like. Then maybe you'll understand a little better. I mean, not to sound mean, but it was really hard having to look at him every day. He gave me nightmares."

I logged on to Facebook and found our class picture, and zoomed in on Auggie's face so she could see. She put her glasses on to look at it and spent a long time studying his face on the computer screen. I thought she would react the way Mom had reacted when she first saw that picture of Auggie, but she didn't. She just nodded to herself. And then she closed the laptop.

"Pretty bad, huh?" I said to her.

She looked at me.

"Julian," she said. "I think maybe your teacher is right. I think you were afraid of this boy."

"What? No way!" I answered. "I'm not afraid of Auggie! I mean, I didn't like him—in fact, I kind of hated him—but not because I was afraid of him."

"Sometimes we hate the things we are afraid of," she said.

I made a face like she was talking crazy.

She took my hand.

"I know what it is like to be afraid, Julian," she said, holding her finger up to my face. "There was a little boy that I was afraid of when I was a little girl."

"Let me guess," I answered, sounding bored. "I bet he looked just like Auggie."

Grandmère shook her head. "No. His face was fine."

"So, why were you afraid of him?" I asked. I tried to make my voice sound as uninterested as possible, but Grandmère ignored my bad attitude.

She just sat back in her chair, her head slightly tilted, and I could tell by looking into her eyes that she had gone somewhere far away.

Grandmère's Story

"I was a very popular girl when I was young, Julian," said Grandmère. "I had many friends. I had pretty clothes. As you can see, I have always liked pretty clothes." She waved her hands down her sides to make sure I noticed her dress. She smiled.

"I was a frivolous girl," she continued. "Spoiled. When the Germans came to France, I hardly took any notice. I knew that some Jewish families in my village were moving away, but my family was so cosmopolitan. My parents were intellectuals. Atheists. We didn't even go to synagogue."

She paused here and asked me to bring her a wine glass, which I did. She served herself a full glass and, as she always did, offered me some, too. And, as I always did, I said, "*Non, merci.*" Like I said, Mom would go ballistic if she knew the stuff Grandmère did sometimes!

"There was a boy in my school called . . . well, they called him Tourteau," she continued. "He was . . . how do you say the word . . . a crippled? Is that how you say it?"

"I don't think people use that word anymore, Grandmère," I said. "It's not exactly politically correct, if you know what I mean."

She flicked her hand at me. "Americans are always coming up with new words we can't say anymore!" she said. "*Alors*, well, Tourteau's legs were deformed from the polio. He needed two canes to walk with. And his back was all twisted. I think that's why he was called *tourteau*, crab: he walked sideways like a crab. I know, it sounds very harsh. Children were meaner in those days."

I thought about how I called August "the freak" behind his back. But at least I never called him that to his face!

Grandmère continued talking. I have to admit: at first I wasn't into her telling me one of her long stories, but I was getting into this one.

"Tourteau was a little thing, a skinny thing. None of us ever talked to him because he made us uncomfortable. He was so different! I never even looked at him! I was afraid of him. Afraid to look at him, to talk to him. Afraid he would accidentally touch me. It was easier to pretend he didn't exist."

She took a long sip of her wine.

"One morning, a man came running into our school. I knew him. Everyone did. He was a Maquis, a partisan. Do you know what that is? He was against the Germans.

He rushed into the school and told the teachers that the Germans were coming to take all the Jewish children away. What? What is this? I could not believe what I was hearing! The teachers in the school went around to all the classes and gathered the Jewish children together. We were told to follow the Maquis into the woods. We were going to go hide. Hurry hurry hurry! I think there were maybe ten of us in all! Hurry hurry hurry! Escape!"

Grandmère looked at me, to make sure I was listening—which, of course, I was.

"It was snowing that morning, and very cold. And all I could think was, *If I go into the woods, I will ruin my shoes!* I was wearing these beautiful new red shoes that Papa had brought me, you see. As I said before, I was a frivolous girl—perhaps even a little stupid! But this is what I was thinking. I did not even stop to think, *Well, where is Maman and Papa? If the Germans were coming for the Jewish children, had they come for the parents already?* This did not occur to me. All I could think about were my beautiful shoes. So, instead of following the Maquis into the woods, I snuck away from the group and went to hide inside the bell tower of the school. There was a tiny room up there, full of crates and books, and there I hid. I remember thinking I would go home in the afternoon after the Germans came, and tell Maman and Papa all about it. This is how stupid I was, Julian!"

I nodded. I couldn't believe I had never heard this story before!

"And then the Germans came," she said. "There was a narrow window in the tower, and I could see them perfectly. I watched them run into the woods after the children. It did not take them very long to find them. They all came back together: the Germans, the children, the Maquis soldier."

Grandmère paused and blinked a few times, and then she took a deep breath.

"They shot the Maquis in front of all the children," she said quietly. "He fell so softly, Julian, in the snow. The children cried. They cried as they were led away in a line. One of the teachers, Mademoiselle Petitjean, went with them—even though she was not Jewish! She said she would not leave her children! No one ever saw her again, poor thing. By now, Julian, I had awakened from my stupidity. I was not thinking of my red shoes anymore. I was thinking of my friends who had been taken away. I was thinking of my parents. I was waiting until it was nighttime so I could go home to them!

"But not all the Germans had left. Some had stayed behind, along with the French police. They were searching the school. And then I realized, they were looking for me! Yes, for me, and for the one or two other Jewish children who had not gone into the woods. I realized then that my friend Rachel had not been among the Jewish children who were marched away.

Nor Jakob, a boy from another village who all the girls wanted to marry because he was so handsome. Where were they? They must have been hiding, just like I was!

"Then I heard creaking, Julian. Up the stairs, I heard footsteps up the stairs, coming closer to me. I was so scared! I tried to make myself as small as possible behind the crate, and hid my head beneath a blanket."

Here, Grandmère covered her head with her arms, as if to show me how she was hiding.

"And then I heard someone whisper my name," she said. "It was not a man's voice. It was a child's voice.

"*Sara?* the voice whispered again.

"I peeked out from the blanket.

"*Tourteau!* I answered, astonished. I was so surprised, because in all the years I had known him, I don't think I had ever said a word to him, nor him to me. And yet, there he was, calling my name.

"*They will find you here,* he said. *Follow me.*

"And I did follow him, for by now I was terrified. He led me down a hallway into the chapel of the school, which I had never really been to before. We went to the back of the chapel, where there was a crypt—all this was new to me, Julian! And we crawled through the crypt so the Germans would not see us through the windows, because they were looking for us still. I heard when they found Rachel. I heard her screaming in the courtyard as they took her away. Poor Rachel!

"Tourteau took me down to the basement beneath

the crypt. There must have been one hundred steps at least. These were not easy for Tourteau, as you can imagine, with his terrible limp and his two canes, but he hopped down the steps two at a time, looking behind him to make sure I was following.

"Finally, we arrived at a passage. It was so narrow we had to walk sideways to get through. And then we were in the sewers, Julian! Can you imagine? I knew instantly because of the smell, of course. We were knee-deep in refuse. You can imagine the smell. So much for my red shoes!

"We walked all night. I was so cold, Julian! Tourteau was such a kind boy, though. He gave me his coat to wear. It was, to this day, the most noble act anyone has ever done for me. He was freezing, too—but he gave me his coat. I was so ashamed for the way I had treated him. Oh, Julian, I was so ashamed!"

She covered her mouth with her fingers, and swallowed. Then she finished the glass of wine and poured herself another.

"The sewers lead to Dannevilliers, a small village about fifteen kilometers away from Aubervilliers. Maman and Papa had always avoided this town because of the smell: the sewers from Paris drained onto the farmland there. We wouldn't even eat apples grown in Dannevilliers! But it's where Tourteau lived. He took me to his house, and we cleaned ourselves by the well, and then Tourteau brought me to the barn behind his house. He wrapped me up in a horse blanket and told me to wait. He was going to get his parents.

"No, I pleaded. *Please don't tell them.* I was so frightened. I wondered if, when they saw me, they would call the Germans. You know, I had never met them before!

"But Tourteau left, and a few minutes later, he returned with his parents. They looked at me. I must have seemed quite pathetic there—all wet and shivering. The mother, Vivienne, put her arms around me to comfort me. Oh, Julian, that hug was the warmest hug I have ever felt! I cried so hard in this woman's arms, because I knew then, I knew I would never cry in my own maman's arms again. I just knew it in my heart, Julian. And I was right. They had taken Maman that same day, along with all the other Jews in the city. My father, who had been at work, had been warned that the Germans were coming and managed to escape. He was smuggled to Switzerland. But it was too late for Maman. She was deported that day. To Auschwitz. I never saw her again. My beautiful maman!"

She took a deep breath here, and shook her head.

Tourteau

Grandmère was silent for a few seconds. She was looking into the air like she could see it all happening again right in front of her. Now I understood why she'd never talked about this before: it was too hard for her.

"Tourteau's family hid me for two years in that barn," she continued slowly. "Even though it was so dangerous for them. We were literally surrounded by Germans, and the French police had a large headquarters in Dannevilliers. But every day, I thanked my maker for the barn that was my home, and the food that Tourteau managed to bring me—even when there was hardly any food to go around. People were starving in those days, Julian. And yet they fed me. It was a kindness that I will never forget. It is always brave to be kind, but in those days, such kindnesses could cost you your life."

Grandmère started to get teary-eyed at this point. She took my hand.

"The last time I saw Tourteau was two months before the liberation. He had brought me some soup. It wasn't even soup. It was water with a little bit of bread and onions in it. We had both lost so much weight. I was in rags. So much for my pretty clothes! Even so, we managed to laugh, Tourteau and I. We laughed about things that happened in our school. Even though I could not go there anymore, of course, Tourteau still went every day. At night, he would tell me everything he had learned so that I would stay smart. He would tell me about all my old friends, too, and how they were doing. They all still ignored him, of course. And he never revealed to any of them that I was still alive. No one could know. No one could be trusted! But Tourteau was an excellent narrator, and he made me laugh a lot. He could do wonderful imitations, and he even had funny nicknames for all my friends. Imagine that, Tourteau was making fun of them!

"I had no idea you were so mischievous! I told him. *All those years, you were probably laughing at me behind my back, too!*

"Laughing at you? he said. *Never! I had a crush on you; I never laughed at you. Besides, I only laughed at the kids who made fun of me. You never made fun of me. You simply ignored me.*

"I called you Tourteau.

"And so? Everyone called me that. I really don't mind. I like crabs!

"Oh, Tourteau, I am so ashamed! I answered, and I remember I covered my face with both my hands."

At this point, Grandmère covered her face with her hands. Although her fingers were bent with arthritis now, and I could see her veins, I pictured her young hands covering her young face so many years ago.

"Tourteau took my hands with his own hands," she continued, slowly removing her hands from her face. "And he held my hands for a few seconds. I was fourteen years old then, and I had never kissed a boy, but he kissed me that day, Julian."

Grandmère closed her eyes. She took a deep breath.

"After he kissed me, I said to him, *I don't want to call you Tourteau anymore. What is your name?*"

Grandmère opened her eyes and looked at me. "Can you guess what he said?" she asked.

I raised my eyebrows as if to say, "No, how would I know?" Then she closed her eyes again and smiled.

"He said, *My name is Julian.*"

Julian

"Oh my God!" I cried. "That's why you named Dad Julian?" Even though everyone called him Jules, that was his name.

"Oui," she said, nodding.

"And I'm named after Dad!" I said. "So I'm named after this kid! That is so cool!"

She smiled and ran her fingers through my hair. But she didn't say anything.

Then I remembered her saying, "The last time I saw Tourteau . . ."

"So what happened to him?" I asked. "To Julian?"

Almost instantaneously, tears rolled down Grand-mère's cheeks.

"The Germans took him," she said, "that same day. He was on his way to school. They were making another sweep of the village that morning. By now, Germany was losing the war and they knew it."

"But . . ." I said, "he wasn't even Jewish!"

"They took him because he was crippled," she said

between sobs. "I'm sorry, I know you told me that word is a bad word, but I don't know another word in English. He was an *invalide*. That is the word in French. And that is why they took him. He was not perfect." She practically spat out the word. "They took all the imperfects from the village that day. It was a purge. The Gypsies. The shoemaker's son, who was . . . simple. And Julian. My *tourteau*. They put him in a cart with the others. And then he was put on a train to Drancy. And from there to Auschwitz, like my mother. We heard later from someone who saw him there that they sent him to the gas chambers right away. Just like that, poof, he was gone. My savior. My little Julian."

She stopped to wipe her eyes with a handkerchief, and then drank the rest of the wine.

"His parents were devastated, of course, M. Beaumier and Mme. Beaumier," she continued. "We didn't find out he was dead until after the liberation. But we knew. We knew." She dabbed her eyes. "I lived with them for another year after the war. They treated me like a daughter. They were the ones who helped track down Papa, although it took some time to find him. So much chaos in those days. When Papa finally was able to return to Paris, I went to live with him. But I always visited the Beaumiers—even when they were very old. I never forgot the kindness they showed me."

She sighed. She had finished her story.

"Grandmère," I said, after a few minutes. "That's like,

the saddest thing I've ever heard! I didn't even know you were in the war. I mean, Dad's never talked about any of this."

She shrugged. "I think it's very possible that I never told your father this story," she said. "I don't like to talk about sad things, you know. In some ways, I am still the frivolous girl I used to be. But when I heard you talking about that little boy in your school, I could not help but think of Tourteau, of how afraid I had once been of him, of how badly we had treated him because of his deformity. Those children had been so mean to him, Julian. It breaks my heart to think of it."

When she said that, I don't know, something just really broke inside of me. Completely unexpected. I looked down and, all of a sudden, I started to cry. And when I say I started to cry, I don't mean a few tears rolling down my cheeks—I mean like, full-scale, snot-filled crying.

"Julian," she said softly.

I shook my head and covered my face with my hands.

"I was terrible, Grandmère," I whispered. "I was so mean to Auggie. I'm so sorry, Grandmère!"

"Julian," she said again. "Look at me."

"No!"

"Look at me, *mon cher*." She took my face in her hands and forced me to look at her. I felt so embarrassed. I really couldn't look her in the eyes. Suddenly, that

95

word that Mr. Tushman had used, that word that everyone kept trying to force on me, came to me like a shout. REMORSE!

Yeah, there it was. That word in all its glory.

REMORSE. I was shaking with remorse. I was crying with remorse.

"Julian," said Grandmère. "We all make mistakes, *mon cher.*"

"No, you don't understand!" I answered. "It wasn't just one mistake. I was those kids who were mean to Tourteau . . . I was the bully, Grandmère. It was me!"

She nodded.

"I called him a freak. I laughed behind his back. *I left mean notes!*" I screamed. "Mom kept making excuses for why I did that stuff . . . but there wasn't any excuse. I just did it! And I don't even know why. I don't even know."

I was crying so hard I couldn't even speak.

Grandmère stroked my head and hugged me.

"Julian," she said softly. "You are so young. The things you did, you know they were not right. But that does not mean you are not capable of doing right. It only means that you chose to do wrong. This is what I mean when I say you made a mistake. It was the same with me. I made a mistake with Tourteau.

"But the good thing about life, Julian," she continued, "is that we can fix our mistakes sometimes. We learn from them. We get better. I never made a mistake like the one I made with Tourteau again, not with anyone in my life. And I have had a very, very long life. You will learn from your mistake, too. You must promise yourself that you will never behave like that with anyone else again. One mistake does not define you, Julian. Do you understand me? You must simply act better next time."

I nodded, but I still cried for a long, long time after that.

My Dream

That night, I dreamt about Auggie. I don't remember the details of the dream, but I think we were being chased by Nazis. Auggie was captured, but I had a key to let him out. And in my dream, I think I saved him. Or maybe that's what I told myself when I woke up. Sometimes, it's hard to know with dreams. I mean, in this dream the Nazis all looked like Darth Vader's Imperial officers anyway, so it's hard to put too much meaning into dreams.

But what was really interesting to me, when I thought about it, is that it had been a dream—not a nightmare. And in the dream, Auggie and I were on the same side.

I woke up super early because of the dream, and didn't go back to sleep. I kept thinking about Auggie, and Tourteau— Julian—the heroic boy I was named for. It's weird: This whole time I had been thinking about Auggie like he was my enemy, but when Grandmère told me that story, I don't know, it all kind of just sank in with me. I kept thinking of how ashamed the original

Julian would be to know that someone who carried his name had been so mean.

I kept thinking about how sad Grandmère was when she told the story. How she could remember all the details, even though it happened like, seventy years ago. Seventy years! Would Auggie remember me in seventy years? Would he still remember the mean things I called him?

I don't want to be remembered for stuff like that. I would want to be remembered the way Grandmère remembers Tourteau!

Mr. Tushman, I get it now! R. E. M. O. R. S. E.

I got up as soon as it was light out, and wrote this note.

> Dear Auggie,
> I want to apologize for the stuff I did last year. I've been thinking about it a lot. You didn't deserve it. I wish I could have a do-over. I would be nicer.
> I hope you don't remember how mean I was when you're eighty years old. Have a nice life.
>
> Julian
>
> PS: If you're the one who told Mr. Tushman about the notes, don't worry. I don't blame you.

When Grandmère woke up that afternoon, I read her the note.

"I'm proud of you, Julian," she said, squeezing my shoulder.

"Do you think he'll forgive me?"

She thought about it.

"That's up to him," she answered. "In the end, *mon cher*, all that matters is that you forgive yourself. You are learning from your mistake. Like I learned with Tourteau."

"Do you think Tourteau would forgive me?" I asked. "If he knew his namesake had been so mean?"

She kissed my hand.

"Tourteau would forgive you," she answered. And I could tell she meant it.

Going Home

I realized I didn't have Auggie's address, so I wrote another email to Mr. Browne asking him if I could send him my note to Auggie and have him mail it to him for me. Mr. Browne emailed me back immediately. He was happy to do it. He also said he was proud of me.

I felt good about that. I mean like, really good. And it felt good to feel good. Kind of hard to explain, but I guess I was tired of feeling like I was this awful kid. I'm not. Like I keep saying over and over again, I'm just an ordinary kid. A typical, normal, ordinary kid. Who made a mistake.

But now, I was trying to make it right.

My parents arrived a week later. Mom couldn't stop hugging and kissing me. This was the longest I'd ever been away from home.

I was excited to tell them about the email from Mr. Browne, and the note I had written to Auggie. But they told me their news first.

"We're suing the school!" said Mom excitedly.

"What?" I cried.

"Dad is suing them for breach of contract," she said. She was practically chirping.

I looked at Grandmère, who didn't say anything. We were all having dinner.

"They had no right to withdraw the enrollment contract," Dad explained calmly, like a lawyer. "Not before we had been placed in another school. Hal told me—in his office—that they would wait to rescind their enrollment offer until *after* we had gotten accepted into another school. And they would return the money. We had a verbal agreement."

"But I was going to another school anyway!" I said.

"Doesn't matter," he said. "Even if they returned the money, it's the principle of the thing."

"What principle?" said Grandmère. She got up from the table. "This is nonsense, Jules. Stupid. Stew-peed! Complete and utter nonsense!"

"Maman!" said Dad. He looked really surprised. So did Mom.

"You should drop this stupidity!" said Grandmère.

"You don't really know the details, Maman," said Dad.

"I know *all* the details!" she yelled, shaking her fist in the air. She looked fierce. "The boy was wrong, Jules! *Your* boy was in the wrong! He knows it. You know it. He did bad things to that other boy and he is sorry for them, and you should let it be."

Mom and Dad looked at each other.

"With all due respect, Sara," said Mom, "I think we know what's best for—"

"No, you don't know anything!" yelled Grandmère. "You don't know. You two are too busy with lawsuits and stupid things like that."

"Maman," said Dad.

"She's right, Dad," I said. "It was all my fault. All that stuff with Auggie. It was my fault. I was mean to him, for no reason. It was my fault Jack punched me. I had just called Auggie a freak."

"What?" said Mom.

"I wrote those awful notes," I said quickly. "I did mean stuff. It was my fault! I was the bully, Mom! It wasn't anyone else's fault but mine!"

Mom and Dad didn't seem to know what to answer.

"Instead of sitting there like two idiots," said Grandmère, who always said things like they were, "you should be praising Julian for this admission! He is taking responsibility! He is owning up to his mistakes. It takes much courage to do this kind of thing."

"Yes, of course," said Dad, rubbing his chin and looking at me. "But . . . I just don't think you understand all the legal ramifications. The school took our tuition and refused to return it, which—"

"Blah! Blah! Blah!" said Grandmère, waving him away.

"I wrote him an apology," I said. "To Auggie. I wrote

him an apology and I sent it to him in the mail! I apologized for the way I acted."

"You what?" said Dad. He was getting mad now.

"And I told Mr. Browne the truth, too," I added. "I wrote Mr. Browne a long email telling him the whole story."

"Julian . . ." said Dad, frowning angrily. "Why did you do that? I told you I didn't want you to write anything that acknowledged—"

"Jules!" said Grandmère loudly, waving her hand in front of Dad's face. "*Tu as un cerveau comme un sandwich au fromage!*"

I couldn't help but laugh at this. Dad cringed.

"What did she say?" asked Mom, who didn't know French.

"Grandmère just told Dad he has a brain like a cheese sandwich," I said.

"Maman!" Dad said sternly, like someone who was about to begin a long lecture.

But Mom reached out and put her hand on Dad's arm.

"Jules," she said quietly. "I think your mom is right."

Unexpected

Sometimes people surprise you. Never in a million years would I have thought my mom would be the one to back down from anything, so I was completely shocked by what she had just said. I could tell Dad was, too. He looked at Mom like he couldn't believe what she was saying. Grandmère was the only one who didn't seem surprised.

"Are you kidding me?" Dad said to Mom.

Mom shook her head slowly. "Jules, we should end this. We should move on. Your mother's right."

Dad raised his eyebrows. I knew he was mad but trying not to show it. "You're the one who got us on this warpath, Melissa!"

"I know!" she answered, taking her glasses off. Her eyes were really shiny. "I know, I know. And I thought it was the right thing to do at the time. I still don't think Tushman was right, the way he handled everything, but . . . I'm ready to put all this behind us now, Jules. I think we should just . . . let go and move forward." She shrugged. She looked at me. "It was very big of Julian to reach out to that boy, Jules. It takes a lot of guts to do that." She looked back at Dad. "We should be supportive."

"I am supportive, of course," said Dad. "But this is such a complete about-face, Melissa! I mean . . ." He shook his head and rolled his eyes at the same time.

Mom sighed. She didn't know what to say.

"Look here," said Grandmère. "Whatever Melissa did, she did it because she wanted Julian to be happy. And that is all. *C'est tout*. And he's happy now. You can see it in his eyes. For the first time in a long time, your son looks completely happy."

"That's exactly right," said Mom, wiping a tear from her face.

I felt kind of sorry for Mom at that moment. I could tell she felt bad about some of the things she had done.

"Dad," I said, "please don't sue the school. I don't want that. Okay, Dad? Please?"

Dad leaned back in his chair and made a soft whistle sound, like he was blowing out a candle in slow motion. Then he started clicking his tongue against the roof of his mouth. It was a long minute that he stayed like that. We just watched him.

Finally he sat back up in his chair and looked at us. He shrugged.

"Okay," he said, his palms up. "I'll drop the lawsuit.

We'll just walk away from the tuition money. Are you sure that's what you want, Melissa?"

Mom nodded. "I'm sure."

Grandmère sighed. "Victory at last," she mumbled into her wine glass.

Starting Over

We went home a week later, but not before Grandmère took us to a very special place: the village she grew up in. It seemed amazing to me, that she had never told Dad the whole Tourteau story. The only thing he knew was that a family in Dannevilliers had helped her during the war, but she had never told him any of the details. She had never told him that his own grandmother had died in a concentration camp.

"Maman, how come you never told me any of this?" Dad asked her while we were driving in the car to her village.

"Oh, you know me, Jules," she answered. "I do not like to dwell on the past. Life is ahead of us. If we spend too much time looking backward, we can't see where we are going!"

Much of the village had changed. Too many bombs and grenades had been dropped. Most of the original houses had been destroyed in the war. Grandmère's school was gone. There was really nothing much to see. Just Starbucks and shoe stores.

But then we drove to Dannevilliers, which is where Julian had lived: that village was intact. She took us to the barn where she had stayed for two years. The old farmer who lived there now let us walk around and take a look. Grandmère found her initials scrawled in a little nook in one of the horse stalls, which is where she would hide under piles of hay whenever the Nazis were nearby. Grandmère stood in the middle of the barn, with one hand on her face as she looked around. She seemed so tiny there.

"How are you doing, Grandmère?" I asked.

"Me? Ah! Well," she said, smiling. She tilted her head. "I lived. I remember thinking, when I was staying here, that the smell of horse manure would never leave my nostrils. But I lived. And Jules was born because I lived. And you were born. So what is the smell of horse manure against all that? Perfume and time make everything easier to bear. Now, there's one more place I want to visit . . ."

We drove about ten minutes away to a tiny cemetery on the outskirts of the village. Grandmère took us directly to a tombstone at the edge of the graveyard.

There was a small white ceramic plaque on the tombstone. It was in the shape of a heart, and it read:

ICI REPOSENT

Vivienne Beaumier
née le 27 avril 1905
décédée le 21 novembre 1985

Jean-Paul Beaumier
né le 15 mai 1901
décédé le 5 juillet 1985

Mère et père de
Julian Auguste Beaumier
né le 10 octobre 1930
tombé en juin 1944
Puisse-t-il toujours marcher le front haut
dans le jardin de Dieu

I looked at Grandmère as she stood looking at the plaque. She kissed her fingers and then reached down to touch it. She was trembling.

"They treated me like their daughter," she said, tears rolling down her cheeks.

She started sobbing. I took her hand and kissed it.

Mom took Dad's hand. "What does the plaque say?" she asked softly.

Dad cleared his throat.

"Here rests Vivienne Beaumier . . ." he translated softly. "And Jean-Paul Beaumier. Mother and father of

Julian Auguste Beaumier, born October 10, 1930. Killed June 1944. May he walk forever tall in the garden of God."

New York

We got back to NYC a week before my new school was scheduled to start. It was nice, being in my room again. My things were all the same. But I felt, I don't know, a little different. I can't explain it. I felt like I really was starting over.

"I'll help you unpack in a minute," said Mom, running off to the bathroom as soon as we stepped through the door.

"I'm good," I answered. I could hear Dad in the living room listening to our answering-machine messages. I started unpacking my suitcase. Then I heard a familiar voice on the machine.

I stopped what I was doing and walked into the living room. Dad looked up and paused the machine. Then he replayed the message for me to hear.

It was Auggie Pullman.

"Oh, hi, Julian," said the message. "Yeah, so . . . umm . . . I just wanted to tell you I got your note. And, um . . . yeah, thanks for writing it. No need to call me back. I just wanted to say hey. We're good. Oh, and by the way, it wasn't me who told Tushman about the notes, just so you know. Or Jack or Summer. I really don't know how he found out, not that it matters anyway. So, okay. Anyway. I hope you like your new school. Good luck. Bye!"

Click.

Dad looked at me to see how I would react.

"Wow," I said. "I didn't expect that at all."

"Are you going to call him back?" asked Dad.

I shook my head. "Nah," I answered. "I'm too chicken."

Dad walked over to me and put his hand on my shoulder.

"I think you've proven that you're anything *but* chicken," he said. "I'm proud of you, Julian. Very proud of you." He leaned over and hugged me. "*Tu marches toujours le front haut.*"

I smiled. "I hope so, Dad."

I hope so.

Contemporary observations are changing our understanding of planetary systems, and it is important that our nomenclature for objects reflect our current understanding. This applies, in particular, to the designation "planets." The word "planet" originally described "wanderers" that were known only as moving lights in the sky. Recent discoveries lead us to create a new definition, which we can make using currently available scientific information.
—International Astronomical Union (IAU), excerpt from Resolution B5

· · ·

I guess there is no one to blame
We're leaving ground
Will things ever be the same?
—Europe, "The Final Countdown"

· · ·

It is such a mysterious place, the land of tears.
—Antoine de Saint-Exupéry, *The Little Prince*

Introductions

I was two days old the first time I met Auggie Pullman. I don't remember the occasion myself, obviously, but my mom told me about it. She and Dad had just brought me home from the hospital for the first time, and Auggie's parents had just brought him home from the hospital for the first time, too. But Auggie was already three months old by then. He had to stay in the hospital, because he needed some surgeries that would allow him to breathe and swallow. Breathing and swallowing are things most of us don't ever think about, because we do them automatically. But they weren't automatic for Auggie when he was born.

My parents took me over to Auggie's house so we could meet each other. Auggie was hooked up to a lot of medical equipment in their living room. My mom picked me up and brought me face to face with Auggie.

"August Matthew Pullman," she said, "this is Christopher Angus Blake, your new oldest friend."

And our parents applauded and toasted the happy occasion.

My mom and Auggie's mom, Isabel, became best friends before we were born. They met at the supermarket on Amesfort Avenue right after my parents moved to the neighborhood. Since both of them were having babies soon, and they lived across the street from each other, Mom and Isabel decided to form a mothers' group. A mothers' group is when a bunch of moms hang out together and have playdates with other kids' moms. There were about six or seven other moms in the mothers' group at first. They hung out together a couple of times before any of the babies were born. But after Auggie was born, only two other moms stayed in the mothers' group: Zachary's mom and Alex's mom. I don't know what happened to the other moms in the group.

Those first couple of years, the four moms in the mothers' group—along with us babies—hung out together almost every day. The moms would go jogging through the park with us in our strollers. They would take long walks along the riverfront with us in our baby slings. They would have lunch at the Heights Lounge with us in our baby chairs.

The only times Auggie and his mom didn't hang out with the mothers' group was when Auggie was back in the hospital. He needed a lot of operations, because, just like with breathing and swallowing, there were other things that didn't come automatically to him. For instance, he couldn't eat. He couldn't talk. He couldn't really even close his mouth all the way. These were things that the doctors had to operate on him so that he could do them. But even after the surgeries, Auggie never really ate or talked or closed his mouth all the way like me and Zack and Alex did. Even after the surgeries, Auggie was very different from us.

I don't think I really understood *how* different Auggie was from everyone else until I was four years old. It was wintertime, and Auggie and I were wrapped in our parkas and scarves while we played outside in the playground. At one point, we climbed up the ladder to the ramp at the top of the jungle gym and waited in line to go down the tall slide. When we were almost next, the little girl in front of us got cold feet about going down the tall slide, so she turned around to let us pass. That's when she saw Auggie. Her eyes opened really wide and her jaw dropped down, and she started screaming and crying hysterically. She was so upset, she couldn't even climb down the ladder. Her mom had to climb up the ramp to get her. Then Auggie started to cry, because he knew the girl was crying because of him. He covered his face with his scarf so nobody could see him, and then his mom had to climb up the ramp to get him, too. I don't remember all the details, but I remember there was a big commotion. A little crowd had formed around the slide. People were whispering. I remember us leaving the playground very quickly. I remember seeing tears in Isabel's eyes as she carried Auggie home.

That was the first time I realized how different Auggie was from the rest of us. It wasn't the last time, though. Like breathing and swallowing, crying comes automatically to most kids, too.

7:08 a.m.

I don't know why I was thinking about Auggie this morning. It's been three years since we moved away, and I haven't even seen him since his bowling party in October. Maybe I'd had a dream about him. I don't know. But I was thinking about him when Mom came into my room a few minutes after I turned off my alarm clock.

"You awake, sweetie?" she said softly.

I pulled my pillow over my head as an answer.

"Time to wake up, Chris," she said cheerfully, opening the curtains of my window. Even under my pillow with my eyes closed, I could tell my room was way too bright now.

"Close the curtains!" I mumbled.

"Looks like it's going to rain all day today," she sighed, not closing the curtains. "Come on, you don't want to be late again today. And you have to take a shower this morning."

"I took a shower, like, two days ago."

"Exactly!"

"Ugh!" I groaned.

"Let's go, honeyboy," she said, patting the top of my pillow.

I pulled the pillow off my face. "Okay!" I yelled. "I'm up! Are you happy?"

"You're such a grump in the morning," she said, shaking her head. "What happened to my sweet fourth grader from last year?"

"Lisa!" I answered.

She hated when I called her by her first name. I thought she'd leave my room then, but she started picking some clothes off my floor and putting them in my hamper.

"Did something happen last night, by the way?" I said, my eyes still closed. "I heard you on the phone with Isabel when I was going to sleep last night. It sounded like something bad . . ."

She sat down on the edge of my bed. I rubbed my eyes awake.

"What?" I said. "Is it really bad? I think I had a dream about Auggie last night."

"No, Auggie's fine," she answered, scrunching up her face a bit. She pushed some hair out of my eyes. "I was going to wait till later to—"

"What!" I interrupted.

"I'm afraid Daisy died last night, sweetie."

"What?"

"I'm sorry, honey."

"Daisy!" I covered my face with my hands.

"I'm sorry, sweetie. I know how much you loved Daisy."

Darth Daisy

I remember the day Auggie's dad brought Daisy home for the first time. Auggie and I were playing Trouble in his room when, all of a sudden, we heard high-pitched squealing coming from the front door. It was Via, Auggie's big sister. We could also hear Isabel and Lourdes, my babysitter, talking excitedly. So we ran downstairs to see what the commotion was about.

Nate, Auggie's dad, was sitting on one of the kitchen chairs, holding a squirming, crazy yellow dog in his lap. Via was kneeling down in front of the dog, trying to pet it, but the dog was kind of hyper and kept trying to lick her hand, which Via kept pulling away.

"A dog!" Auggie screamed excitedly, running over to his dad.

I ran over, too, but Lourdes grabbed me by the arm.

"Oh no, *papi*," she said to me. She had just started babysitting me in those days, so I didn't know her very well. I remember she used to put baby powder in my

125

sneakers, which I still do now because it reminds me of her.

Isabel's hands were on the sides of her face. It was obvious that Nate had just come through the door. "I can't believe you did this, Nate," she was saying over and over again. She was standing on the other side of the room next to Lourdes.

"Why can't I pet him?" I asked Lourdes.

"Because Nate says three hours ago this dog lived on the street with a homeless man," she answered quickly. "Is disgusting."

"She's not disgusting—she's beautiful!" said Via, kissing the dog on her forehead.

"In my country, dogs stay outside," said Lourdes.

"He's so cute!" Auggie said.

"It's a *she*!" Via said quickly, nudging Auggie.

"Be careful, Auggie!" said Isabel. "Don't let her lick you in the face."

But the dog was already licking Auggie all over his face.

"The vet said she's perfectly healthy, guys," Nate said to both Isabel and Lourdes.

"Nate, she was living on the street!" Isabel answered quickly. "Who knows what she's carrying."

"The vet gave her all her shots, a tick bath, checked for worms," answered Nate. "This puppy's got a clean bill of health."

"That is *not* a puppy, Nate!" Isabel pointed out.

126

That was true: The dog was definitely not a puppy. She wasn't little, or soft and round, like puppies usually are. She was skinny and pointy and wild-eyed, and she had this crazy, long black tongue kind of pouring out of the side of her mouth. And she wasn't a small dog, either. She was the same size as my grandmother's labradoodle.

"Okay," said Nate. "Well, she's puppy*like*."

"What kind of dog is she?" asked Auggie.

"The vet thinks a yellow lab mix," answered Nate. "Maybe some chow?"

"More like pit bull," said Isabel. "Did he at least tell you how old she is?"

Nate shrugged. "He couldn't tell for sure," he answered. "Two or three? Usually they judge from the teeth, but hers are in bad shape because, you know, she's probably been eating junk food all her life."

"Garbage and dead rats," Lourdes said, like it was for sure.

"Oh God!" Isabel muttered, rubbing her hand over her face.

"Her breath does smell pretty bad," said Via, waving her hand in front of her nose.

"Isabel," said Nate, looking up at her. "She was destined for us."

"Wait, you mean we're *keeping* her?" Via said excitedly, her eyes opening up really wide. "I thought we were just babysitting her until we could find her a home!"

"I think *we* should be her home," said Nate.

"Really, Daddy?" cried Auggie.

Nate smiled and pointed his chin at Isabel. "But it's up to Mommy, guys," he said.

"Are you kidding me, Nate?" cried Isabel as Via and Auggie ran over to her and started pleading with her, putting their hands together, like they were praying in church.

"Please please please please please please please please?" they kept saying over and over again. "Please pretty please please please please?"

"I can't believe you're doing this to me, Nate!" said Isabel, shaking her head. "Like our lives aren't complicated enough?"

Nate smiled and looked down at the dog, who was looking at him. "Look at her, honey! She was starving and cold. The homeless guy offered to sell her to me for ten bucks. What was I going to do, say no?"

"Yes!" said Lourdes. "Very easy to do."

"It's good karma to save a dog's life!" answered Nate.

"Don't do it, Isabel!" said Lourdes. "Dogs are dirty, and smelly. And they have germs. And you know who will end up walking her all the time, picking up all the poo-poo?" She pointed at Isabel.

"That's not true, Mommy!" said Via. "I promise I'll walk her. Every day."

"Me too, Mommy!" said Auggie.

"We'll take care of her completely," continued Via. "We'll feed her. We'll do everything."

"Everything!" added Auggie. "Please please please, Mommy?"

"Please please please, Mommy?" Via said at the same time.

Isabel was rubbing her forehead with her fingers, like she had a headache. Finally she looked at Nate and shrugged. "I think this is crazy, but . . . Okay. Fine."

"Really?" shrieked Via, hugging Isabel tightly. "Thank you, Mommy! Thank you so much! I promise we'll take care of her."

"Thank you, Mommy!" repeated Auggie, hugging Isabel.

"Yay! Thank you, Isabel!" said Nate, clapping the dog's two front paws together.

"Can I please pet her now?" I said to Lourdes, pulling away from her grip before she could stop me again. I slid over between Auggie and Via.

Nate put the dog down on the rug then, and she literally turned over onto her back so that we would all scratch her tummy. She closed her eyes like she was smiling, her long black tongue hanging from the side of her mouth onto the rug.

"That's exactly how I found her today," Nate pointed out.

"I've never seen a longer tongue in my life," said Isabel, crouching down next to us. She still hadn't pet the dog yet, though. "She looks like the Tasmanian Devil."

"I think she's beautiful," said Via. "What's her name?"

"What do you want to name her?" asked Nate.

"I think we should name her Daisy!" answered Via without any hesitation at all. "She's yellow, like a daisy."

"That's a nice name," said Isabel, who started petting the dog. "Then again, she looks a little like a lion. We could call her Elsa."

"I know what you should name her," I said, nudging Auggie. "You should call her Darth Maul!"

"That is the stupidest name in the world for a dog!" Via answered, disgusted.

I ignored her. "Do you get it, Auggie? Darth . . . *maul*? Get it? Because dogs maul . . ."

"Ha ha!" Auggie said. "That's so funny! Darth *Maul*!"

"We're not calling her that!" Via said snottily to the two of us.

"Hi, Darth Maul!" Auggie said to the dog, kissing her on her pink nose. "We can call her Darth for short."

Via looked at Nate. "Daddy, we're not calling her that!"

"I think it's kind of a fun name," Nate answered, shrugging.

"Mommy!" Via said angrily, turning to Isabel.

130

"I agree with Via," said Isabel. "I don't think we should use the word 'maul' for a dog . . . especially one that looks like this one."

"Then we'll just name her Darth," Auggie insisted.

"That's idiotic," said Via.

"I think, since Mommy's letting us keep the dog," answered Nate, "she should be the one who decides what to name her."

"Can we call her Daisy, Mommy?" asked Via.

"Can we call her Darth Maul?" asked Auggie.

Isabel gave Nate a look. "You really are killing me, Nate."

Nate laughed.

And that was how they ended up calling her Darth Daisy.

7:11 a.m.

"How did she die?" I asked Mom. "Was she hit by a car?"

"No." She stroked my arm. "She was old, sweetie. It was her time."

"She wasn't that old."

"She was sick."

"What, so they put her to sleep?" I asked, incensed. "How could they do that?"

"Sweetie, she was in pain," she answered. "They didn't want her to suffer. Isabel said that she died very peacefully in Nate's arms."

I tried to picture what that would look like, Daisy dying in Nate's arms. I wondered if Auggie had been there, too.

"As if that family hasn't been through enough already," Mom added.

I didn't say anything. I just blinked and looked up at the glow-in-the-dark stars on my ceiling. Some of them were coming unstuck, hanging on by just one or two points. A few had fallen down on me, like little pointy raindrops.

"You never fixed the stars, by the way," I said without thinking.

She had no idea what I was talking about. "What?"

"You said you were going to glue them back on," I said, pointing to the ceiling. "They keep falling down on me."

She looked up. "Oh, right," she said, nodding. I think she hadn't expected the conversation about Daisy to be over so quickly. But I didn't want to talk about it anymore.

She got up on top of my bed, took one of the lightsabers leaning on my bookcase, and tried to jam one of the larger stars back into place with the end of the lightsaber.

"They need to be glued, Lisa," I said just as the plastic star fell down on her head.

"Right," she answered, picking the star out of her hair. She jumped down off my bed. "Can you not call me Lisa, please?"

"Okay, Lisa," I answered.

She rolled her eyes and pointed the lightsaber at me, like she was going to jab me.

"Thanks for waking me up with really bad news, by the way," I said sarcastically.

"Hey, you're the one who asked me about it," she

answered, putting the lightsaber back. "I was going to wait until this afternoon to tell you."

"Why? I'm not a baby, Lisa," I answered. "I mean, sure, I love Daisy, but it's not like she was my dog. It's not like I see her anymore."

"I thought you'd be really upset," she answered.

"I am!" I said. "I'm just not, like, going to start crying or anything."

"Okay," she answered, nodding and looking at me.

"What?" I said impatiently.

"Nothing," she answered. "You're right, you're not a baby." She looked at the plastic star that was still stuck on her thumb and then, without saying anything else, leaned down and stuck it on my forehead. "You should call Auggie this afternoon, by the way."

"Why?" I asked.

"Why?" She raised her eyebrows. "To tell him how sorry you are about Daisy. To pay your condolences. Because he's your best friend."

"Oh, right," I mumbled, nodding.

"Oh, right," she repeated.

"Okay, Lisa. I get it!" I said.

"Grumpity grump grump," she said on her way out. "You have three minutes, Chris. Then you've got to get up. I'll turn on the shower for you."

"Close the door behind you!" I called out after her.

"Please!" she yelled from the hallway.

"Close the door behind you, PLEASE!" I groaned.

134

She slammed the door shut.

She could be so annoying sometimes!

I picked the star off my forehead and looked at it. Mom had put those stars on the ceiling when we first moved in. That was back when she was trying to do everything she could to get me to like our new house in Bridgeport. She had even promised that we would get a dog after we got settled in. But we never got a dog. We got a hamster. But that's hardly a dog. That's not even one quarter of a dog. A hamster is basically just a warm potato with fur. I mean, it moves and it's cute and all, but don't let anyone try to fool you that it's the same as a dog. I called my hamster Luke. But he's no Daisy.

Poor Daisy! It was hard to believe she was gone.

But I didn't want to think about her now.

I started thinking of all the things I had to do this afternoon. Band practice right after school. Study for the math test tomorrow. Start my book report for Friday. Play some *Halo*. Maybe catch up on *The Amazing Race* tonight.

I flicked the plastic star in the air and watched it spin across the room. It landed on the edge of my rug by the door.

Lots of stuff to do. It was going to be a long day.

But even as I was ticking off all the things I had to do today, I knew calling Auggie wasn't going to be one of them.

Friendships

I don't remember exactly when Zack and Alex stopped hanging out with me and Auggie. I think it was about the time we started kindergarten.

Before that, we all used to see each other almost every day. Our moms would usually bring us over to Auggie's house, since there were a lot of times when he couldn't go out because he was sick. Not a contagious kind of sick or anything, but the kind where he couldn't go outside. But we liked going to his house. His parents had turned their basement into a giant playroom. So, basically, it was like a toy store down there. Board games, train sets, air hockey and foosball tables, even a mini trampoline in the back. Zack and Alex and Auggie and I would literally spend hours running around down there, having all-day lightsaber duels and hop ball races. We would have balloon wars. We would pile cardboard bricks into giant mountains and play avalanche. Our moms called us the Four Musketeers, since we did everything together. And even after all the moms—except

136

Isabel—went back to work, our babysitters got us together every day. They would take us on day trips to the Bronx Zoo, or to see the pirate ships at the South Street Seaport. We'd have picnics in the park. We even went all the way down to Coney Island a few times.

But once we started kindergarten, Zack and Alex started having playdates with other kids. They went to a different school than I did, since they lived on the other side of the park, so we didn't see them as much anymore. Auggie and I would bump into them in the park sometimes—Zack and Alex, hanging out with their new buddies—and we tried hanging out with them a couple of times. But their new friends didn't seem to like us. Okay, that's not exactly true. Their new friends didn't like *Auggie*. I know that for a fact, because Zack told me this. I remember telling this to my mom, and she explained that some kids might feel "uncomfortable" around Auggie because of the way he looks. That's how she put it. Uncomfortable. That's not how Zack and Alex had put it, though. They used the word "scared."

But I knew that Zack and Alex weren't uncomfortable or scared of Auggie, so I didn't understand why *they* stopped hanging out with us. I mean, I had new friends from my school, too, but I didn't stop hanging out with Auggie. Then again, I never hung out with Auggie and my new friends together, because, well, mixing friends can be a weird thing even under the best circumstances.

I guess the truth is, I didn't want anyone to feel uncomfortable or scared, either.

Auggie had his own group of friends, too, by the way. These were kids who belonged to an organization for kids with "craniofacial differences," which is what Auggie has. Every year, all the kids and their families hang out together at Disneyland or some other fun place like that. Auggie loved going on these trips. He'd made friends all over the country. But these friends didn't live near us, so he hardly ever got to hang out with them.

I did meet one of his friends once, though. A kid named Hudson. He had a different syndrome than Auggie has. His eyes were spaced very far apart, and they kind of bulged out a bit. He and his parents were staying with Auggie's family for a couple of days while they were in the city meeting with doctors at Auggie's hospital. Hudson was the same age as me and Auggie. He was really into Pokémon, I remember.

Anyway, I had an okay time playing with him and Auggie that day, though Pokémon has never really been my thing. But then we all went out to dinner together—and that's when things got bad for me. I can't believe how much we got stared at! Like, usually when it was just me and Auggie, people would look at him and not even notice me. I was used to that. But with Hudson there, for some reason, it was just so much worse. People would look at Auggie first, and then they'd look at Hudson, and then they'd automatically look at me like they were wondering what was wrong with me, too. I saw one teenager staring at me like he was trying to figure out what was out of place on my face. It was so annoying! It made me want to scream. I couldn't wait to go home.

The next day, since I knew Hudson was still going to be there, I asked Lourdes if I could have a playdate over at Zack's house after school instead of going to Auggie's house. It's not that I didn't like Hudson, because I did. But I wasn't into Pokémon, and I definitely didn't want to get stared at again if we all went out somewhere.

I ended up having lots of fun at Zack's house. Alex came over, and the three of us played Four Square in front of his stoop. It really felt like old times again— except for the fact that Auggie wasn't there with us. But it was nice. No one stared at us. No one felt uncomfortable. No one got scared. Hanging out with Zack and Alex was just easy. That's when I realized why they didn't hang out with us anymore. Being friends with Auggie could be hard sometimes.

Luckily, Auggie never asked me why I didn't come over to his house that day. I was glad about that. I didn't know how to tell him that being friends with him could be hard for me sometimes, too.

8:25 a.m.

I don't know why, but it's almost impossible for me to get to school on time. Honestly, I don't know why. Every day, it's the same thing. I sleep through my alarm. Mom or Dad wakes me up. Whether I take a shower or not, whether I have a big breakfast or a Pop-Tart, we end up scrambling before we leave, Mom or Dad yelling at me to hurry up and get my coat, hurry up and tie my shoe-laces. And even in those rare moments when we do get out the door on time, I'll forget something, so we end up having to turn back anyway. Sometimes it's my home-work folder I forget. Sometimes it's my trombone. I don't know why, I really don't. It's just the way it is. Whether I'm sleeping at my mom's house or my dad's house, I'm always running late.

Today, I took a quick shower, got dressed super fast, popped my Pop-Tart, and managed to get out the door on time. It wasn't until we had driven the fifteen minutes it takes to get to school and had pulled into the school parking lot that I realized I had forgotten my science paper, my gym shorts, *and* my trombone. A new record for forgetting things.

"You're kidding, right?" said Mom when I told her. She was looking at me in the rearview mirror.

"No!" I said, biting my nails nervously. "Can we go back?"

"Chris, you're already running late! In this rain, it'll take forty minutes by the time we get home and back. No. You go to class, and I'll write you a note or something."

"I can't show up without my science paper!" I argued. "I have science first period!"

"You should have thought of that before you left the house this morning!" she answered. "Now come on, get out or you'll be late on top of everything. Look, even the school buses are leaving!" She pointed to where the school buses had started driving out of the parking lot.

"Lisa!" I said, panicked.

"What, Chris?" she shot back. "What do you want me to do? I can't teleport."

"Can't you go home and get them for me?"

She passed her fingers through her hair, which had gotten wet from the rain. "How many times have I told you to pack up your stuff the night before so you don't forget anything, huh?"

"Lisa!"

"Fine," she said. "Just go to class, and I'll bring you your stuff. Now go, Chris."

"But you have to hurry!"

"Go!" She turned around and gave me that look she gives me sometimes, when her eyeballs get super big and she kind of looks like an angry bird. "Get out of the car and go to school already!"

"Fine!" I said. I stomped out of the car. It had started raining harder, and of course I didn't have an umbrella.

She lowered the driver's side window. "Be careful walking to the sidewalk!"

"Trombone, science paper, gym shorts," I said to her, counting on my fingers.

"Careful where you're walking," she said, nodding. "This is a parking lot, Chris!"

"Mrs. Kastor will deduct five points off my grade if I don't hand my paper in by the end of first period!" I answered. "You have to be back before first period ends!"

"I know, Chris," she answered quickly. "Now walk to the sidewalk, sweetie."

"Trombone, science paper, gym shorts!" I said, walking backward toward the sidewalk.

"Watch where you're walking, Chris!" she shrieked just as a bike swerved around to avoid hitting me.

"Sorry!" I said to the bicyclist, who had a baby bundled up in the front bike carrier. The guy shook his head and pedaled away.

"Chris! You have to watch where you're going!" Mom screamed.

"Will you stop yelling?" I yelled.

She took a deep breath and rubbed her forehead. "Walk. To. The. Sidewalk. PLEASE." This she said through gritted teeth.

I turned around, looked both ways in an exaggerated way, and crossed the parking lot to the path leading to the school entrance. By now, the last of the school buses was pulling out of the parking lot.

"Happy now?" I said when I reached the sidewalk.

I could hear her sighing from twenty feet away. "I'll leave your stuff at the front desk in the main office," she answered, turning on the ignition and looking behind her as she started slowly backing out of the parking space. "Bye, honey. Have a nice—"

"Wait!" I ran over to the car while it was still moving.

The car screeched to a stop. "Chris!"

"I forgot my backpack," I said, opening the car door to get the backpack that I had left on the backseat. I could see her shaking her head out of the corner of my eye.

I closed the door, looked both ways in a super-obvious way again, and sprinted back toward the sidewalk. By now, the rain was coming down really hard. I pulled my hood over my head.

"Trombone! Science paper! Gym shorts!" I shouted, not looking back at her. I started jogging up the side-walk to the school entrance.

"Love you!" I heard her call out.
"Bye, Lisa!"
I made it inside just before first bell rang.

9:14 a.m.

I kept looking at the clock all through science class. Then, about ten minutes before the bell, I asked for the bathroom pass. I ran over to the main office as fast as I could and asked Ms. Denis, the nice old lady behind the main desk, for the stuff my mother had dropped off.

"Sorry, Christopher," she said. "Your mother hasn't dropped anything off."

"What?" I said.

"Was she supposed to come at a certain time?" she asked, looking at her watch. "I've been here all morning. I'm sure I haven't missed her."

She must have seen the expression on my face, because she waved me to come to the other side of her desk. She pointed to the phone. "Why don't you give her a call, honey?"

I called Mom's cell phone and got her voice mail.

"Hi, Mom. It's me and . . . um, you're not here and it's . . ." I looked at the big clock on the wall. "It's nine-fourteen. I'm totally screwed if you don't show up in the next ten minutes, so, yeah. Thanks a lot, Lisa."

I hung up.

"I'm sure she'll be here any minute now," said Ms. Denis. "There's a lot of traffic on the highway because of all the construction. And it's really pouring outside now . . ."

"Yeah." I nodded and headed back to class.

At first, I thought maybe I'd gotten lucky. Mrs. Kastor didn't mention anything about the paper for the rest of the class. Then, just as the bell rang, she reminded us to drop off our science papers at her desk on the way out.

I waited until everyone else had left and walked over to her at the whiteboard.

"Um, Mrs. Kastor?" I said.

"Yes, Christopher?"

"Yeah, um, sorry, but I left my science paper at home this morning?"

She continued erasing the whiteboard.

"My mom's bringing it to school, but she got caught in the rain?" I said.

I don't know why, but when I talk to teachers and get a little nervous, my voice goes up at the end of every sentence.

"That's the fourth time this semester you've forgotten an assignment, Christopher," she said.

"I know," I answered. Then I raised my shoulders and smiled. "But I didn't know *you* knew! Ha."

She didn't even crack a smile at my attempt at humor.

"I just meant I didn't know you were keeping track . . ." I started to say.

"It's five points off, Chris," she said.

"Even if I get it to you next period?" I know I sounded whiny at this point.

"Rules are rules."

"So unfair," I muttered under my breath, shaking my head.

The second bell rang, and I ran to my next class before she could respond.

10:05 a.m.

Mr. Wren, my music teacher, was just as annoyed at me for forgetting my trombone as Mrs. Kastor had been about my science paper. For one thing, I had told Mr. Wren that Katie McAnn, the first trombonist, could take my trombone home today to practice her solo for the spring concert on Wednesday night. Katie's trombone was getting repaired, and the only other spare trombone was so banged up, you couldn't even push the slide past fourth position. So not only was Mr. Wren angry, but Katie was, too. And Katie is the kind of girl you don't want getting mad at you. She's a head taller than everyone else, and she gives really scary dirty looks to people she's mad at.

Anyway, I told Katie that my mom was on her way back to school with my trombone, so she didn't give me the dirty look right away. Mr. Wren gave her the dented trombone to use during class, so she didn't even have to sit out of music. When people forget their instruments, Mr. Wren usually makes them sit quietly off to the side and watch the orchestra rehearse. You're not allowed to read anything, or do homework. You just have to sit and listen to the orchestra rehearse. Not exactly the most thrilling experience in the world. I, of course, did have to sit music out today, since there was no trombone left for me to play.

During break, I ran over to the main office to pick up the stuff Mom should have dropped off by now. But she still hadn't shown up.

"I'm sure she just got stuck in traffic," offered Ms. Denis.

I shook my head. "No, I think I know what happened," I answered grumpily.

It had occurred to me while I was watching the band rehearse.

Isabel.

Duh, of course! Daisy just died. Something else must have happened. Maybe something to do with Auggie. And Isabel called Mom. And Mom, like she always does, dropped whatever she was doing to go help the Pullmans.

For all I knew, she was probably at the Pullman house right now! I bet she'd been on her way back to school with my trombone, science paper, and gym shorts on the backseat of the car when Isabel called, and bam, Mom completely forgot about me. Duh, of course that's what happened! It wouldn't be the first time, either.

"You want to call her again?" said Ms. Denis sweetly, handing me the phone.

"No thanks," I mumbled.

Katie came over to me when I got back to music class.

"Where's the trombone?" she said. Her eyebrows were practically touching in the middle of her forehead. "You said your mom was bringing it!"

"She's stuck in traffic?" I said apologetically. "She'll have it when she picks me up from school today, though?" I guess Katie made me as nervous as teachers did. "Can you meet me after school at five-thirty?"

"Why would I want to wait around till five-thirty?" she answered, making a clucking sound with her tongue. She gave me the same look she gave me when I accidentally emptied my spit valve in her Dixie cup a few weeks ago. "Gee, thanks, Chris! Now I'm going to totally mess up my solo at the spring concert. And it's totally going to be your fault!"

"It's not my fault?" I said. "My mother was supposed to bring me my stuff?"

"You're such a . . . moron," she mumbled.

"No, you are" was my brilliant comeback.

"Your ears stick out." She made both her hands into little fists and walked away with her arms straight at her sides.

"Ugh!" I answered her, rolling my eyes.

And for the rest of the class, she shot me the dirtiest looks you can imagine over her music stand. If looks really could kill, Katie McAnn would be a serial murderer.

All of this could have been avoided if Mom hadn't abandoned me today! I was so mad at her for that. Boy, was she going to be sorry tonight. I could picture it already, how she would pick me up after school and be all, "I'm so sorry, honey! I had to drive over to the Pullmans', because they needed help with yadda yadda yadda."

And I would be like, "Yadda yadda yadda."

And she would be like, "Come on, honey. You know they need our help sometimes."

"Yadda! Yadda! Yadda!"

Space

When Auggie turned five, someone gave him an astronaut helmet as a birthday present. I don't remember who. But Auggie started wearing that helmet all the time. Everywhere. Every day. I know people thought it was because he wanted to cover his face—and maybe part of it *was* that. But I think it was more because Auggie really loved outer space. Stars and planets. Black holes. Anything to do with the *Apollo* missions. He started telling everyone he was going to be an astronaut when he grew up. In the beginning, I didn't get why he was so obsessed with this stuff. But then one weekend, our moms took us to the planetarium at the natural history museum—and that's when I got sucked into it, too. That was the beginning of what we called our space phase.

Auggie and I had gone through a lot of phases by then. ZoobiePlushies. PopBopBots. Dinosaurs. Ninjas. Power Rangers (I'm embarrassed to say). But, until then, nothing had been as intense as our space phase. We watched every DVD we could find about the universe. Space videos. Picture books about the Milky Way. Making 3-D solar systems. Building model rocket ships. We would spend hours playing pretend games about missions to deep space, or landing on Pluto. That became our favorite planet to travel to. Pluto was our Tatooine.

We were still deep into our space phase when my sixth birthday rolled around, so my parents decided to have my party at the planetarium. Auggie and I were so excited! The new space show had just come out, and we hadn't seen it yet. I invited my entire first-grade class. And Zack and Alex, of course. I even invited Via, but she couldn't come because she had a different birthday party to go to that same day.

But then, the morning of my birthday, Isabel called Mom and told her that she and Nate had to take Auggie to the hospital. He had woken up with a high fever, and his eyelids were swollen shut. A few days before, he had had a "minor" surgery to correct a previous surgery to make his lower eyelids less droopy, and now it had become infected. So Auggie had to go to the hospital instead of going to my sixth birthday party.

I was so bummed! But I got even more bummed when Mom told me that Isabel had asked her if she would be able to drop Via off at the other birthday party before going to my party.

Before even checking with me first, Mom had said,

"Yes, of course, whatever we can do to help!" Even though that meant that she might end up being a little late to *my* birthday party!

"But why can't Nate drop Via off at the other party?" I asked Mom.

"Because he's driving Auggie to the hospital, along with Isabel," Mom answered. "It's not a big deal, Chris. I'll take Via in a taxi and then hop on a train."

"But can't someone else take Via? Why does it have to be you?"

"Isabel doesn't have the time to start calling other moms, Chris! So if we don't take Via, she'll have to just go with them to the hospital. Poor Via is always missing out—"

"Mommy!" I interrupted. "I don't care about Via! I don't want you to be late to my birthday party!"

"Chris, what do you want me to say?" Mom answered. "They're our friends. Isabel is my good friend, just like Auggie is your good friend. And when good friends need us, we do what we can to help them, right? We can't just be friends when it's convenient. Good friendships are worth a little extra effort!"

When I didn't say anything, she kissed my hand.

"I promise I'll only be a few minutes late," she said.

But she wasn't just a few minutes late. She ended up being more than an hour late.

"I'm so sorry, honey . . . The A train was out of service . . . No taxis anywhere . . . So sorry . . ."

I knew she felt terrible. But I was so angry. I remember even Dad was annoyed.

She was so late, she even missed the space show.

3:50 p.m.

The rest of the day ended up being pretty much as bad as the beginning of the day. I had to sit out of gym, because I didn't have my gym shorts and I didn't have a spare set in my locker. Katie McAnn's entire table kept shooting me dirty looks at lunch. I don't even remember my other classes. Then math was the last class of the day. I knew we were having a big math test tomorrow, which I hadn't studied for over the weekend like I was supposed to. But it wasn't until Ms. Medina started going over the material for tomorrow's test that I realized I was in deep trouble. I didn't understand what the heck we were doing. I mean, seriously, it was like Ms. Medina was suddenly talking in a made-up language that everyone else in class seemed to understand but me. *Gadda badda quotient. Patta beeboo divisor.* At the end of class, she offered to meet with any kids who needed a little extra help studying right after school. *Um, that would be me, thank you!* But I had band practice then, so I couldn't go.

I raced down to the auditorium right after dismissal. The after-school rock band meets every Monday and Tuesday afternoon. I had only joined a few months ago, at the beginning of the spring semester, but I was really into it. I'd been taking guitar lessons since last summer, and my dad, who's a really good guitar player, had been teaching me all these great guitar licks. So when *Santa* gave me an electric guitar for Christmas, I figured I was ready to join the after-school rock band. I was a little nervous in the beginning. I knew the three guys who were already in the band were really good musicians. But then I found out there was a fourth grader named John who was also joining the band in the spring semester, so I knew I wouldn't be the only new kid. John played guitar, too. He wore John Lennon glasses.

The other three guys in the band were Ennio, who plays the drums and is considered to be this prodigy drummer, Harry on lead guitar, and Elijah on bass guitar. Elijah's also the lead singer, and he's kind of the leader of the band. The three of them are all in the sixth grade. They've been in the after-school rock band since they were in the fourth grade, so they're a pretty tight group.

I can't say they were thrilled when John and I first joined the band. Not that they weren't *nice*, but they weren't *nice* nice. They didn't treat us like we were equal members of the band. It was pretty obvious that they didn't think we played as well as they did—and, to be truthful, we really didn't. But still, we were trying really hard to get better.

"So, Mr. B," Elijah said after we had all jammed on our own a bit. "We're thinking we want to play 'Seven Nation Army' for the spring concert on Wednesday."

Mr. Bowles was the after-school rock band adviser. He had gray hair that he kept in a ponytail, and had been a member of a famous folk-rock band in the '80s that my dad, for one, had never heard of. But Mr. Bowles was super nice, and he was always trying to get the other guys to include me and John. This, of course, just got the other guys even more annoyed at us. And it also made them really dislike Mr. Bowles. They made fun of the way he sometimes talked with his eyes closed. They made fun of his ponytail and his taste in music.

"'Seven Nation Army'?" answered Mr. Bowles, like he was impressed by the song choice. "That's an awesome song, Elijah."

"Is that by Europe, too?" John asked, since we'd all agreed a few weeks ago—after much arguing—to play "The Final Countdown" by Europe at the spring concert.

Elijah snickered and made a face. "Dude," he answered, not looking at John or me. "It's the White Stripes."

Elijah had long blond hair that he was really good at talking through.

"Never heard of them!" John said cheerfully, which I

158

wished he hadn't said. Truth is, I hadn't heard of them, either, but I knew enough to pretend I knew them—at least until I could download the song tonight. John wasn't so great at the social stuff that goes on inside a rock band. Lots of group dynamic stuff to sort out. You have to kind of just nod and go along if you want to fit in. Then again, John wasn't very good at fitting in that way.

Elijah laughed and turned around to tune his guitar.

John looked at me over his little round glasses and made an "Is it me, or are they crazy?" face.

I shrugged in response.

John and I had become our own little group inside this rock band. We hung out together during breaks and made jokes, especially since the other three guys hung out together and made their own jokes. Every Thursday after school, I'd go over to John's house and we'd practice together, or we'd listen to some classic rock songs so we could sound like we knew as much about rock music as the other guys. And then we'd make suggestions about what songs we could play. So far, we had suggested "Yellow Submarine" and "Eye of the Tiger." But Elijah, Harry, and Ennio had nixed them both.

That was fine, though, because I was really into "The Final Countdown," which had been Mr. Bowles's suggestion. *It's the final countdown!*

"I don't know, guys," Mr. Bowles said. "I'm not sure there's going to be enough time between today and

Wednesday to learn a brand-new song. Maybe we should stick to 'The Final Countdown' for now?" He played the opening notes of that song on the keyboard, and John started bopping his head.

Then Elijah started playing a great riff on his bass, which turned out to be the opening of "Seven Nation Army." As if on cue, Harry and Ennio started playing, too. It was pretty obvious that they had practiced the song a lot of times before today. I have to say, they sounded amazing.

Somewhere in the second chorus, Mr. Bowles put his hand up for them to stop jamming.

"Okay, dudes," he said, nodding. "You're sounding absolutely awesome. Killer bass, Elijah. But everyone's got to be able to play the song for the spring concert, right? These two dudes need a chance to learn the song, too." He pointed at me and John.

"But it's just basic chords!" said Elijah. "Like C and G! B. D. You do know D, right?" He looked at us like we were an alien species. "You seriously can't do that?"

"I can do that," I answered quickly, forming the chords with my fingers.

"I hate the B chord!" said John.

"It's so easy!" said Elijah.

"But what about 'The Final Countdown'?" John whined. "I've been practicing that for weeks!"

He started playing the same opening part that Mr. B had just played, but he honestly didn't sound that good.

"Dude, that was awesome!" said Mr. B, high-fiving John.

I noticed Elijah smiled at Harry, who looked down like he was trying not to laugh.

"Guys, we have to be fair here," said Mr. B to Elijah.

"Here's the thing," answered Elijah. "We can only play one song at the spring concert, and we want it to be 'Seven Nation Army.' Majority rules."

"But it's not what we *said* we were going to play!" yelled John. "It's not fair that you guys agreed to play 'The Final Countdown,' and me and Chris have spent a lot of time learning it . . ."

I have to admit, John had guts talking back to a sixth grader like that.

"Sorry, dude," said Elijah, fiddling with his amp. But he didn't seem sorry.

"Okay, let's settle down, guys," said Mr. B with his eyes closed.

"Mr. B?" said Ennio, holding up his hand like he was in class. "The thing is, this is going to be our last spring concert before the three of us graduate." He pointed his drumstick at Harry and Elijah and himself.

"Yeah, we're going to middle school next year!" agreed Elijah.

"We want to play a song that we feel really good about," Ennio finished. "'The Final Countdown' doesn't represent us musically."

"But that's not fair!" said John. "This is an after-*school* rock band. Not just *your* band! You can't just do that!"

"Dude, you can play whatever you want next year," Elijah answered. He looked like he wanted to flick John's glasses off his face. "You can play 'Puff the Magic Dragon' for all I care."

This made the other guys laugh.

Mr. Bowles finally opened his eyes. "Okay, guys, enough," he said, holding up his hands. "Here's what we're going to do. Let's see how well you two pick up 'Seven Nation Army' today and tomorrow." He said this while pointing at me and John. "We'll practice it a little today. We'll also tighten up 'The Final Countdown.' Then, tomorrow, we'll see which song sounds better. But I'm going to be the one to make the final decision which song we play, okay? Sound good?"

John nodded yes eagerly, but Elijah rolled his eyes.

"So, let's start with 'The Final Countdown,'" said Mr. Bowles. He clapped his hands twice. "From the beginning. Let's go, guys. 'The Final Countdown'! From the top. Ennio, wake up! Harry! Elijah, get us going, man! On four. A one. Two. Three . . ."

We played the song. Even though Elijah and the other guys weren't into it, they totally rocked it. In fact, we sounded pretty amazing together, I thought.

"That sounded awesome!" said John when it was over. He held his hand in the air to high-five me, which I did a little reluctantly.

"Whatever," said Elijah, shaking his hair off his face.

We spent the rest of the class running through "Seven Nation Army." But John kept making mistakes and asking us to start over. It didn't sound good at all.

"You guys sound terrific!" said John's mother, who had just come in the band room. She tried to clap while holding her wet umbrella.

Mr. B looked at his watch. "Whoa, it's five-thirty? Oh man! Dudes, I've got a gig tonight. We have to wrap this up. Let's go. Everything in the lock room."

I started putting my guitar in the case.

"Step on it, guys!" said Mr. B, putting the mics away.

We all hurried up and put our instruments in the lock room.

"See you tomorrow, Mr. B!" said John, who was the first to be ready to leave. "Bye, Elijah, bye, Ennio, bye, Harry!" He waved at them. "See you tomorrow!"

I saw the three of them shoot each other looks, but they nodded goodbye to John.

"Bye, Chris!" John said loudly from the door.

"Bye," I mumbled. I liked the guy, I really did. One on one he was awesome. But he could be so clueless, too. It was like being friends with SpongeBob.

After John and his mother had left, Elijah went up to Mr. Bowles, who was wrapping up the mic cords.

"Mr. B," he said, ultra politely. "Can we please play 'Seven Nation Army' on Wednesday night?"

At that moment, Ennio's mom arrived to pick up the three of them.

"We'll see tomorrow, dude," Mr. Bowles answered distractedly, throwing the last of the equipment into the lock room.

"Yeah, you're just gonna choose 'The Final Countdown,'" said Elijah, and then he walked out the door.

"Bye, guys," I said to Harry and Ennio as they followed Elijah out.

"Bye, dude," they both said to me.

Mr. B turned the key in the lock room. Then he looked at me, like he was surprised I was still there.

"Where's your mom?"

"I guess she's running late."

"Don't you have a cell phone?"

I nodded, fished my phone out of my backpack, and turned it on. There were no texts or missed calls from Mom.

"Just call her!" he said after a few minutes. "I've got to get out of here, dude."

5:48 p.m.

Just as I was about to call, my dad knocked on the band-room door. I was totally surprised. He's never picked me up from school on a Monday before.

"Dad!" I said.

He smiled and walked in. "Sorry I'm late," he said, shaking out his umbrella.

"This is Mr. Bowles," I said to him.

"Nice to meet you!" said Mr. B quickly, but he'd already started out the door. "Sorry, I can't stay and chat. You've got a nice kid there!" Then he left.

"Don't forget to lock the door behind you, Chris!" he yelled out a second later from down the hallway.

"I will!" I said, loud enough for him to hear me.

I turned to Dad. "What are you doing here?"

"Mom asked me to get you," he answered, picking up my backpack.

"Let me guess," I said sarcastically, putting on my jacket. "She went to Auggie's house today, right?"

Dad looked surprised. "No," he said. "Everything is

fine, Chris. Pull your hood up—it's raining hard." We started walking out the door.

"Then where is she? Why didn't she bring me my stuff?" I said angrily.

He put his hand on my shoulder as we kept walking. "I don't want you to worry at all, but . . . Mommy got in a little car accident today."

I stopped walking. "What?"

"She's totally fine," he said, squeezing my shoulder. "Nothing to worry about. Promise." He motioned for me to keep walking.

"So, where is she?" I asked.

"She's still in the hospital."

"Hospital?" I yelled. Once again, I stopped walking.

"Chris, she's fine, I promise," he answered, pulling me by the elbow. "She broke her leg, though. She has a huge cast."

"Seriously?"

"Yes." He held the exit door open for me while opening his umbrella. "Pull your hood up, Chris."

I pulled my hood over my head as we hurried across the parking lot. It was really pouring. "Was she hit by a car?"

"No, she was driving," he answered. "Apparently, the rain caused some flooding on the parkway, and a construction truck hit a ditch, and Mom swerved to avoid hitting it but then got sideswiped by the car in the left lane. The woman in the other car was fine, too. Mommy's fine. Her leg will be fine. Everyone is fine, thank God."

He stopped at a red hatchback I had never seen before.

"Is this new?" I said, confused.

"It's a rental," he answered quickly. "Mom's car got totaled. Come on, get in."

I got into the backseat. By now my sneakers were soaking wet. "Where's your car?"

"I went to the hospital straight from the train station," he answered.

"We should sue whoever was driving that construction truck," I said, putting my seat belt on.

"It was a freak accident," he muttered. He started driving out of the parking lot.

"When did it happen?" I asked.

"This morning."

"What time this morning?"

"I don't know. About nine? I had just gotten to work when they called me from the hospital."

"Wait, did the person who called you know that you and Mom are getting a divorce?"

He looked at me in the rearview mirror. "Chris," he said. "Your mom and I will always be there for one another. You know that."

"Right," I said, shrugging.

I looked out the window. It was that time of day when the sun's gone down but the streetlights haven't come on yet. The streets were black and shiny because of the rain. You could see the reflections of all the red and white lights of the cars in the puddles along the highway.

I pictured Mom driving in the rain this morning. Did it happen right after she dropped me off, or when she was driving back to school with my stuff?

"Why did you think she was on her way to Auggie's house?" Dad asked.

"I don't know," I answered, still looking out the window. "Because Daisy died. I thought maybe—"

"Daisy died?" he said. "Oh no, I didn't know that. When did that happen?"

"They put her to sleep last night."

"Had she been sick?"

"Dad, I don't know any details!"

"Okay, don't bite my head off."

"It's just . . . I wish you had told me about the accident earlier in the day! Someone should have told me."

Dad looked at me in the rearview mirror again. "There was no need to alarm you, Chris. Everything was under control. There was nothing you could have done anyway."

"I was waiting for Mom to come back with my stuff all morning!" I said, crossing my arms.

"It was a crazy day for all of us, Chris," he answered. "I spent the day dealing with accident reports and insurance forms, rental cars, going back and forth to the hospital . . ."

"I could have gone to the hospital with you," I said.

"Well, you're in luck," he said, drumming the steering wheel. "Because that's where we're going right now."

"Wait, we're going to the hospital?" I said.

"Mom just got discharged, so we're picking her up." He looked at me in the mirror again, but I looked away. "Isn't that great?"

"Yeah."

We drove quietly for a few seconds. The rain was coming down in sheets. Dad made the windshield wipers go faster. I leaned my head against the window.

"This day sucked," I said quietly. I blew some hot air on the window and drew a sad face with my finger.

"You okay, Chris?"

"Yes," I mumbled. "I hate hospitals, that's all."

The Hospital Visit

The first and only time I'd ever been to a hospital before was to visit Auggie. This was when we were about six years old. Auggie had had like a million surgeries before then, but this was the first time my mom thought I was old enough to go and visit him.

The surgery had been to remove the "buttonhole" on his neck. This is what he used to call his trach tube, a little plastic thingy that was literally inserted into his neck below his Adam's apple. The "buttonhole" is what the doctors put inside Auggie when he was born to allow him to breathe. The doctors were removing it now, because they were pretty sure Auggie could breathe on his own.

Auggie was really excited about this surgery. He hated his buttonhole. And when I say he hated it, I mean he *haaaated* it. He hated that it was so noticeable, since he wasn't allowed to cover it up. He hated that he couldn't go swimming in a pool because of it. Most of all, he hated how sometimes it would get blocked up, for no reason, and he would start to cough like he was choking, like he couldn't breathe. Then Isabel or Nate would have to jab a tube into the hole, to suction it, so that he could breathe again. I watched this happen a couple of times, and it was pretty scary.

I remember I was really happy about visiting Auggie after his surgery. The hospital was downtown, and Mom surprised me by stopping off at FAO Schwarz so I could pick out a nice big present to bring to Auggie (a *Star Wars* Lego set) and a small present for me (an Ewok plushie). After we bought the toys, Mom and I got lunch at my favorite restaurant, which makes the best foot-long hot dogs and iced hot chocolate milk shakes on the planet.

And then, after lunch, we went to the hospital.

"Chris, there are going to be other kids who are having facial surgeries," Mom told me quietly as we walked through the hospital doors. "Like Auggie's friend Hudson, okay? Remember not to stare."

"I would never stare!" I answered. "I hate when kids stare at Auggie, Mommy."

As we walked down the hall to Auggie's room, I remember seeing lots of balloons everywhere, and posters of Disney princesses and superheroes taped to the hallway walls. I thought it was cool. It felt like a giant birthday party.

I peeked into some of the hospital rooms as we passed, and that's when I realized what my mom meant. These were kids like Auggie. Not that they looked like him, though a couple of them did, but they had other facial differences. Some of them had bandages on their faces. One girl, I saw quickly, had a huge lump on her cheek that was the size of a lemon.

I squeezed my mom's hand and remembered not to stare, so I looked down at my feet as we walked and held on tight to my Ewok plushie.

When we reached Auggie's room, I was glad to see that Isabel and Via were already there. They both came over to the door when they saw us and kissed us hello happily.

They walked us over to Auggie, who was in the bed by the window. As we passed the bed closest to the door, I got the impression that Isabel was trying to block me from looking at the kid lying in that bed. So I took a quick peek behind me after we had passed. The boy in the bed, who was probably only about four, was watching me. Under his nose, where the top of his mouth was supposed to be, was an enormous red hole, and inside the hole was what looked like a piece of raw meat. There seemed to be teeth stuck into the meat, and pieces of jagged skin hanging over the hole. I looked away as quickly as I could.

Auggie was asleep. He seemed so tiny in the big hospital bed! His neck was wrapped up in white gauze, and there was blood on the gauze. He had some tubes sticking out of his arm, and one sticking into his nose.

His mouth was wide open, and his tongue was kind of hanging out of his mouth onto his chin. It looked a little yellow and was all dried up. I've seen Auggie asleep before, but I'd never seen him sleep like that.

I heard my mom and Isabel talking about the surgery in their quiet voices, which they used when they didn't want me or Auggie to hear what they were saying. Something about "complications" and how it had been "touch and go" for a while. My mom hugged Isabel. I stopped listening.

I stared at Auggie, wishing he would close his mouth in his sleep.

Via came over and stood next to me. She was about ten years old then. "It was nice of you to come visit Auggie," she said.

I nodded. "Is he going to die?" I whispered.

"No," she whispered back.

"Why is he bleeding?" I asked.

"It's where they operated on him," she answered. "It'll heal."

I nodded. "Why is his mouth open?"

"He can't help it."

"What's wrong with the little boy in the other bed?"

"He's from Bangladesh. He has a cleft lip and palate. His parents sent him here to have surgery. He doesn't speak any English."

I thought of the big empty red hole in the boy's face. The jagged flap of skin.

"Are you okay, Chris?" Via asked gently, nudging me. "Lisa? Lisa, I don't think Chris is looking so good . . ."

That's when the foot-long hot dog and iced hot chocolate milk shake kind of just exploded out of me. I threw up all over myself, the giant Lego box I'd gotten for Auggie, and most of the floor in front of his bed.

"Oh my goodness!" cried Mom as she looked around for paper towels. "Oh, sweetie!"

Isabel found a towel and started cleaning me with it. My mom, meanwhile, was frantically wiping the floor with a newspaper.

"No, Lisa! Don't worry about that," said Isabel. "Via, sweetie, go find a nurse and tell her we need a cleanup here." She said this as she was picking hot-dog chunks off my chin.

Via, who looked like she might throw up herself, turned around calmly and headed out the door. Within a few minutes, some nurses had come into the room with mops and buckets.

"Can we go home, Mommy?" I remember saying, the vomit taste still fresh in my mouth.

"Yes, honey," said Mom, taking over from Isabel and cleaning me off.

"I'm so sorry, Lisa," said Isabel, wetting another towel at the sink. She dabbed my face with it.

By now, I was sweating profusely. I turned to leave even before Mom and Isabel had finished cleaning me off. But then I accidentally caught a glimpse of the little boy in the bed, who was still looking at me. I started to cry when I looked into the big empty red hole above his mouth.

At that point, Mom kind of hugged me and glided me out the door at the same time. When we got outside the room, she half carried me to the lobby by the elevators. My face was buried in her coat, and I was crying hysterically.

Isabel and Via followed us out.

"I'm so sorry," Isabel said to us.

"I'm so sorry," said Mom. They were both kind of mumbling sorries to each other at the same time. "Please tell Auggie we're sorry we couldn't stay."

"Of course," said Isabel. She knelt down in front of me and started wiping my tears. "Are you okay, honey? I'm so sorry. I know it's a lot to process."

I shook my head. "It's not Auggie," I tried to say.

Her eyes got very wet suddenly. "I know," she whispered. Then she put both her hands on my face, like she was cradling it. "Auggie's lucky to have a friend like you."

The elevator came, Isabel hugged me and Mom, and then we got inside the elevator.

I saw Via waving at me as the elevator doors closed. Even though I was only six at the time, I remember thinking I felt sorry for her that she couldn't leave with us.

As soon as we were outside, Mom sat me down on a

bench and hugged me for a long time. She didn't say anything. She just kissed the top of my head over and over again.

When I finally calmed down, I handed her the Ewok.

"Can you go back and give it to him?" I said.

"Oh, honey," she answered. "That's so sweet of you. But Isabel can clean the Lego set. It'll be good as new for Auggie, don't worry."

"No, for the other kid," I answered.

She looked at me for a second, like she didn't know what to say.

"Via said he doesn't speak any English," I said. "It must be really scary for him, being in the hospital."

She nodded slowly. "Yeah," she whispered. "It must be."

She closed her eyes and hugged me again. And then she took me over to the security desk, where I waited until she went back up the elevator and, after about five minutes, came back down again.

"Did he like it?" I asked.

"Honeyboy," she said softly, brushing the hair out of my eyes. "You made his day."

7:04 p.m.

When we got to Mom's hospital room, we found her sitting up in a wheelchair watching TV. She had a huge cast that started from her thigh and went all the way down to her ankle.

"There's my guy!" she said happily as soon as she saw me. She held her arms out to me, and I went over and hugged her. I was relieved to see that Daddy had told the truth: except for the cast and a couple of scratches on her face, Mom looked totally fine. She was dressed and ready to go.

"How are you feeling, Lisa?" said Dad, leaning over and kissing her cheek.

"Much better," she answered, clicking off the TV set. She smiled at us. "Totally ready to go home."

"We got you these," I said, giving her the vase of flowers we had bought downstairs in the gift store.

"Thank you, sweetie!" she said, kissing me. "They're so pretty!"

I looked down at her cast. "Does it hurt?" I asked her.

"Not too much," she answered quickly.

"Mommy's very brave," said Dad.

"What I am is very lucky," Mom said, knocking the side of her head.

"We're all very lucky," added Dad quietly. He reached over and squeezed Mom's hand.

For a few seconds, no one said anything.

"So, do you need to sign any discharge papers or anything?" asked Dad.

"All done," she answered. "I'm ready to go home."

Dad got behind the wheelchair.

"Wait, can I push her?" I said to Dad, grabbing one of the handles.

"Let me just get her out the door here," answered Dad. "It's a little hard to maneuver with her leg."

"How was your day, Chris?" asked Mom as we wheeled her into the hallway.

I thought about what an awful day it had been. All of it, from beginning to end. Science, music, math, rock band. Worst day ever.

"Fine," I answered.

"How was band practice? Is Elijah being any nicer these days?" she asked.

"It was good. He's fine." I shrugged.

"I'm sorry I didn't bring your stuff," she said, stroking my arm. "You must have been wondering what happened to me!"

"I figured you were running errands," I answered.

"He thought you went to Isabel's house," laughed Dad.

"I did not!" I said to him.

We had reached the nurses' station and Mom was saying goodbye to the nurses, who were waving back, so she didn't really hear what Dad had said.

"Didn't you ask me if Mom had gone to—" Dad said to me, confused.

"Anyway!" I interrupted, turning to Mom. "Band was fine. We're playing 'Seven Nation Army' for the spring concert on Wednesday. Can you still come?"

"Of course I can!" she answered. "I thought you were playing 'The Final Countdown.'"

"'Seven Nation Army' is a great song," said Dad. He started humming the bass line and playing air guitar as we waited for the elevator.

Mom smiled at him. "I remember you playing that at the Parlor."

"What's the Parlor?" I asked.

"The pub down the road from our dorm," answered Mom.

"Before you were born, buddy," said Dad.

The elevator doors opened, and we got in.

"I'm starving," I said.

"You guys haven't eaten dinner yet?" Mom asked, looking at Dad.

"We came straight here from school," he answered. "When were we going to stop for dinner?"

"Can we stop for some McDonald's on the way home?" I asked.

"Sounds good to me," answered Dad.

We reached the lobby, and the elevator doors opened.

"Now can I push the wheelchair?" I said.

"Yep," he answered. "You guys wait for me over there, okay?" He pointed to the farthest exit on the left. "I'll pull the car around."

He jogged out the front entrance toward the parking lot. I pushed Mom's wheelchair to where he'd pointed.

"I can't believe it's still raining," said Mom, looking out the lobby windows.

"I bet you could pop a wheelie on this thing!" I said.

"Hey, hey! No!" Mom screamed, squeezed the sides of the wheelchair as I tilted it backward. "Chris! I've had enough excitement for the day."

I put the wheelchair down. "Sorry, Mom." I patted her head.

She rubbed her eyes with the palms of her hand. "Sorry, it's just been a really long day."

"Did you know that a day on Pluto is 153.3 hours long?" I asked.

"No, I didn't know that."

We didn't say anything for a few minutes.

"Hey, did you give Auggie a call, by the way?" she said out of the blue.

"Mom," I groaned, shaking my head.

"What?" she said. She tried to turn around in her

180

wheelchair to look at me. "I don't get it, Chris. Did you and Auggie have a fight or something?"

"No! There's just so much going on right now."

"Chris . . ." She sighed, but she sounded too tired to say anything else about it.

I started humming the bass line of "Seven Nation Army."

After a few minutes, the red hatchback pulled up in front of the exit, and Dad came jogging out of the car, holding an open umbrella. I pushed Mom outside the front doors. Dad gave her the umbrella to hold, and then he pushed her down the wheelchair ramp and around to the passenger side of the car. The wind was picking up now, and the umbrella Mom was holding went inside out after a strong gust.

"Chris, get inside!" said Dad. He started picking Mom up under her arms to transfer her to the front seat of the car.

"Kind of nice being waited on," Mom joked. But I could tell she was in pain.

"Worth a broken femur?" Dad joked back, out of breath.

"What's a femur?" I asked, scooching into the back-seat.

"The thighbone," answered Dad. He was soaking wet by now as he tried to help Mom find her seat belt.

"Sounds like an animal," I answered. "Lions and tigers and femurs."

Mom tried to laugh at my joke, but she was sweating.

Dad hurried around to the back of the car and spent a few minutes trying to figure out how to fold the wheelchair to get it inside. Then he came around to the driver's seat, sat down, and closed the door. We all kind of sat there quietly for a second, the wind and rain howling outside the windows. Then Dad started the car. We were all soaking wet.

"Mommy," I said after we'd been driving a few minutes, "when you got in the accident this morning, were you on your way home after dropping me off? Or were you driving back to school with my stuff?"

Mom took a second to answer. "It's actually kind of a blur, honey," she answered, reaching her arm behind her so that I would take her hand. I squeezed her hand.

"Chris," said Dad, "Mommy's kind of tired. I don't think she wants to think about it right now."

"I just want to know."

"Chris, now's not the time," said Dad, giving me a stern look in the rearview mirror. "The only thing that's important is that everything worked out okay and that Mommy's safe and sound, right? We have a lot to be thankful for. Today could have been so much worse."

It took me a second to realize what he meant. And then when I did, I felt a shiver go up my spine.

FaceChat

The first year after we moved to Bridgeport, our parents tried really hard to get Auggie and me together at least a couple of times a month—either at our place or at Auggie's. I had a couple of sleepovers at Auggie's house, and Auggie tried a sleepover at my place once, though that didn't work out. But it's a long car ride between Bridgeport and North River Heights, and eventually we only got together every couple of months or so. We started FaceChatting each other a lot around that time. Like, practically every day in third grade, Auggie and I would hang out together on FaceChat. We had decided to grow our Padawan braids before I moved away, so it was a great way to check how long they had gotten. Sometimes we wouldn't even talk: we'd just keep the screens on while we both watched a TV show together or built the same Lego set at the same time. Sometimes we would trade riddles. Like, what has a foot but no leg? Or, what does a poor man have, a rich man need, and you would die if you ate it? Stuff like that could keep us going for hours.

Then, in the fourth grade, we started FaceChatting less. It wasn't a thing we did on purpose. I just started having more things to do in school. Not only did I get more homework now, but I was doing a lot of after-school stuff. Soccer a couple of times a week. Tennis lessons. Robotics in the spring. It felt like I was always missing Auggie's Face-Chat requests, so finally we decided to schedule our chats for right before dinner on Wednesdays and Saturdays.

And that worked out fine, though it ended up being only Wednesday nights because Saturdays I had too much going on. It was somewhere toward the end of the fourth grade that I told Auggie I had cut off my Padawan braid. He didn't say it, but I think that hurt his feelings.

Then this year, Auggie started going to school, too.

I almost couldn't imagine Auggie at school, or how it would be for him. I mean, being a new kid is hard enough. But being a new kid that looks like Auggie? That would be insane. And not only was he starting school, he was starting *middle* school! That's how they do it in his school—fifth graders walking down the same hallways as ninth graders! Crazy! You have to give Auggie his props—that takes guts.

The only time I FaceChatted with Auggie in September was a few days after school had started, but he didn't seem to want to talk. I did notice he had cut off his Padawan braid, but I didn't ask him about it. I figured it was for the same reason I had cut mine off. I mean, you know, nerd alert.

I was curious to go to Auggie's bowling party a few weeks before Halloween. I got to meet his new friends, who seemed nice enough. There was this one kid named Jack Will who was pretty funny. But then I think something happened with Jack and Auggie, because when I FaceChatted with Auggie after Halloween, he told me they weren't friends anymore.

The last time I FaceChatted with Auggie was right after winter break had ended. My friends Jake and Tyler were over my place and we were playing *Age of War II* on my laptop when Auggie's FaceChat request came up on my screen.

"Guys," I said, turning the laptop toward me. "I need to take this."

"Can we play on your Xbox?" asked Jake.

"Sure," I said, pointing to where they could find the extra controllers. And then I kind of turned my back to them, because I didn't want them to see Auggie's face. I tapped "accept" on the laptop, and a few seconds later, Auggie's face came on the screen.

"Hey, Chris," he said.

"Sup, Aug," I answered.

"Long time no see."

"Yeah," I answered.

Then he started talking about something else. Something about a war at his school? Jack Will? I didn't really follow what he was saying, because I was completely distracted by Jake and Tyler, who had started nudging one another, mouths open, half laughing, the moment Auggie had come on-screen. I knew they had seen Auggie's face. I walked to the other side of the room with the laptop.

"Mm-hmm," I said to Auggie, trying to tune out the things Jake and Tyler were whispering to each other. But I heard this much:

"Did you see that?"

"Was that a mask?"

". . . a fire?"

"Is there someone there with you?" asked Auggie.

I guess he must have noticed that I wasn't really listening to him.

I turned to my friends and said, "Guys, shh!"

That made them crack up. They were very obviously trying to get a closer look at my screen.

"Yeah, I'm just with some friends," I mumbled quickly, walking to yet another side of my room.

"Hi, Chris's friend!" said Jake, following me.

"Can we meet your friend?" asked Tyler loudly so Auggie would hear.

I shook my head at them. "No!"

"Okay!" said Auggie from the other side of the screen.

Jake and Tyler immediately came on either side of me so the three of us were facing the screen and seeing Auggie's face.

"Hey!" Auggie said. I knew he was smiling, but sometimes, to people who didn't know, his smile didn't look like a smile.

"Hey," both Jake and Tyler said quietly, nodding politely. I noticed that they were no longer laughing.

"So, these guys are my friends Jake and Tyler," I said to Auggie, pointing my thumb back and forth at them. "And that's Auggie. From my old neighborhood."

"Hey," said Auggie, waving.

"Hey," said Jake and Tyler, not looking at him directly.

"So," said Auggie, nodding awkwardly. "So, yeah, what are you guys doing?"

"We were just turning on the Xbox," I answered.

"Oh, nice!" answered Auggie. "What game?"

"*House of Asterion.*"

"Cool. What level are you on?"

"Um, I don't know exactly," I said, scratching my head. "Second maze, I think."

"Oh, that's a hard one," Auggie answered. "I've almost unlocked Tartarus."

"Cool."

I noticed out of the corner of my eye that Jake was poking Tyler behind my back.

"Yeah, well," I said, "I think we're going to start playing now."

"Oh!" said Auggie. "Sure. Good luck with the second maze!"

"Okay. Bye," I said. "Hope the war thing works out."

"Thanks. Nice meeting you guys," Auggie added politely.

"Bye, Auggie!" Jake said, smirking.

Tyler started laughing, so I elbowed him out of screen view.

"Bye," Auggie said, but I could tell he noticed them laughing. Auggie always noticed stuff like that, even though he pretended not to.

I clicked off. As soon as I did, both Jake and Tyler started cracking up.

"What the heck?" I said to them, annoyed.

"Oh, dude!" said Jake. "What was up with that kid?"

"I've never seen anything that ugly in my life," said Tyler.

"Hey!" I answered defensively. "Come on."

"Was he in a fire?" asked Jake.

"No. He was born like that," I explained. "He can't help the way he looks. It's a disease."

"Wait, is it contagious?" asked Tyler, pretending to be afraid.

"Come on," I answered, shaking my head.

"And you're friends with him?" asked Tyler, looking at me like I was a Martian. "Whoa, dude!" He was snickering.

"What?" I looked at him seriously.

He opened his eyes wide and shrugged. "Nothing, dude. I'm just saying."

I saw him look at Jake, who squeezed his lips together like a fish. There was an awkward silence.

"Are we playing or not?" I asked after a few seconds. I grabbed one of the controllers.

We started playing, but it wasn't a great game. I was in a bad mood, and they just continued being goofballs. It was irritating.

After they left, I started thinking about Zack and Alex, how they had ditched Auggie all those years ago.

Even after all this time, it can still be hard being friends with Auggie.

8:22 p.m.

As soon as Dad wheeled Mom into our house, I plopped down on the sofa in front of the TV with my half-finished McDonald's Happy Meal. I clicked the TV on with the remote.

"Wait," said Dad, shaking out the umbrella. "I thought you had homework to do."

"I just want to watch the rest of *Amazing Race* while I eat," I answered. "I'll do my homework when it's over."

"Is it okay for him to do that?" Dad said to Mom.

"It's almost over anyway, Mommy!" I said to Mom. "Please?"

"So long as you start right after the show's over," she answered, but I knew she wasn't really paying attention. She was looking up at the staircase, shaking her head slowly. "How am I going to do this, Angus?" she said to Dad. She looked really tired.

"That's what I'm here for," Dad answered. He turned her wheelchair around toward him, reached under her, wrapped his other arm around her back, and lifted her out of the wheelchair. This made Mom scream in a giggly sort of way.

"Wow, Dad, you're strong!" I said, popping a french fry in my mouth as I watched them. "You guys should be on *The Amazing Race*. They're always having divorced couples."

Dad started climbing the staircase with Mom in his arms. They were both laughing as they bumped into the railing and the walls on the way up. It was nice seeing them like this. Last time we were all together, they were screaming at each other.

I turned around and watched the rest of the show. Just as Phil the host was telling the last couple to arrive at the pit stop that they have been eliminated, my phone buzzed.

It was a text from Elijah.

Yo chris. so me and the guys decided we're dropping out of after school rock band. we're starting our own band. we're playing 7NationArmy on Wednesday.

I reread the text. My mouth was literally hanging open. Dropping out of the band? Could they do that? John would go ballistic when none of them showed up at band practice tomorrow. And what did that mean for the after-school rock band? Would it be just me and John playing "The Final Countdown"? That would be awful!

Then another text came through.

do you want to join our band? we want YOU to join. but

ABSOLUTLY NOT john. He sucks. We're practicing at my place tomorrow after school. Bring your guitar.

Dad came downstairs. "Time for homework, Chris," he said quietly. Then he saw my face. "What's the matter?"

"Nothing," I said, clicking off the phone. I was kind of in a state of shock. They want me in their band? "I just remembered, I need to practice for the spring concert."

"Okay, but it needs to be quiet," answered Dad. "Mom is out like a light, and we have to let her rest, okay? Don't make a lot of noise going up the stairs. I'm in the guest room if you need anything."

"Wait, you're staying here tonight?" I asked.

"For a few days," he answered. "Until your mom can get around herself."

He started walking back upstairs with the crutches they had given Mom in the hospital.

"Can you print out the chords for 'Seven Nation Army' for me?" I asked. "I have to learn them by tomorrow."

"Sure," he said at the top of the stairs. "But remember, keep it down!"

North River Heights

Our new house is much bigger than our old house in North River Heights. Our old house was actually a brownstone, and we lived on the first floor. We only had one bathroom, and a tiny yard. But I loved our apartment. I loved our block. I missed being able to walk everywhere. I even missed the ginkgo trees. If you don't know what ginkgo trees are, they're the trees that drop these little squishy nuts that smell like dog poop mixed with cat pee mixed with some toxic waste when you step on them. Auggie used to say they smelled like orc vomit, which I always thought was funny. Anyway, I missed everything about our old neighborhood, even the ginkgo trees.

When we lived in North River Heights, Mom owned a little floral shop on Amesfort Avenue called Earth Laughs in Flowers. She worked really long hours, which is why they hired Lourdes to babysit me. That was another thing I missed: Lourdes. I missed her empanadas. I missed how she used to call me *papi*. But we didn't need Lourdes after we moved to Bridgeport, because Mom had sold her floral shop and no longer worked full-time. Now Mom picks me up from school on Mondays through Wednesdays. On Thursday nights, she picks me up from John's house and drops me off at Dad's place, which is where I stay until Sunday.

When we lived in North River Heights, Dad was usually home by seven p.m. But now he can't get home before nine p.m. because of the long commute from the city. Originally the plan was that that was only going to be a temporary thing, because he was going to be transferred to a Connecticut office, but it's been three years and he still has his old job in Manhattan. Mom and Dad used to argue about that a lot.

On Fridays, Dad leaves work early so that he can pick me up from school. We usually order Chinese food for dinner, jam a little on our guitars, and watch a movie. Mom gets annoyed with Dad that he doesn't make me do my homework over the weekend when I'm with him, so by the time I go back home on Sunday night, I'm always kind of grumpy as I scramble to finish my homework with her. This weekend, for instance, I should have been studying for my math test, but Dad and I went bowling and I just never got around to doing that. My bad.

I got used to the new house in Bridgeport, though. My new friends. Luke the hamster that's not a dog. But what I miss the most about North River Heights is that my parents seemed together then.

Dad moved out of our house last summer. My parents had been fighting a lot before that, but I don't know why he moved out over the summer. Just that one day, out of nowhere, they told me that they were separating. They "needed some time apart" to figure out if they wanted to continue living together. They told me that this had nothing to do with me, and they would "both go on loving me" and seeing me as much as before. They said they still loved each other, but that sometimes marriages are like friendships that get tested, and people have to work through things.

"Good friendships are worth a little extra effort," I remember saying to them.

I don't think Mom even remembered that she's the one who told me that once.

9:56 p.m.

I listened to "Seven Nation Army" while I did my home-work. And I tried not to think too much about how John would react tomorrow when I told him I was joining the other band. I mean, I didn't think I really had a choice. If I stayed in the after-school rock band, it'd just be me and John playing "The Final Countdown" at the spring concert, with Mr. B playing drums, and we'd look like the world's biggest dweebs. We were just not good enough to play by ourselves. I remembered how Harry was trying not to laugh when John played the guitar solo today. If it was just the two of us up there, *all* the kids in the audience would be trying not to laugh.

What I couldn't figure out was what John would do when he found out. Any sane person would just forget about playing in the spring concert on Wednesday at all. But knowing John, I could pretty much bet that he would go ahead and play "The Final Countdown." He didn't care about making a fool of himself that way. I could picture him singing his heart out, strumming the guitar, with Mr. Bowles rocking out behind him on the keyboards. *Ladies and gentlemen, the after-school rock band!* Just the thought of it made me cringe for him. He would never live that down.

It was hard to concentrate on my homework, so it took me a lot longer than I thought it would. I didn't even start studying for the math test until almost ten p.m. That's when I remembered that I was totally screwed in math. I waited to the last minute to study, and I didn't understand any of it.

Dad was in bed working on his laptop when I opened the door of the guest bedroom. I was holding my ridiculously heavy fifth-grade math textbook in my hands.

"Hey, Dad."

"You're not in bed yet?" he asked, looking at me over his reading glasses.

"I need some help studying for my math test tomorrow."

He glanced over at the clock on the bedside table. "Kind of late to be discovering this, no?"

"I had so much homework," I answered. "And I had to learn the new song for the spring concert, which is the day after tomorrow. There's so much going on, Dad."

He nodded. Then he put his laptop down and patted the bed for me to sit next to him, which I did. I turned to page 151.

"So," I said, "I'm having trouble with word problems."

"Oh, well, I'm great at word problems!" he answered, smiling. "Lay it on me."

I started reading from the textbook. "Jill wants to buy honey at an outdoor market. One vendor is selling a twenty-six-ounce jar for $3.12. Another vendor is selling a sixteen-ounce jar for $2.40. Which is the better deal, and how much money per ounce will Jill save by choosing it?"

I put the textbook down and looked at Dad, who looked at me blankly.

"Okay, um . . ." he said, scratching his ear. "So, that was twenty-six ounces for . . . what again? I'm going to need a piece of paper. Pass me my notebook over there?"

I reached over to the other end of the bed and passed him his notebook. He started scribbling in it, asked me to repeat the question again, and then kept scribbling.

"Okay, okay, so . . ." he said, turning his notebook around for me to look at his scribbled numbers. "So, first you want to divide the numbers to figure out what the cost per ounce is, then you want . . ."

"Wait, wait," I said, shaking my head. "That's the part I don't get. When do you know you have to divide? What do you need to do? How do you know?"

He looked down at the scribbles on his notebook again, as if the answer were there.

"Let me see the question?" he said, pushing his

reading glasses back up on his nose and looking at where I pointed in the textbook. "Okay, well, you know you have to divide, because, um, well, you want to figure out the price per ounce . . . because it says so right here." He pointed to the problem.

I looked quickly at where he pointed but shook my head. "I don't get it."

"Well, look, Chris. Right there. It asks how much the cost per ounce is."

I shook my head again. "I don't get it!" I said loudly. "I hate this. I suck at this."

"No, you don't, Chris," he answered calmly. "You just have to take a deep breath and—"

"No! You don't understand," I said. "I don't get this at all!"

"Which is why I'm trying to explain it to you."

"Can I ask Mom?"

He took his eyeglasses off and rubbed his eyes with his wrist. "Chris, she's asleep. We should just let her rest tonight," he answered slowly. "I'm sure we can figure this out ourselves."

I started poking my knuckles into my eyes, so he pulled my hands down off my face gently. "Why don't you call one of your friends at school? How about John?"

"He's in the fourth grade!" I said impatiently.

"Okay, well, someone else," he said.

"No!" I shook my head. "There's no one I can call.

I'm not friends with anyone like that this year. I mean, my *friend* friends aren't in the same math class I'm in. And I don't know the kids in this math class that well."

"Then call your other friends, Chris," he said, reaching over for his cell phone. "What about Elijah and those guys in the band? I'm sure they've all taken that class."

"No! Dad! Ugh!" I covered my face with my hands. "I'm totally going to fail this test. I don't get it. I just don't get it."

"Okay, calm down," he said. "What about Auggie? He's kind of a math whiz, isn't he?"

"Never mind!" I said, shaking my head. I took the textbook from him. "I'll figure it out myself!"

"Christopher," he said.

"It's fine, Dad," I said, getting up. "I'll just figure it out. Or I'll text someone. It's fine."

"Just like that?"

"It's fine. Thanks, Dad." I closed the textbook and got up.

"I'm sorry I couldn't help you," he answered, and for a second, I felt sorry for him. He sounded a little defeated. "I mean, I think we can figure it out together if you give me another chance."

"No, it's okay!" I answered, walking toward the door.

"Good night, Chris."

"Night, Dad."

I went to my room, sat at my desk, and opened the

textbook to page 151 again. I tried rereading the word problem, but all I could hear in my head were the words to "Seven Nation Army." And those made no sense to me, either.

No matter how hard I stared at the problem, I just couldn't think of what to do.

Pluto

A few weeks before we moved to Bridgeport, Auggie's parents were over at our house helping my parents pack for the big move. Our entire apartment was filled with boxes.

Auggie and I were having a Nerf war in the living room, turning the boxes into hostile aliens on Pluto. Occasionally, one of our Nerf darts would hit Via, who was trying to read her book on the sofa. Okay, maybe we were doing it a little bit on purpose, *tee-hee*.

"Stop it!" she finally screamed when one of my darts zinged her book. "Mom!" she yelled.

But Isabel and Nate were all the way on the other side of the apartment with my parents, taking a coffee break in the kitchen.

"Can you guys please stop?" Via said to us seriously.

I nodded, but Auggie shot another Nerf dart at her book.

"That's a fart dart," said Auggie. This made us both crack up.

Via was furious. "You guys are such geeks," she said, shaking her head. "*Star Wars*."

"Not *Star Wars*. Pluto!" answered Auggie, pointing his Nerf blaster at her.

"That's not even a real planet," she said, opening her book to read.

Auggie shot another Nerf dart at her book. "What are you talking about? Yes, it is."

"Stop it, Auggie, or I swear I'll . . ."

Auggie lowered his Nerf blaster. "Yes, it is," he repeated.

"No, it's not," answered Via. "It *used* to be a planet. I can't believe you two geniuses don't know that after all the space videos you've watched!"

Auggie didn't answer right away, like he was processing what she just said. "But my very educated mother just showed us nine planets! That's how Mommy said people remember the planets in our solar system."

"My very educated mother just served us nachos!" answered Via. "Look it up. I'm right." She started looking it up on her phone.

It may be that in all our reading science books and watching videos, this information had made its way to us before. But I guess we never really understood what it meant. We were still little kids when we were in our space phase. We barely knew how to read.

Via started reading aloud from her phone: "From Wikipedia: 'The understanding that Pluto is only one of several large icy bodies in the outer solar system prompted the International Astronomical Union (IAU) to formally define "planet" in 2006. This definition excluded Pluto and reclassified it as a member of the new "dwarf planet" category (and specifically as a plutoid).' Do I need to go on? Basically what that means is that Pluto was considered too puny to be a real planet, so there. I'm right."

Auggie looked really upset.

"Mommy!" he yelled out.

"It's not a big deal, Auggie," said Via, seeing how upset he was getting.

"Yes, it is!" he said, running down the hallway.

Via and I followed him to the kitchen, where our parents were sitting around the table over a bagel and cream cheese spread.

"You said it was 'my very educated mother just showed us nine planets'!" said Auggie, charging over to Isabel.

Isabel almost spilled her coffee. "What—" she said.

"Why are you making such a big deal about this, Auggie?" Via interrupted.

"What's going on, guys?" asked Isabel, looking from Auggie to Via.

"It *is* a big deal!" Auggie screamed at the top of his lungs. It was so loud and unexpected, that scream, that everyone in the room just looked at one another.

"Whoa, Auggie," said Nate, putting his hand on Auggie's shoulder. But Auggie shrugged it off.

"You told me Pluto was one of the nine planets!" Auggie yelled at Isabel. "You said it was the littlest planet in the solar system!"

"It is, sweetness," Isabel answered, trying to get him to calm down.

"No, it's not, Mom," Via said. "They changed Pluto's planetary status in 2006. It's no longer considered one of the nine planets in our solar system."

Isabel blinked at Via, and then she looked at Nate. "Really?"

"I knew that," Nate answered seriously. "They did the same thing to Goofy a few years ago."

This made all the adults laugh.

"Daddy, this isn't funny!" Auggie shrieked. And then, out of the blue, he started to cry. Big tears. Sobbing crying.

No one understood what was happening. Isabel wrapped her arms around Auggie, and he sobbed into her neck.

"Auggie Doggie," Nate said, gently rubbing Auggie on the back. "What's going on here, buddy?"

"Via, what happened?" Isabel asked sharply.

"I have no idea!" said Via, opening her eyes wide. "I didn't do anything!"

"Something must have happened!" said Isabel.

"Chris, do you know why Auggie's so upset?" asked Mom.

"Because of Pluto," I answered.

"But what does that mean?" asked Mom.

I shrugged. I understood why he was so upset, but I couldn't explain it to them exactly.

"You said . . . it was . . . a planet . . ." Auggie finally said in between gulps. Even under ordinary circumstances, Auggie could be hard to understand sometimes. In the middle of a crying fit, it was even harder.

"What, sweetness?" whispered Isabel.

"You said . . . it was . . . a planet," Auggie repeated, looking up at her.

"I thought it was, Auggie," she answered, wiping his tears with her fingertips. "I don't know, sweetness. I'm not a real science teacher. When I was growing up, there were nine planets. It never even occurred to me that that could change."

Nate knelt down beside him. "But even if it's not considered a planet anymore, Auggie, I don't understand why that should upset you so much."

Auggie looked down. But I knew he couldn't explain his Plutonian tears.

10:28 p.m.

By about ten-thirty, I was getting desperate about the math test tomorrow. I had texted Jake, who's in my math class, and messaged a few other kids on Facebook. When my phone buzzed, I assumed it was one of these kids, but it wasn't. It was Auggie.

Hey, Chris. Just heard about your mom being in hospital. Sorry, hope she's ok.

I couldn't believe he was texting me, just when I'd been thinking about him. Kind of psychic.

Hey, Aug, I texted back. *Thx. She's ok. She broke her femur. She has this huge cast.*

He texted me a sad-face emoticon.

I texted: *My dad had to carry her up the stairs! They kept bumping into the wall.*

Ha ha. He texted me a laughing-face icon.

I texted: *I was going to call u today. To tell u sorry about Daisy.* :(((((

Oh yeah. Thx. He texted a string of crying-face emoticons.

Hey, remember the Galactic Adventures of Darth Daisy? I texted.

This was a comic strip we used to draw together about two astronauts named Gleebo and Tom who lived on Pluto and had a dog named Darth Daisy.

Ha ha. Yeah, Major Gleebo.

Major Tom.

Good times good times, he texted back.

Daisy was the GR8EST DOG IN UNIVERSE! I thumbed loudly. I was smiling.

He texted me a picture of Daisy. It had been such a long time since I had seen her. In the picture, her face had gotten completely white, and her eyes were kind of foggy. But her nose was still pink and her tongue was still super long as it hung out of her mouth.

So cute! Daisy!!!!!!! I texted.

DARTH Daisy!!!!!!!!!!!!!!!

Ha ha. Take that, Via! I wrote.

Remember those fart darts?

Hahahahahaha. I was smiling a lot at this point. It was the happiest part of my day, to be truthful. *That was when we were still into Pluto.*

Were we into Star Wars yet?

Getting into it. Do you still have all your miniatures?

Yeah but I put some away too. So anyway, Gleebo, my mom's telling me I gots to go to bed now. Glad your mom is okay.

I nodded. There was no way I could ask him for help

in math at this point. It would just be too lame. I sat down on the edge of my bed and started responding to his text.

Before I could finish, he texted: *my mom actually wants to talk to you. she wants to FaceChat. R U free?*

I stood up. *Sure.*

Two seconds later, I got a request to FaceChat. I saw Isabel on the phone.

"Oh, hey, Isabel," I said.

"Hi, Chris!" she answered. I could tell she was in her kitchen. "How are you? I talked to your mom earlier. I wanted to make sure you guys got home okay."

"Yeah, we did."

"And she's doing okay? I didn't want to wake her if she's sleeping."

"Yeah, she's sleeping," I answered.

"Oh good. She needs her rest. That was a big cast!"

"Dad's staying here tonight."

"Oh, that's so great!" she answered happily. "I'm so glad. And how are you doing, Chris?"

"I'm good."

"How's school?"

"Good."

Isabel smiled. "Lisa told me you got her beautiful flowers today."

"Yeah," I answered, smiling and nodding.

"Okay. Well, I just wanted to check in on you and say

hello, Chris. I want you to know we're thinking about you guys, and if there's anything we can do—"

"I'm sorry about Daisy," I blurted out.

Isabel nodded. "Oh. Thank you, Chris."

"You guys must be so sad."

"Yeah, it's sad. She was such a presence in our house. Well, you know. You were there when we first got her, remember?"

"She was so skinny!" I said. I was smiling, but suddenly, out of the blue, my voice got a little shaky.

"With that long tongue of hers!" She laughed.

I nodded. I felt a lump in my throat, like I was going to cry.

She looked at me carefully. "Oh, sweetie, it's okay," she said quietly.

Auggie's mom had always been like a second mom to me. I mean, aside from my parents, and maybe my grandmother, Isabel Pullman knew me better than anyone.

"I know," I whispered. I was still smiling, but my chin was trembling.

"Sweetie, where's your dad?" she asked. "Can you put him on the phone?"

I shrugged. "I think . . . he might be asleep by now."

"I'm sure he won't care if you wake him up," she answered softly. "Go get him. I'll wait on the phone."

Auggie nudged his way into view on the screen.

"What's the matter, Chris?" he asked.

I shook my head, fighting back tears. I couldn't talk. I knew if I did, I'd start to cry.

"Christopher," Isabel said, coming close to the screen. "Your mom is going to be fine, sweetie."

"I know," I said, my voice cracking, but then it just came out of me. "But she was in the car because of me! Because I forgot my trombone! If I hadn't forgotten my stuff, she wouldn't have gotten into an accident! It's my fault, Isabel! She could have died!"

This all came pouring out of me in a string of messy crying bursts.

10:52 p.m.

Isabel put Auggie on the phone while she called Dad's cell phone to let him know I was crying hysterically in my room. A minute later, Dad came into my room and I hung up on Auggie. Dad put his arms around me and hugged me tightly.

"Chris," said Dad.

"It was my fault, Daddy! It was my fault she was driving."

He untangled himself from my hug and put his face in front of my face.

"Look at me, Chris," he said. "It's not your fault."

"She was on her way back to school with my stuff." I sniffled. "I told her to hurry. She was probably speeding."

"No, she wasn't, Chris," he answered. "I promise you. What happened today was just an accident. It wasn't anyone's fault. It was a fluke. Okay?"

I looked away.

"Okay?" he repeated.

I nodded.

"And the most important thing is that no one got seriously hurt. Mom is fine. Okay, Chris?"

He was wiping my tears away as I nodded.

"I kept calling her Lisa," I said. "She hates when I do that. The last thing she said to me was 'Love you!' and all I answered was 'Bye, Lisa.' And I didn't even turn around!"

Dad cleared his throat. "Chris, please don't beat yourself up," he said slowly. "Mom knows you love her so much. Listen, this was a scary thing that happened today. It's natural for you to be upset. When something scary like this happens, it acts like a wake-up call, you know? It makes us reassess what's important in life. Our family. Our friends. The people we love." He was looking at me while he was talking, but I almost felt like he was talking to himself. His eyes were very moist. "Let's just be grateful she's fine, okay, Chris? And we'll take really good care of her together, okay?"

I nodded. I didn't try to say anything, though. I knew it would just come out as more tears.

Dad pulled me close to him, but he didn't say anything, either. Maybe for the same reason.

10:59 p.m.

After Dad had gotten me to calm down a bit, he called Isabel back to let her know everything was fine. They chatted, and then Dad handed the phone to me.

It was Auggie on the line.

"Hey, your dad told my mom you need some help with math," he said.

"Oh yeah," I answered shyly, blowing my nose. "But it's so late. Don't you need to go to bed?"

"Mom's totally fine with my helping you. Let's Face Chat."

Two seconds later, he was on-screen.

"So, I'm having trouble with word problems," I said, opening my textbook. "I just . . . I'm not getting how you know what operation to use. When do you multiply and when do you divide? It's so confusing."

"Oh, that." He nodded. "Yeah, I definitely had trouble with that, too. Have you memorized the clue words, though? That helped me a lot."

I had no idea what he was talking about.

214

"Let me send you a PDF," he said.

Two seconds later, I printed out the PDF he sent me, which listed a whole bunch of different math words.

"If you know what clue words to look for in the word problem," Auggie explained, "you know what operation to use. Like 'per' or 'each' or 'equally' means you have to divide. And 'at this rate' or 'doubled' means multiplication. See?"

He went over the whole list of words with me, one by one, until it finally began to make some sense. Then we went over all the math problems in the textbook. We started with the sample problems first, and it turned out he was right: once I found the clue word in each problem, I knew what to do. I was able to do most of the worksheet problems on my own, though we went over each and every one of them after I was done, just to be sure I had really gotten it.

11:45 p.m.

My favorite types of books have always been mysteries. Like, you don't know something at the beginning of the book. And then at the end of the book, you know it. And the clues were there all along, you just didn't know how to read them. That's what I felt like after talking to Auggie. Like this colossal mystery I couldn't understand before was now completely, suddenly solved.

"I can't believe I'm finally getting this now," I said to him after we had gone over the last problem. "Thank you so much, Aug. Seriously, thank you."

He smiled and got in close to the screen. "It's cool beans," he said.

"I totally owe you one."

Auggie shrugged. "No problem. That's what friends are for, right?"

I nodded. "Right."

"G'night, Chris. Talk soon!"

"Night, Aug! Thanks again! Bye!"

He hung up. I closed my textbook.

I went to the guest room to tell Dad that Auggie had helped me figure out all the math stuff, but he wasn't in the room. I knocked on the bathroom door, but he wasn't in there, either. Then I noticed Mom's bedroom door was open. I could see Dad's legs stretched out on the chair next to the dresser. I couldn't see his face from the hallway, so I walked in quietly to let him know that I was finished talking with Auggie.

That's when I saw that he had fallen asleep in the chair. His head was drooping to one side. His glasses were on the edge of his nose, and his computer was on his lap.

I tiptoed to the closet, got a blanket, and placed it over his legs. I did it really softly so he wouldn't wake up. I took the computer from his lap and put it on the dresser.

Then I walked over to the side of the bed where Mom was sleeping. When I was little, Mom used to fall asleep reading to me at bedtime. I would nudge her awake if she fell asleep before finishing the book, but sometimes, she just couldn't help it. She'd fall asleep next to me, and I would listen to her soft breathing until I fell asleep, too.

It had been a long time since I'd seen her sleeping, though. As I looked at her now, she seemed kind of little to me. I didn't remember the freckle on her cheek. I'd never noticed the tiny lines on her forehead.

I watched her breathing for a few seconds.

"I love you, Mommy."

I didn't say this out loud, though, because I didn't want to wake her up.

11:59 p.m.

It was almost midnight by the time I went back to my room. Everything was exactly the way I had left it this morning. My bed was still unmade. My pajamas were jumbled up on the floor. My closet door was wide open. Usually, Mom would make my room look nice after she dropped me off at school in the morning, but today, of course, she never got the chance to do that.

It felt like days had passed since Mom woke me up this morning.

I closed the closet door, and that's when I noticed the trombone resting against the wall. So the accident didn't happen as she was bringing me my stuff this morning! I don't know why exactly, but this made me feel so much better.

I put the trombone right next to the bedroom door so I wouldn't forget it again on my way to school tomorrow, and I packed my science paper and gym shorts inside my backpack.

Then I sat down at my desk.

Without thinking anything more about it, I replied to Elijah's text.

Hey, Elijah. Thanks for the offer to join your band. But I'm going to stick with John at the spring concert. Good luck with Seven Nation Army.

Even if I looked like a total dweeb at the spring concert, I couldn't let John down like that. That's what friends are for, right? *It's the final countdown!*

Sometimes friendships are hard.

I put my pajamas on, brushed my teeth, and got into bed. Then I turned off the lamp on my nightstand. The stars on my ceiling were glowing bright neon green now, as they always did right after I turned the lights off.

I turned over on my side, and my eyes fell on a small star-shaped green light on my floor. It was the star Mom had placed on my forehead this morning, which I had flicked across the room.

I got out of bed, picked it up, and stuck it on my forehead. Then I got back in my bed and closed my eyes.

We're leaving together
But still it's farewell
And maybe we'll come back
To Earth, who can tell

I guess there is no one to blame
We're leaving ground
Will things ever be the same again?

It's the final countdown . . .

But every Spring
It groweth young again,
And fairies sing.
—Cicely Mary Barker, "Flower
Fairies of the Spring", 1923

• • •

Nobody can do the shingaling like I do.
—The Isley Brothers, "Nobody But Me"

How I Walked to School

There was a blind old man who played the accordion on Main Street, who I used to see every day on my way to school. He sat on a stool under the awning of the A&P supermarket on the corner of Moore Avenue, his seeing-eye dog lying down in front of him on a blanket. The dog wore a red bandanna around its neck. It was a black Labrador. I know because my sister Beatrix asked him one day.

"Excuse me, sir. What kind of dog is that?"

"Joni is a black Labrador, missy," he answered.

"She's really cute. Can I pet her?"

"Best not. She's working right now."

"Okay, thank you. Have a good day now."

"Bye, missy."

My sister waved at him. He had no way of knowing this, of course, so he didn't wave back.

Beatrix was eight then. I know because it was my first year at Beecher Prep, which means I was in kindergarten.

I never talked to the accordion-man myself. I hate to admit it, but I was kind of afraid of him back then. His eyes, which were always open, were kind of glazed and cloudy. They were cream-colored, and looked like white-and-tan marbles. It spooked me. I was even a little afraid of his dog, which really made no sense because I usually love dogs. I mean, I *have* a dog! But I was afraid of his dog, who had a gray muzzle and whose eyes were kind of gloopy, too. But—and here's a big but—even though I was afraid of both of them, the accordion-man *and* his dog, I always dropped a dollar bill into the open accordion case in front of them. And somehow, even though he was playing the accordion, and no matter how quietly I crept over, the accordion-man would always hear the *swoosh* of the dollar bill as it fell into the accordion case.

"God bless America," he would say to the air, nodding in my direction.

That always made me wonder. How could he hear that? How did he know what direction to nod at?

My mom explained that blind people develop their other senses to make up for the sense they've lost. So, because he was blind, he had super hearing.

That, of course, got me wondering if he had other superpowers, too. Like, in the winter when it was freezing cold, did his fingers have a magical way of keeping warm while they pressed the keys? And how did the rest of him stay warm? On those really frigid days when my teeth would start to chatter after walking just a few blocks against the icy wind, how did he stay warm enough to play his accordion? Sometimes, I'd even see little rivers of ice forming in parts of his mustache and beard, or I'd see him reach down to make sure his dog was covered by the blanket. So I knew he *felt* the cold, but how did he keep playing? If that's not a superpower, I don't know what is!

In the wintertime, I always asked my mom for *two* dollars to drop into his accordion case instead of just one.

Swoosh. Swoosh.

"God bless America."

He played the same eight or ten songs all the time. Except at Christmastime, when he'd play "Rudolph the Red-Nosed Reindeer" and "Hark! The Herald Angels Sing." But otherwise, it was the same songs. My mom knew the names of some of them. "Delilah." "Lara's Theme." "Those Were the Days." I downloaded all the titles she named, and she was right, those *were* the songs. But why just those songs? Were they the only songs he ever learned to play, or were they the only songs he remembered? Or did he know a whole bunch of other songs, but chose to play just those songs?

And all that wondering got me wondering even more! When did he learn to play the accordion? When he was a little boy? Could he see back then? If he couldn't see, how could he read music? Where did he grow up?

Where did he live when he wasn't on the corner of Main Street and Moore Avenue? I saw him and his dog walking together sometimes, his right hand holding the dog's harness and his left hand holding the accordion case. They moved so slowly! It didn't seem like they could get very far. So where *did* they go?

There were a lot of questions I would have asked him if I hadn't been afraid of him. But I never asked. I just gave him one-dollar bills.

Swoosh.

"God bless America."

It was always the same.

Then, when I got older and wasn't *that* afraid of him anymore, the questions I used to have about him didn't seem to matter as much to me. I guess I got so accustomed to seeing him, I didn't really think about his foggy eyes or if he had superpowers. It's not like I stopped giving him a dollar when I passed by him or anything. But it was more like a habit now, like swiping a MetroCard through a subway turnstile.

Swoosh.

"God bless America."

By the time I started fifth grade, I stopped seeing him completely because I no longer walked past him on my way to school. The Beecher Prep middle school is a few blocks closer to my house than the lower school was, so now I walk *to* school with Beatrix and my oldest sister, Aimee, and I walk home *from* school with my best friend, Ellie, as well as Maya and Lina, who live near me. Once in a while, at the beginning of the school year, we would go get snacks at the A&P after school before heading home, and I'd see the accordion-man and give him a dollar and hear him bless America. But as the weather got colder, we didn't do that as much. Which is why it wasn't until a few days into winter break, when I went to the A&P with my mom one afternoon, that I realized that the blind old man who played the accordion on Main Street wasn't there anymore.

He was gone.

How I Spent My Winter Vacation

People who know me always say I'm so dramatic. I have no idea why they say that, because I'm really, really, really *not* dramatic. But when I found out the accordion-man was gone, I kind of lost it! I really don't know why, but I just couldn't stop obsessing about what had happened to him. It was like a mystery that I had to solve! What in the world happened to the blind old man who played the accordion on Main Street?

Nobody seemed to know. My mom and I asked the cashiers in the supermarket, the lady in the dry cleaner's, and the man in the eye shop across the street if they knew anything about him. We even asked the policeman who gave out parking tickets on that block. Everyone knew who he was, but no one knew what had happened to him, just that one day—*poof!*—he wasn't there anymore. The policeman told me that on really cold days, homeless people are actually taken to the city shelters so they won't freeze to death. He thought that's probably what happened to the accordion-man.

But the dry-cleaning lady said that she knew for a fact that the accordion-man wasn't homeless. She thought he lived somewhere up in Riverdale because she'd see him getting off the Bx3 bus early in the mornings with his dog. And the eye-shop man said that he was certain that the accordion-man had been a famous jazz musician once and was actually loaded, so I shouldn't worry about him.

You would think these answers would have helped me, right? But they didn't! They just raised a whole bunch of other questions that made me even *more* curious about him. Like, was he in a homeless shelter for the winter? Was he living in his own beautiful house in Riverdale? Had he really been a famous jazz musician? Was he rich? If he was rich, why was he playing for money?

My whole family got sick and tired of my talking about this, by the way.

Beatrix was like: "Charlotte, if you talk about this one more time, I'm going to throw up all over you!"

And Aimee said, "Charlotte, will you just *drop* it already?"

My mom's the one who suggested that a good way to "channel" my energy would be to start a coat drive in our neighborhood to benefit homeless people. We put up flyers asking people to donate their "gently worn" coats by dropping them off in plastic bags in a giant bin we left in front of our brownstone. Then, after we'd collected about ten huge garbage bags full of coats, my mom and dad and I drove all the way downtown to the Bowery Mission to donate the coats. I have to say, it felt really good to give all those coats to people who really needed them! I looked around when I was inside the mission with my parents to see if maybe the accordion-man was there, but he wasn't. Anyway, I knew he had a nice coat already: a bright orange Canada Goose parka that made my mom hopeful that the rumors about his being rich might actually be true.

"You don't see many homeless people wearing Canada Goose," observed Mom.

When I got back to school after winter break, Mr. Tushman, the middle school director, congratulated me on having started a coat drive. I'm not sure how he knew, but he knew. It was generally agreed upon that Mr. Tushman had some kind of secret surveillance drone keeping tabs on everything going on at Beecher Prep: there was no other way he could know all the stuff he seemed to know.

"That's a beautiful way to spend your winter vacation, Charlotte," he said.

"Aw, thank you, Mr. Tushman!"

I loved Mr. Tushman. He was always really nice. What I liked was that he was one of those teachers that never talks to you like you're some little kid. He always uses big words, assuming you know and understand them, and he never looks away when you're talking to him. I also loved that he wore suspenders and a bow tie and bright red sneakers.

"Do you think you could help me organize a coat drive here at Beecher Prep?" he asked. "Now that you're an expert at it, I would love your input."

"Sure!" I answered.

Which is how I ended up being part of the first annual Beecher Prep Coat Drive.

In any case, between the coat drive and all the other drama going on at school when I got back from winter vacation (more on that soon!), I didn't really get a chance to solve the mystery of what happened to the blind old man who played the accordion on Main Street. Ellie didn't seem the least bit interested in helping me solve the mystery, though it was the kind of thing that she might have been into just a few months before. And neither Maya nor Lina seemed to remember him at all. In fact, no one seemed to care about what happened to him in the least, so finally, I just dropped the subject.

I still thought about the accordion-man sometimes, though. Every once in a while, one of the songs he used to play on his accordion would come back to me. And then I'd hum it all day long.

How the Boy War Started

The only thing everybody *could* talk about when we got back from winter break was "the war," also referred to as "the boy war." The whole thing started right before winter break. A few days before recess, Jack Will had gotten suspended for punching Julian Albans in the mouth. *Talk about drama!* Everyone was gossiping about it. But no one knew exactly why Jack did it. Most people thought it had something to do with Auggie Pullman. To explain that a bit, you have to know that Auggie Pullman is this kid at our school who was born with very severe facial issues. And by severe, I mean *severe*. Like, *really* severe. None of his features are where they're supposed to be. And it's kind of shocking when you see him at first because it's like he's wearing a mask or something. So when he started at Beecher Prep, *everybody* noticed him. He was impossible not to notice.

A few people—like Jack and Summer and *me*—were nice to him from the beginning. Like, when I would pass him in the hall, I'd always say, "Hey, Auggie, how're you doing?" and stuff like that. Now, sure, part of that was because Mr. Tushman had asked me to be a welcome buddy to Auggie before school had started, but I would have been nice to him even if he hadn't asked me to do that.

Most people, though—like Julian and his group— were not at *all* nice to Auggie, especially in the beginning. I don't think people were even trying to be mean necessarily. I think they were just a little weirded out by his face, is all. They said stupid things behind his back. Called him *Freak*. Played this game called The Plague, which I did *not* participate in, by the way! (If I've never touched Auggie Pullman, it's only because I've never had a reason to—that's all!) Nobody ever wanted to hang out with him or get partnered up with him on a class project. At least in the beginning of the year. But after a couple of months, people did start getting used to him. Not that they were really nice or anything, but at least they stopped being mean. Everyone, that is, *except* for Julian, who continued to make such a big deal about him! It's like he couldn't get over the fact that Auggie looks the way he looks! As if the poor guy could help it, right?

Anyway, so what everyone thinks happened is that Julian said something horrible about Auggie to Jack. And Jack—being a good friend—punched Julian. *Boom.*

And then Jack got suspended. *Boom.*

And now he's back from suspension! *Boom!*

And that's the *drama*!

But that's not all there is to it!

Because then what happened is this: over winter break, Julian had this huge party and, basically, turned everyone in the fifth grade against Jack. He spread this rumor that the school psychologist had told his mom that Jack was emotionally unstable. And that the pressure of being friends with Auggie had made him snap and turn into an angry maniac. Crazy stuff! Of course, none of it was true, and most people knew that, but it didn't stop Julian from spreading that lie.

And now the boys are all in this war. And that's how it started. And it's so *stupid*!

How I Stayed Neutral

I know one thing people say about me is that I'm a goody two-shoes. I have no idea why they say that. Because I'm really *not* that much of a goody two-shoes. But I'm also not someone who's going to be mean to *someone* just because *someone* else says I should be mean to them. I hate when people do stuff like that.

So, when all the boys started giving Jack the cold shoulder, and Jack didn't know why, I thought the least I could do was tell him what was going on. I mean, I've known Jack since we were in kindergarten. He's a good kid!

The thing is, I didn't want anyone to *see* me talking to him. Some of the girls, like Savanna's group, had started taking sides with the Julian boys, and I really wanted to stay neutral because I didn't want any of them to get mad at *me*. I was still hoping that maybe, one of these days, I'd work my way into that group myself. The last thing I wanted was to do anything to mess up my chances with them.

So, one day right before last period, I slipped Jack a note to meet me in room 301 after school. Which he did. And then I told him everything that was going on. You should have seen Jack's face! It was bright red! Seriously! The poor kid! We pretty much agreed that this whole thing was *so* messed up! I really felt sorry for him.

Then, after we were done talking, I sneaked out of the room without anyone seeing me.

How I Wanted to Tell Ellie About My Talk with Jack Will

At lunch the next day, I was going to tell Ellie that I'd talked to Jack. Ellie and I both had had a tiny *secret* crush on Jack Will going back to the fourth grade, when he played the Artful Dodger in *Oliver!* and we thought he looked adorable in a top hat.

I went over to her when she was emptying her lunch tray. We don't sit at the same lunch table anymore, ever since she switched to Savanna's lunch table around Halloween. But I still trusted Ellie. We've been BFFs since first grade! That counts for a lot!

"Hey," I said, nudging into her with my shoulder.

"Hey!" she said, nudging me back.

"Why weren't you in chorus yesterday?"

"Oh, didn't I tell you?" she said. "I switched electives when I came back from winter break. I'm in band now."

"*Band?* Seriously?" I said.

"I'm playing the clarinet!" she answered.

"Wow," I said, nodding. "Sweet."

This bit of news was really surprising to me, for a lot of reasons.

"Anyhow, what's up with you, Charly?" she said. "I feel like I've hardly seen you since we got back from winter break!" She picked up my wrist to inspect my new bangle.

"I know, right?" I answered, though I didn't point out that that was because she had canceled on me every single time we'd made plans to hang out after school.

"How's Maya's dots tournament going?"

She was referring to Maya's obsession with making the world's largest dot game to play at lunchtime. We kind of made fun of it behind her back.

"Good," I answered, smiling. "I keep meaning to ask you about this whole boy-war thing. It's so lame, isn't it?"

She rolled her eyes. "It's totally out of control!"

"Right?" I said. "I feel kind of sorry for Jack. Don't you think Julian should just call it quits already?"

Ellie started twisting a strand of hair around her finger. She took a fresh juice box off the counter and popped the straw into the hole. "I don't know, Charly," she answered. "Jack's the one who punched *him* in the mouth. Julian has every right to be mad." She took a long sip. "I'm actually starting to think that Jack has serious anger-management issues."

Hold up. What? I've known Ellie since forever, and the Ellie I know would never use a phrase like "anger-management issues." Not that Ellie isn't smart, but she's not *that* smart. *Anger-management issues?* That sounded more like something Ximena Chin would say in that sarcastic way of hers. Ever since Ellie started hanging out with Ximena and Savanna, she's been acting weirder and weirder!

Wait a minute! I just remembered something: Ximena plays clarinet! *That* explains why Ellie switched electives! Now it's all making sense!

"Either way," said Ellie, "I don't think we should get involved. It's a boy thing."

"Yeah, whatever," I answered, deciding it was better if I didn't tell Ellie I had spoken with Jack.

"So are you ready for the dance tryouts today?" she asked cheerfully.

"Yeah," I answered, pretending to get excited. "I think Mrs. Atanabi is—"

"Ready, Ellie?" said Ximena Chin, who had just appeared out of nowhere. She nodded a quick hello my way without really looking at me, and then turned around and headed to the lunchroom exit.

Ellie dropped her unfinished juice box into the trash can, clumsily heaved her backpack onto her right shoulder, and trotted after Ximena. "See you later, Charly!" she mumbled halfway across the lunchroom.

"Later," I answered, watching her catch up to Ximena. Together, they joined Savanna and Gretchen, a sixth grader, who were waiting for them by the exit.

The four of them were all about the same height, and they all had super-long hair, with wavy curls at the ends. Their hair colors were different, though. Savanna's was golden blond. Ximena's was black. Gretchen's was red. And Ellie's was brown. I actually wondered sometimes if Ellie hadn't gotten into that popular group because of her hair, which was just the right color and length to fit in.

My hair is white-blond, and so straight and flat, there's no way it would ever end in a curl without massive doses of hair spray. And it's short. Like me.

How to Use Venn Diagrams (Part 1)

In Ms. Rubin's science class, we learned about Venn diagrams. You draw Venn diagrams to see the relationships between different groups of things. Like, if you want to see the common characteristics between mammals, reptiles, and fish, for instance, you draw a Venn diagram and list all the attributes of each one inside a circle. Where the circles intersect is what they have in common. In the case of mammals, reptiles, and fish, it would be that they all have backbones.

Anyway, I love Venn diagrams. They're so useful for explaining so many things. I sometimes draw them to explain friendships.

in first grade

Charlotte — Ellie

·short
·prefers dogs
·favorite animal horse
·blond hair
·Elsa

♥ dance!
♥ Flower Fairies!
♥ favorite ice cream: vanilla
♥ Big Time Rush
♥ friends with Maya

·tall
·prefers cats
·favorite animal koala
·brown hair
·Anna

Ellie and me in first grade.

As you can see, Ellie and I had a lot in common. We've been friends since the first day of first grade, when Ms. Diamond put us both at the same table. I remember that day very clearly. I kept trying to talk to Ellie, but she was shy and didn't want to talk. Then, at snack time, I started ice-skating with my fingers on the top of the desk we shared. If you don't know what that is, it's when you make an upside-down peace sign and let your fingers glide over the glossy desk, like they were figure skaters. Anyway, Ellie watched me do that for a little while, and then she started ice-skating with her fingers, too. Pretty soon, we were both making figure eights all over the desk. After that, we were inseparable.

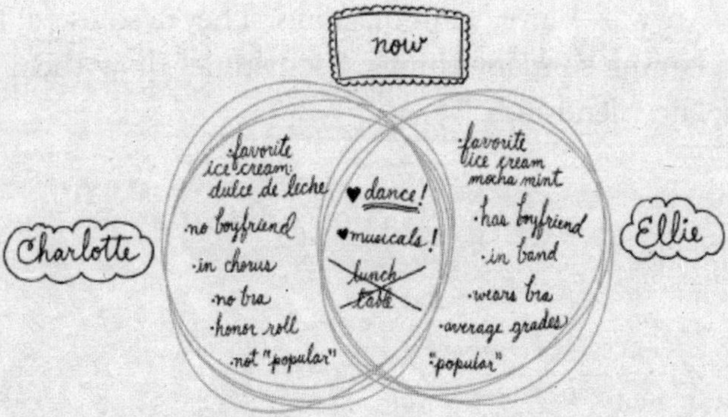
now
Charlotte
Ellie
·favorite ice cream dulce de leche
·no boyfriend
·in chorus
·no bra
·honor roll
·not "popular"
♥dance!
♥musicals!
lunch table
·favorite ice cream mocha mint
·has boyfriend
·in band
·wears bra
·average grades
·"popular"

Ellie and me now.

How I Continued to Stay Neutral

Ellie, Savanna, and Ximena were hanging out in front of the lockers outside the performance space when I showed up for the dance tryouts after school. I knew the moment they looked at me that they'd just been talking about me.

"You're not really taking *Jack's* side in the boy war, are you?" said Savanna, making an *eww* expression with her lips.

I glanced at Ellie, who had obviously shared some of my lunch conversation with Savanna and Ximena. She chewed a strand of hair and looked away.

"I'm not on Jack's side," I said calmly. I popped open my locker and shoved my backpack inside. "All I said is that I think this whole boy-war thing is dumb. *All* the boys are just being so jerky."

"Yeah, but Jack started it," said Savanna. "Or are you saying it's okay that he punched Julian?"

"No, it's definitely not okay that he did that," I answered, pulling out my dance gear.

"So how could you be on Jack's side?" Savanna asked quickly, still making that *eww* face with her mouth.

"Is it because you *like* him?" asked Ximena, smiling mischievously.

Ximena, who probably hasn't said more than thirty words to me all year long, is asking me if I *like* Jack?

"No," I answered, but I could feel my ears turning red. I glanced up at Ellie as I sat down to put on my jazz sneakers. She was twirling yet another part of her hair in preparation for putting it into her mouth. I can't believe she told them about Jack! What a traitor!

At that moment, Mrs. Atanabi came into the room, clapping to get everyone's attention in her usual, theatrical way. "Okay, girls, if you haven't signed your name on the tryout sheet, please do so now," she said, pointing to the clipboard on the table next to her. There were about eight other girls standing in line to sign in. "And if you've already signed in, please take a spot on the dance floor and start doing your stretches."

"I'll sign in for you," Ximena said to Savanna, walking over to the table.

"Do you want me to sign in for you, Charly?" Ellie asked me. I knew that was her way of checking to see if I was mad at her. *Which I was!*

"I already signed in," I answered quietly, not looking at her.

"Of course she signed in," Savanna said quickly, rolling her eyes. "Charlotte's *always* the first to sign in."

How (and Why) I Love to Dance

I've been taking dance lessons since I was four. Ballet. Tap. Jazz. Not because I want to be a prima ballerina when I grow up, but because I intend on becoming a Broadway star someday. To do that, you really have to learn how to sing and dance and perform. Which is why I work so hard on my dance lessons. And my singing lessons. I take them very seriously, because I know that someday, when I get my big break, I'll be ready for it. And why will I be ready for it? Because I've worked hard for it—my whole life! People seem to think that Broadway stars just come out of nowhere—but that's not true! They practice until their feet hurt! They rehearse like maniacs! If you want to be a star, you have to be willing to work harder than everyone else to achieve your goals and dreams! The way I see it, a dream is like a drawing in your head that comes to life. You have to imagine it first. Then you have to work extremely hard to make it come true.

So, when Savanna says, "Charlotte's *always* the first

to sign in," on the one hand it's kind of a compliment because she's saying, "Charlotte's always on top of things, which is why her hard work pays off for her." But when she says, "Charlotte's *always* the first to sign in," with that *eww* expression on her face, it's more like she's saying, "Charlotte only gets what she wants because she's first in line." Or at least that's what I hear. A put-down.

Savanna's really good at those kinds of put-downs, where it's all in the eyes and the corners of the mouth. It's too bad, because she didn't used to be like that. In lower school, Savanna and Ellie and me and Maya and Summer: we were all friends. We played together after school. We had tea parties. It's only been since we started middle school—ever since she got popular—that Savanna's become less nice than she used to be.

How Mrs. Atanabi
Introduced Her Dance

"Okay, ladies," said Mrs. Atanabi, clapping her hands and motioning for us to walk toward her, "everybody on the dance floor, please! Take your positions. Everybody spread out. So what we're going to do today is, I'm going to show you a couple of different dances from the sixties that I'd like you to try. The twist. The Hully Gully. And the mambo. Just those three. Sound good?"

I had taken up a position behind Summer, who smiled and waved one of her cute happy hellos at me. When I was little and still into Flower Fairies, I used to think that Summer Dawson looked exactly like the Lavender Fairy. Like she should have been born with violet wings.

"Since when have you been into dance?" I asked her, because she had never been one of the girls I'd see at dance recitals.

Summer shrugged shyly. "I started taking classes this summer."

"Sweet!" I answered, smiling encouragingly.

"Mrs. Atanabi?" said Ximena, raising her hand. "What is this audition even for?"

"Oh my goodness!" answered Mrs. Atanabi, tapping her forehead with her fingers. "Of course. I completely forgot to tell you guys what we're doing here."

I, personally, have always loved Mrs. Atanabi—with her long flowy dresses and scarves and the messy bun. I love that she always has the breathless appearance of someone who's just come back from a great journey. I like that. But a lot of people think she's flaky and weird. The way she throws her head back when she laughs. The way she mumbles to herself sometimes. People have said she looks exactly like Mrs. Puff in *SpongeBob SquarePants*. They call her Mrs. Fatanabi behind her back, which I think is incredibly mean.

"I've been asked to put together a dance piece to perform at the Beecher Prep Benefit Gala," she started explaining. "Which is in mid-March. It's not a performance that other students will ever see. It's for the parents, faculty, and alumni. But it's kind of a big deal. They're having it at Carnegie Hall this year!"

Everyone made little excited chirpy sounds.

Mrs. Atanabi laughed. "I thought you'd all like that!" she said. "I'm adapting a piece I choreographed years ago, which had gotten considerable attention at the time, I don't mind saying. And it should be a lot of fun. But it will take plenty of work! Which reminds me: if you're chosen for this dance, it will require a *big* time

252

commitment! I want to be clear about that right from the start, ladies. Ninety minutes of rehearsal, after school, three times a week. From now, through March. So if you can't commit to that, don't even try out. Okay?"

"But what if we have soccer practice?" asked Ruby, in the middle of a *plié*.

"Ladies, sometimes in life you have to choose," Mrs. Atanabi answered. "You can't have soccer practice *and* be in this dance. It's as simple as that. I don't want to hear any excuses about homework assignments or tests or anything else. Even one missed rehearsal is too much! Remember, this is *not* something you're required to do for school! You don't *have* to be here, girls. You won't be getting extra credit. If the appeal of dancing on one of the world's most famous stages isn't enough for you, then please *don't* try out." She extended her arm all the way and pointed to the exit. "I won't take it personally."

We all looked at each other. Ruby and Jacqueline both smiled apologetically at Mrs. Atanabi, waved goodbye, and left. I couldn't believe anyone would do that! To give up the chance to dance at Carnegie Hall? That's as famous as Broadway!

Mrs. Atanabi blinked but didn't say anything. Then she rubbed her head, like she was warding off a headache. "One last thing," she said. "If you're not selected for this particular routine, please remember there's still the big dance number in the spring variety show—and *everyone* can dance in that one. So if you don't make this performance, *please don't* have your mom email me. There are only spots for three girls."

"Only *three?*" cried Ellie, covering her mouth with her hand.

"Yes, *only* three," Mrs. Atanabi responded, sounding exactly like Mrs. Puff sounds when she says, *Oh, SpongeBob.*

I knew what Ellie was thinking: *Please let it be me, Ximena, and Savanna.*

But even as she wished that, she probably knew it wasn't going to work out that way. The thing is, everybody knows that Ximena is the best dancer in the whole school. She got selected for the summer intensives at the School of American Ballet. She's at *that* level. So it was a pretty safe bet that Ximena would make it in.

And everybody knows that Savanna made the finals in two different regionals last year, and had come close to placing at a national—so there was a good chance that she would make it in.

And everybody knows that— Well, not to brag, but dance is kind of my thing, and I have a bunch of huge trophies on my shelf that prove it.

Ellie, though? Sorry, but she's just not in the same league as either Ximena or Savanna. Or me. Sure, she's been into dance all these years, but she's always been kind of lazy about it. I don't know, maybe if there were room for four girls. But not if there can only be *three*.

254

Nope, it seemed pretty clear as I looked around the room at the competition: the final three would be Ximena, Savanna. And me! *Sorry, Ellie!*

And maybe, just *maybe*, this would be my chance to finally work my way into the Savanna group, once and for all. I could go back to having Ellie as my best friend. Savanna could have Ximena. It could all work out.

The twist. The Hully Gully. And the mambo.

Got it.

How to Use Venn Diagrams (Part 2)

In middle school, your lunch-table group isn't always the same as your friend group. Like, it's very possible—in fact, it's *probable!*—that you may end up sitting at a lunch table with a bunch of girls that you're friends with—but who aren't necessarily your *friend* friends. How you ended up at that table is completely random: Maybe there wasn't enough room at the table with the girls you really wanted to sit with. Or maybe you just happened to end up with a group of girls because of the class you had right before lunch. That's actually what happened to me. On the first day of school, Maya, Megan, Lina, Rand, Summer, Ellie, and I were all in Ms. Petosa's advanced math class together. When the lunch bell rang, we flew down the stairs in a big huddle, not knowing exactly how to get to the cafeteria. When we finally did find it, we all just sat down at a table in a pack. It was like we were playing musical chairs, with everyone scrambling to get a seat. There were actually only supposed to be six kids to a table, but the seven of us squeezed in and made it work.

Lina Summer Megan Rand

Ellie Charlotte Maya

At first, I thought it was the greatest table in the whole lunchroom! I was sitting right between Ellie, my best friend from first grade, and Maya, my other best friend from lower school. I was sitting directly across from Summer and Megan, both of whom I knew from lower school, too, even if we weren't necessarily good friends. *And* I knew Lina from the Beecher Prep Summer Camp program. The only person I didn't know at all was Rand, but she seemed nice enough. So, all in all, it looked like a totally awesome lunch table!

But then, that very first day, Summer switched tables to go sit with Auggie Pullman. It was so shocking! One second we were all sitting there, talking about him, watching him eat his lunch. Lina said something really mean that I won't repeat. And the next second, Summer, without saying anything to *anyone*, just picked up her lunch tray and walked over to him. It was so unexpected! Lina, I remember, looked like she was watching a car accident.

"Stop staring!" I said to her.

"I can't believe she's *eating* with him," she whispered, horrified.

"It's not *that* big a deal," I said, rolling my eyes.

"Then why aren't *you* having lunch with him?" she answered. "Aren't you supposed to be his welcome buddy?"

"That doesn't mean I have to sit with him at lunch," I answered quickly, regretting that I'd told anyone that Mr. Tushman had chosen me to be Auggie's welcome buddy. Yes, it was an honor that he had asked me, along with Julian and Jack—but I didn't want anyone throwing it in my face!

All around the cafeteria, people were doing the exact same thing we were doing at our lunch table: staring at Auggie and Summer eating together. We were literally only a few hours into middle school, but people had already started calling him the *Zombie Kid* and *Freak*.

Beauty and the Freak. That's what people were whispering about Summer and Auggie.

No way was I going to have people whisper stuff behind my back, too!

"Besides," I said to Lina, taking a bite of my Caesar salad. "I like *this* table. I don't want to switch."

And that was true! I *did* like this table!

At least, at first I did.

But then, as I got to know everyone a little better, I realized that maybe I didn't have as much in common with them as I would have liked. It turned out that Lina, Megan, and Rand were *all* super into sports (Maya played soccer, but that was all). So there was this whole world of soccer games and swim meets and "away games" that Ellie and I couldn't really talk to them about. Another thing is that they had all chosen to be in orchestra, while Ellie and I had chosen chorus. And the last thing, very simply, was that they weren't into a lot of the stuff *we* were into! They never watched *The Voice* or *American Idol*. They weren't into movie stars or old movies. They had never even seen *Les Misérables*, for crying out loud! I mean, how could I have a serious friendship with someone who had no interest in seeing *Les Mis*?

But as long as I had Ellie to talk to, with Maya there to round us out, everything was totally fine by me. The three of us would chat about the stuff *we* wanted to talk about on our side of the table, and Megan, Lina, and Rand would chat about the stuff *they* wanted to talk about on their side of the table. And then we'd all catch up about the stuff we had in common—schoolwork, homework, teachers, tests, bad cafeteria food—in the middle of the table.

Which is why everything was good. Until Ellie switched tables!

259

And now it's just me. And Maya.

Maya, who was only really fun to talk to when Ellie was there. Or if you wanted to play a rousing game of dots.

Look, I'm not mad at Ellie for switching tables. I honestly *don't* blame her. Ever since we heard that Amos had a crush on her, it was like she'd gotten a free pass into the popular group. Savanna had asked her to sit with them at lunch, and then arranged it so Amos and Ellie sat next to each other. That's how all the "couples" in the grade got together. Ximena and Miles. Savanna and Henry. And now, Amos and Ellie. In arranged group huddles. The popular boys and the popular girls. It was natural that they'd all want to stick together. Nobody else in our grade is dating or even *close* to dating! I know for a fact that the girls at *my* lunch table still act like boys have cooties! And, from what I can tell, most of the boys act like girls don't exist.

So, yeah, I totally get why Ellie switched lunch tables. I really do. And I'm not about to be super-mad at her, like Maya is. It's hard when you've been invited to a better lunch table. There's kind of no looking back.

All I can do is sit and wait, talk to Maya, and hope that Savanna will ask me to join them at the popular table someday.

In the meanwhile, I draw Venn diagrams. And play lots and lots of dots.

Charlotte
- loves dance
- hates sports
- in chorus
- prefers dogs
- no bra
- ♥Les Mis
- on honor roll

Lina, Megan, & and
- hate dance
- love sports
- in band
- on soccer team
- hate musicals
- don't care about grades that much
- prefer cats
- sports bra

- dots
- "not popular"

Maya
- neutral about dance
- neutral about sports
- in orchestra
- prefers vampires

How a New Subgroup Was Formed

The next day, right before lunch, this note was tacked to the announcement board outside of the library:

Congratulations to the girls listed below! You've been chosen to participate in Mrs. Atanabi's 1960s dance performance. I've posted a rehearsal schedule on the website. Mark your calendars! No absences. No excuses. Our first rehearsal is tomorrow at 4:00 p.m. in the performance space. DO NOT DARE TO BE LATE!—Mrs. Atanabi

Ximena Chin
Charlotte Cody
Summer Dawson

OMG, I got in! Yay!!!!!! I was so happy when I read my name on the list! Overjoyed! Ecstatic! Woo-hoo!

So it was me, Ximena—and *Summer*?

Whaaat! *Summer*? That was such a surprise! I was so positively sure it was going to be Savanna! I mean,

Summer had just started taking dance! Did she really beat out Savanna?

Oh boy: I could only imagine how mad Savanna was at that. I bet her *eww* frown stretched clear across her face when she saw the list! And Ellie? Actually, I bet Ellie was somewhat relieved. She would have had a hard time keeping up with Ximena and Savanna, and Ellie never *really* loved dancing that much. I always kind of thought she was only into it because *I'd* always been into it. I was happy it worked out for her this way. I mean, she might not act like it, but she's still *my* BFF.

And I was happy for me, too! Because even though I was hoping to get a bit closer to the Savanna group, I had also been a little stressed wondering if the Savanna and Ximena pairing would have iced me out.

But having Summer in the group along with Ximena? That was going to be awesome! Maybe the combined power of Summer's niceness and my niceness would turn Ximena into one of us. At the very least, it might keep her from being the mean girl everyone seems to think she is. Not that I think she's a mean girl. In fact, I barely know her! Either way, having Summer be the third girl in the dance made me so happy. I almost couldn't stop smiling all day.

How I Saw Savanna

At lunch, I squeezed in next to Maya and Rand, who were hunched over yet another one of Maya's giant dot games, which were getting more and more elaborate.

"So!" I said happily. "Good news, guys! I got picked to be in Mrs. Atanabi's sixties dance show for the benefit in March! Yay!"

"Yay!" Maya answered, not looking up from the dot game. "That's great, Charlotte."

"Yay," echoed Rand. "Congrats."

"Summer got in, too."

"Oh yay, good for her," said Maya. "I like Summer. She's always so nice."

Rand, who was marking a row of boxes she had just closed off with her initial, looked up at Maya and smiled. "Fifteen!" she said.

"Argh!" said Maya, grinding her teeth. She had just gotten braces, and was making a lot of funny movements with her mouth these days.

I flicked my eraser at them. "That sure is one intense

game of dots you're playing there," I said sarcastically.

"Ha-ha!" said Maya, leaning into me with her shoulder. "That's so funny I forgot to laugh."

"The mean-girl table is looking at you," said Rand.

"What?" I said. Both Maya and I turned around in the direction she was staring.

But Savanna, Ximena, Gretchen, and Ellie turned away the moment I glanced in their direction.

"They were *so* just talking about you!" said Maya, giving them her dirtiest look through her black-framed glasses.

"Stop that, Maya," I said to her.

"Why? I don't care," she answered. "Let them see me."

She bared her teeth at them like some kind of crazy ferret.

"Stop looking at them, Maya!" I whispered through my own gritted teeth.

"Fine," she said.

She went back to playing her colossal game of dots with Rand, and I concentrated on eating my ravioli. At one point, I could feel someone's eyes burning into my back, so I turned around to sneak a peek at the Savanna table again. This time around, Ximena, Gretchen, and Ellie were talking together, completely oblivious to me. But Savanna was glaring right at me! And she didn't look away when our eyes met. She just continued staring me down. Then, right before she finally stopped, she poked her tongue out at me. It happened so fast, no one else would have seen it. And it seemed so childish, I almost couldn't believe it!

That's when I realized that I got it wrong before, about Summer taking the third spot in Mrs. Atanabi's dance piece. I had thought that spot should have gone to Savanna, *not* Summer. But in Savanna's view, it wasn't Summer who had taken that spot from her. It was *me*! "Charlotte's *always* the first to sign in," she had said.

Savanna blamed *me* for taking her rightful spot in the dance!

How We Got Off to an Awkward Start

All the next day, the threat of a snowstorm made everyone kind of giddy and uncertain, since there was talk that the school would close early if it came down as bad as the forecast predicted. Luckily—because the last thing in the world I wanted was for our first rehearsal to be canceled!—the snow only started falling in the late afternoon. Not hard at all. So I made my way up to the performance space as quickly as I could after the last bell. Given that Mrs. Atanabi had issued such a threatening warning about being late, I wasn't surprised that both Summer and Ximena were already there, too.

We said hello to one another before changing into our dance clothes. It was a little awkward at first, I guess. The three of us had never really hung out together before. We were from different groups, our own version of mammals, reptiles, and fish. Summer and I only had one class together. And, like I said before, I *barely* knew Ximena. The longest conversation we'd ever had was back in December, in Ms. Rubin's class, when she asked me—without a shred of remorse—if I would mind switching partners with her so she could be paired up with Savanna. Which is how I ended up with Remo as my science fair project partner, but that's a whole other story not worth telling.

We started doing warm-ups and stretches to pass the time. Mrs. Atanabi was now almost half an hour late!

"Do you think this is how it's always going to be?" said Ximena, mid-*battement*. "Mrs. Atanabi being late?"

"She's *never* on time to theater class," I said, shaking my head.

"Right?" Ximena said. "That's what I'm afraid of."

"Maybe she just got stuck in the snow?" Summer said, somewhat hopefully. "It's starting to come down pretty hard now, I think."

Ximena made a face. "Yeah, maybe she needs a dog-sled," she answered quickly.

"Ha-ha-ha!" I laughed.

But I could tell I sounded dorky.

Please, God, please don't let me seem dorky in front of Ximena Chin.

The truth is: Ximena Chin made me a little nervous. I don't know why exactly. It was just that she was *so* cool, and *so* pretty, and everything about her was always *so* perfect. The way she wrapped her scarf. The way her jeans fit her. The way she fastened her hair into the neatest twist. Everything was so flawless with her!

I remember from the moment Ximena started at

Beecher Prep this year, *everybody* had wanted to be her friend. Including me! I'm sure she didn't even remember this, but I was the one who helped her find her locker on the first day of school. I was the one who let her borrow a pencil in third period (which she never returned to me, come to think of it). But Savanna was the one who became her best friend. Savanna managed to zoom in on her within the first nanosecond of school. And then, forget it. It was like the Big Bang of friendships. It just exploded into an instantaneous universe of knowing looks and giggles and clothes and secrets.

There was really no chance of getting to know Ximena better after that. The truth is, she didn't make much of an effort to expand beyond the Savanna group anyway. Maybe she felt like she didn't actually have to. People said she was kind of a snob.

All I really knew about her was that she had the most amazing leg extension I'd ever seen, the highest scores in our grade, and she was snarky. Meaning, she made a lot of "clever observations" about people behind their backs. There were a bunch of people—like Maya, for instance—who couldn't stand her. But I couldn't wait to get to know her better. To be friends with her, maybe! To laugh at her sarcastic gibes. More than anything, though, I just really really *really* wanted her to like me!

"I hope this is all going to be worth the time-suck," Ximena was saying. "I mean, we've got so many other things going on this month! That science fair project?"

"I haven't even started mine," said Summer.

"Me, neither!" I said, though that actually wasn't true at all. Remo and I had finished our diorama of a cell the first week back from winter break.

"I just want to make sure we get enough rehearsal time for this dance," Ximena said, looking at her phone. "I don't want to be onstage at *Carnegie* Hall looking like a *total* idiot because we didn't rehearse enough—all because Mrs. Atanabi was too flaky to show up on time."

"You know," I said, trying to sound casual, "if we ever need a place to rehearse away from school, you guys could come over to my house. I have a mirrored wall in my basement and a barre. My mom used to teach ballet out of our house."

"I remember your basement!" said Summer cheerfully. "You had that Flower Fairy birthday party there once!"

"Back in the second grade," I answered, a little embarrassed she would mention Flower Fairies in front of Ximena.

"Do you live far from here?" Ximena asked me, scrolling through her texts.

"Just ten blocks away."

"Okay, text me your address," she said.

"Sure!" I said, whipping out my phone, thinking *I'm texting Ximena Chin my address* like the big dork that I am. "Umm, sorry, what's your number?"

She didn't look up from her phone but held her hand up to my face, like a crossing guard. There, running vertically down the side of her palm, was her phone number written in neat block letters in dark blue pen. I keyed her number into my contacts and texted her my address.

"Hey, you know," I said as I was texting, "you guys could come over tomorrow after school, if you want. We can start rehearsing then."

"Okay," Ximena mumbled casually, which made me want to gasp. *Ximena Chin is coming over to my house tomorrow!*

"Oh, I actually *can't*," said Summer, squinting her eyes apologetically. "I'm hanging out with Auggie tomorrow."

"What about Friday, then?" I asked.

"Can't," said Ximena. She had obviously finished texting now and looked up.

"Then maybe next week?" I said.

"We'll figure out some other time," Ximena answered indifferently. She started running her fingers through her hair. "I forget you're friends with the freak," she said to Summer, smiling. "What's that like?"

I don't think she was even trying to be mean when she said this. That's really just how a lot of people automatically referred to Auggie Pullman.

I looked at Summer. *Don't say anything*, I thought.

But I knew she would.

How Nobody Gets Mad at the Lavender Fairy

Summer sighed. "Could you please not call him that?" she asked, almost shyly.

Ximena acted like she didn't get it. "Why? He's not here," she said, pulling her hair into a ponytail. "It's just a nickname."

"It's an awful nickname," Summer answered. "It makes me feel bad."

Here's the thing with Summer Dawson: she has this way of talking where she can say stuff like this, and people don't seem to mind. If I had said something like this? Forget it, people would be all over me about being a goody two-shoes! But when the Lavender Fairy does it, with her cute little eyebrows raised like smiles on her forehead, she doesn't come off as preachy. She just seems sweet.

"Oh, okay, I'm sorry," answered Ximena apologetically, her eyes open wide. "I honestly wasn't trying to be mean, Summer. But I won't call him that again, I promise."

She sounded like she was genuinely sorry, but there was something about her expression that always made you wonder if she was being completely sincere. I think it had something to do with the dimple in her left cheek. She almost couldn't help looking mischievous.

Summer looked at her doubtfully. "It's fine."

"I really am sorry," said Ximena, almost like she was trying to smooth out her dimple.

Now Summer smiled. "Totally cool beans," she said.

"I've said it before and I'll say it again," answered Ximena, giving Summer a little squeeze. "You really are a saint, Summer."

For a second, I felt a quick pang of jealousy that Ximena seemed to like Summer so much.

"I don't think anyone should call him a freak, *either*," I said absently.

Now, here I have to stop and say something in my defense—I HAVE NO IDEA WHY I SAID THAT! It literally just came out of me, this stupid string of words hurling from my mouth like vomit! I knew immediately how obnoxious it made me sound.

"So *you've* never called him that," Ximena said, raising one eyebrow high. The way she was looking at me, it was like she was daring me to blink.

"I, um—" I said. I could feel my ears turning red.

No, I'm sorry I said it. Don't hate me, Ximena Chin!

"Let me ask you something," she said quickly. "Would you go out with him?"

It was so out of the blue, I almost didn't know what to say.

"What? No!" I answered immediately.

"Exactly," she said, like she had just proved a point.

"But not because of how he looks," I said, flustered. "Just because we don't have anything in common!"

"Oh, come on!" laughed Ximena. "That's *so* not true."

I didn't know what she was getting at.

"Would *you* go out with him?" I asked.

"Of course not," she answered calmly. "But I'm not about to be hypocritical about it."

I glanced at Summer, who gave me an *ouch, that hurts* look.

"Hey, I don't want to be mean," continued Ximena matter-of-factly. "But when you say, *Oh, I would never call him a freak*, it totally makes me look like a jerk because I had obviously just called him that, and it's kind of annoying because everyone knows that Mr. Tushman *asked* you to be his welcome buddy and *that's* why you don't call him a freak like everybody else does. Summer became friends with him without anyone forcing her to be his welcome buddy, which is why she's a saint."

"I'm not a saint," Summer answered quickly. "And I don't think Charlotte would have called him that, even if Mr. Tushman hadn't asked her to be a welcome buddy."

"See? You're being a saint even now," said Ximena.

"I don't think I would have called him a freak," I said quietly.

Ximena crossed her arms. She was looking at me with a knowing smile.

"You know, you're nicer to him when you're in front of teachers," she said very seriously. "It's been noticed."

Before I could answer—not that I even knew what I *would* have answered—Mrs. Atanabi burst into the performance space through the double doors in the back of the auditorium.

"So sorry I'm late, so sorry I'm late!" she announced breathlessly, covered in snow. She looked like a little snowman as she walked down the stairs carrying four ridiculously full tote bags.

Ximena and Summer ran up the stairs to help her, but I turned around and walked out to the hallway. I pretended to drink at the water fountain, but what I really needed to gulp down was air. Ice-cold air. Because I could feel my cheeks burning, like they were on fire. It felt like I'd just gotten slapped in the face. I could see out the hallway window that the snow really was coming down hard now, and a part of me just wanted to run outside and ice-skate away.

Is that how *other* people saw me? Like I was this hypocritical fake or something? Or was that just Ximena being her typical snarky self?

You're nicer to him when you're in front of teachers. It's been noticed.

Is that true? Has it been noticed? I mean, have there been a couple of times when I was being especially nice to Auggie Pullman because I knew it would get back to Mr. Tushman that I was being a good welcome buddy? Maybe. I don't know!

But even if that were the case, at least I can say I've *been* nice to him! That's more than most people can say! That's more than Ximena can say! I still remember that time she was partnered with Auggie in dance class and looked like she was about to throw up. I've never done anything like that to Auggie!

Okay, so maybe I *am* a little nicer to Auggie when teachers are around. Is that *so* horrible?

It's been noticed? What does that even mean? Noticed by *who*? Savanna? Ellie? Is that what they say about me? Is that what they were talking about in the lunchroom yesterday, when they were so obviously talking about me that even Maya—who can be so clueless about social stuff—felt sorry for me?

Here this whole time I had assumed that Ximena Chin didn't even know who I was! And now, it turns out, *I've been noticed*. More than I ever wanted to be.

How I Received My First Surprise of the Day

I walked back inside the performance space as Mrs. Atanabi finished unwrapping herself from all her wintry layers. Her coat, her scarf, and her sweater were all scattered around her on the floor, which was wet from the snow she had brought inside with her.

"Oh my gosh, oh my gosh!" she kept saying over and over again, fanning herself with both hands. "It's really starting to come down now."

She plopped onto the piano bench in front of the stage and caught her breath. "Oh my gosh, I do hate being late!"

I saw Ximena and Summer exchange knowing looks.

"When I was little," Mrs. Atanabi continued, talking in that chatterbox way of hers that some people loved and some people thought made her seem crazy, "my mother actually used to charge my sister and me one dollar every time we were late for something. Literally, *every* time I was late—even if it was just for dinner—I had to pay my mom a dollar!" She laughed and started redoing her bun, holding a couple of bobby pins in her teeth while she talked. "When your entire allowance for the week is only three bucks, you learn to budget your time! That's why I'm conditioned to *hate* being late!"

"And yet," Ximena pointed out, smiling in that sly way of hers, "you were still late today. Maybe we should charge you a dollar from now on?"

"Ha-ha-ha!" laughed Mrs. Atanabi good-naturedly, flicking off her boots. "Yes, I was late, Ximena! And that's actually not a bad idea. Maybe I *should* give all three of you a dollar!"

Ximena kind of laughed, assuming she was joking.

"In fact," Mrs. Atanabi said, reaching for her pocketbook, "I think I'm going to give *each* one of you girls a dollar bill *every* time I'm late to a rehearsal. From now on! That'll force me to be on time!"

Summer shot me a quizzical look. We started to realize that Mrs. Atanabi, who had pulled out her wallet, was serious.

"Oh no, Mrs. Atanabi," said Summer, shaking her head. "You don't have to do that."

"I know! But I'm going to!" answered Mrs. Atanabi, smiling. "Now, here's the rub. I'll agree to give each of you a dollar every time *I'm* late to a rehearsal if you agree to give me a dollar every time *you're* late for a rehearsal."

278

"Are you allowed to do that?" Ximena asked incredulously. "Take money from a student?"

I was thinking the same thing.

"Why not?" answered Mrs. Atanabi. "You're in private school. You can afford it! *Probably more than I can.*" This last part she muttered. And then she started cracking up.

Mrs. Atanabi was kind of famous for laughing at her own jokes. You pretty much had to get used to it.

She pulled three crisp dollar bills out of her wallet and held them up in the air for us to see.

"So, what do you girls say?" she said. "Is it a deal?"

Ximena looked at both of us. "I know *I'm* never going to be late," she said to us.

"I'm not going to be late, either!" said Summer.

I shrugged, still unable to look Ximena in the eyes. "Me, neither," I said.

"Then it's a deal!" said Mrs. Atanabi, walking over to us.

"For you, *mademoiselle*," she said to Ximena, handing her a spanking-new dollar bill.

"*Merci!*" said Ximena, shooting us a quick smile, which I pretended not to see.

Then Mrs. Atanabi walked over to me and Summer.

"For you, and for you," she said, handing us each a dollar bill.

"God bless America," we both answered at the same time.

Wait. What?

We looked at each other, our mouths and eyes open wide. Suddenly everything that occurred in the last half-hour seemed to lose any importance—if what I *think* just happened *did* just happen.

"The accordion-man?" I whispered excitedly.

Summer gasped and nodded happily. "The accordion-man!"

How We Went to Narnia

It's funny how you can know someone your whole life, but not *really* know them at all. Here, this whole time, I've been living in a parallel world to Summer Dawson, a nice girl I've known since kindergarten who I've always thought looked like the Lavender Fairy. But we'd never actually become *friend* friends! Not for any particular reason. It just worked out that way. The same way that Ellie and I were *destined* to be friends because Ms. Diamond had sat us next to each other on the first day of school, Summer and I were *destined* not to get to know each other because we were never in the same classes. Except for PE and swim, and assembly and concerts and stuff like that, our paths never crossed in lower school. Our moms weren't really friends, so we never had playdates. Sure, I invited her to my Flower Fairy birthday party once. But it really was because Ellie and I thought she looked like the Lavender Fairy! And sure, we'd hang out a bit at other people's bowling parties and at sleepovers and stuff. We were Facebook friends. We had lots of people in common. We were totally *friendly*.

But we were never actually *friends*.

So, when she said "God bless America," it almost felt like I was meeting her for the first time in my life. Imagine finding out that there was someone else in the world who knew a secret that only you knew! It was like an invisible bridge had instantly been built connecting us. Or, like we had stumbled onto a tiny door in the back of a wardrobe and an accordion-playing faun had welcomed us to Narnia.

How I Received My Second Surprise of the Day

Before Summer and I could say anything else on the subject of the accordion-man, Mrs. Atanabi brushed her hands together and said it was time to "get to work." We spent the rest of the rehearsal time, since there was only half an hour left, listening to Mrs. Atanabi give us a quick overview of the dance while also periodically checking the weather app on her phone. We didn't really do any actual dancing: just some basic steps and a little rough blocking.

"We'll start getting into it next time!" Mrs. Atanabi assured us. "I promise I won't be late! See you Friday! Stay warm! Be careful going home!"

"Bye, Mrs. Atanabi!"

"Bye!"

As soon as she was gone, Summer and I came together like magnets, talking excitedly at the same time.

"I can't believe you know who I'm talking about," I said.

"God bless America!" she answered.

"Do you have any idea what happened to him?"

"No! I asked around and everything."

"I did, too! No one knows what happened to him."

"It's like he just vanished off the face of the earth!"

"It's like *who* vanished off the face of the earth?" asked Ximena, looking at us curiously. I guess the way we were squealing and carrying on, it did seem like something major had *just* happened.

I was still kind of keeping my distance from her because of before, so I let Summer answer.

"This guy who used to play the accordion on Main Street," said Summer. "In front of the A&P on Moore? He was always there with his guide dog? I'm sure you must have noticed him. Whenever you'd drop money into his accordion case, he'd say, 'God bless America.'"

"God bless America," I chimed in at the exact same time.

"Anyway," she continued, "he's been there for *forever*, but a couple of months ago, he just wasn't there anymore."

"And no one knows what happened to him!" I added. "It's like this *mystery*."

"Wait, so this is a *homeless* person you're talking about?" asked Ximena, kind of making the same *eww* face Savanna makes sometimes.

"I don't know if Gordy's homeless, actually," Summer answered.

"You know his name?" I asked, completely surprised.

"Yeah," she answered matter-of-factly. "Gordy Johnson."

"How do you know that?"

"I don't know. My dad used to talk to him," she answered, shrugging. "He was a veteran, and my dad was a marine, and was always like, *That gentleman's a hero, Summer. He served his country.* We used to bring him coffee and a bagel on the way to school sometimes. My mom gave him my dad's old parka."

"Wait, was it an orange Canada Goose parka?" I said, pointing at her.

"Yes!" Summer answered happily.

"I remember that parka!" I screamed, grabbing her hands.

"OMG, you guys are totally geeking out," Ximena laughed. "All this over a homeless guy in an orange parka?"

Summer and I looked at each other.

"It's hard to explain," said Summer. But I could tell she felt it, too: our connection over this. Our bond. It was our version of the Big Bang.

"Oh my God, Summer!" I said, grabbing her arm. "Maybe we could track him down! We could find out where he is and make sure he's okay! If you know his name, we should be able to do that!"

"You think we could?" asked Summer, her eyes doing that little dancing thing they did when she was super-happy. "I would *love* that!"

"Wait, wait, wait," said Ximena, shaking her head. "Are you guys serious? You want to track down some homeless dude you barely know?" She acted like she couldn't believe what she was hearing.

"Yes," we both said, looking at each other happily.

"Who barely knows *you?*"

"He'll know me!" Summer said confidently. "Especially if I tell him I'm Sergeant Dawson's daughter."

"Will he know you, Charlotte?" Ximena asked me, her eyes narrowing doubtfully.

"Of course not!" I answered her quickly, just wanting her to stop talking. "He's blind, *stupid!*"

The moment I said it, everything got quiet. Even the radiator, which had been making all these loud banging noises in the performance space until then, suddenly fell silent. As if the performance space wanted to hear my words echo in the air.

He's blind, stupid. He's blind, stupid. He's blind, stupid.

Another vomit of words. It's almost like I was *trying* to get Ximena Chin to hate me!

I waited for her to hit me with a sarcastic comeback, something that would slap me like an invisible hand across the face.

But, instead, to my utter and complete amazement, she started to laugh.

Summer started to laugh, too. "He's blind, *stupid!*" she said, imitating the way I had said it exactly.

"He's blind, *stupid!*" Ximena repeated.

They both started cracking up. I think the horrified look on my face made it even funnier for them. Every time they looked at me, they laughed harder.

"I'm so sorry I said that, Ximena," I whispered quickly.

Ximena shook her head, wiping her eyes with the palm of her hand.

"It's fine," she answered, catching her breath. "I kind of had that coming."

There wasn't a trace of snarkiness to her right now. She was smiling.

"Look, I didn't mean to insult you earlier," she said. "What I said about Auggie. I know you're not *only* nice to him in front of teachers. I'm sorry I said that."

I couldn't believe she was apologizing.

"No, it's fine," I answered, fumbling.

"Really?" she asked. "I don't want you to be mad at me."

"I'm not!"

"I can be a total jerk sometimes," she said regretfully. "But I really want us to be friends."

"Okay."

"Awww," said Summer, stretching her arms out to us. "Come on, guys. Group hug."

She wrapped her fairy wings around us, and for a few seconds, we came together in an awkward embrace that lasted a second too long and ended in more giggles. This time, I was laughing, too.

That turned out to be the biggest surprise of the day. Not finding out that people have *noticed* me. Not finding out that Summer knew the accordion-man's name.

But realizing that Ximena Chin, under her layers and layers and layers of snarkiness and mischief, could actually be kind of sweet. When she wasn't being kind of mean.

How We Got to Know
Each Other Better

The next few weeks flew by! A crazy blur of snowstorms, and dance rehearsals, and science fair projects, and studying for tests, *and* trying to solve the mystery of what had happened to Gordy Johnson (more on that later).

Mrs. Atanabi turned out to be quite the little drill sergeant! Lovable, in her own cute, waddly way, but *really* pushy. Like, we could *never* practice enough for her. Drills, drills, drills. *En pointe!* Shimmy! Hip roll! Classical ballet! Modern dance! A little bit of jazz! No tap! Downbeat! Half toe! Everything done her way, because she had a lot of very specific dance quirks. Things she obsessed about. The dances themselves weren't hard. The twist. The monkey. The Watusi. The pony. The hitchhike. The swim. The hucklebuck. The shingaling. But it was doing them exactly the way she wanted us to do them that was hard. Doing them as part of a larger choreographed piece. And doing them in sync. That's what we spent most of our time working on. The way we carried our arms. The way we snapped our fingers. Our turnouts. Our jumps. We had to work hard on learning how to dance *alike*—not just together!

The dance we spent the most time working on was the shingaling. It was the centerpiece of Mrs. Atanabi's whole dance number, what she used to transition from one dance style to the next. But there were so many variations to it—the Latin one, the R&B one, the funk shingaling—it was hard not to mix them up. And Mrs. Atanabi was *so* particular about the way each one was danced! Funny how she could be so loosey-goosey about some things—like never *once* getting to a rehearsal on time!—and yet be so strict about other things—like, God forbid you do a diagonal *chassé* instead of a sideways *chassé*! *Uh-oh, careful, the world as you know it might end!*

I'm not saying that Mrs. Atanabi wasn't nice, by the way. I want to be fair. She *was* super-nice. Reassuring us if we were having trouble with a new routine: "Small steps, girls! Everything starts with small steps!" Surprising us with brownies after a particularly intense workout. Driving us home when she kept us rehearsing too late. Telling us funny stories about other teachers. Personal stories about her own life. How she'd grown up in the Barrio. How some of her friends had gone down a "wrong" path. How watching *American Bandstand* had saved her life. How she'd met her husband, who was also a dancer, while performing with Cirque du Soleil in

Quebec. "We fell in love doing arabesques on a tightrope thirty feet in the air."

But it was intense. When I would go to sleep at night, I had so much information bouncing around my head! Bits of music. Things to memorize. Math equations. To-do lists. Mrs. Atanabi saying in her smooth East Harlem accent: *"It's the shingaling, baby!"* There were times when I would just put my headset on to drown out the chatter in my brain.

I was having so much fun, though, I wouldn't have changed a thing. Because the best part about all the crazy rehearsing and Mrs. Atanabi's drills and every-thing else—*and I don't want to sound corny*—was that Ximena, Summer, and I were really starting to get to know each other. Okay, that *does* sound corny. But it's true! Look, I'm not saying we became best friends or anything. Summer still hung out with Auggie. Ximena still hung out with Savanna. I still played dots with Maya. But we were becoming friends. Like, *friend* friends.

Ximena's snarkiness, by the way, was completely put on. Something she could take off whenever she wanted to. Like a scarf you wear as an accessory until it starts feeling itchy around your neck. When she was with Savanna, she wore the scarf. With us, she took it off. That's not to say I didn't still get nervous around her sometimes! OMG. The first time she came over to my house? I was a complete wreck! I was nervous that my mom would embarrass me. I was nervous that the stuffed animals on my bed were too pink. I was nervous about the *Big Time Rush* poster on my bedroom door. I was nervous that my dog, Suki, would pee on her.

But, of course, everything turned out fine! Ximena was totally nice. Said I had a cool room. Offered to do the dishes after dinner. Made fun of a particularly hilarious photo of me when I was three, which was fair because I look like a sock puppet in it! At some point during that afternoon, I don't even know when it was, I actually stopped thinking *Ximena Chin is in my house! Ximena Chin is in my house!* and just started having fun. That was huge for me because it was a turning point, the moment I stopped acting like an idiot around Ximena. No more word vomits. I guess that was when I took my "scarf" off, too.

Anyway, February was intense, but awesome. And by the end of February, we were pretty much hanging out at my place every day after school, dancing in front of the mirrored walls, self-correcting, matching our moves. Whenever we'd get tired, or discouraged, one of us would say in Mrs. Atanabi's accent, "It's the shingaling, baby!" And that would keep us going.

And sometimes we didn't rehearse. Sometimes we just chilled in my living room by the fire doing homework together. Or hanging out. Or, occasionally, searching for Gordy Johnson.

How I Prefer Happy Endings

One of the things I miss the most about being a little kid is that when you're little, all the movies you watch have happy endings. Dorothy goes back to Kansas. Charlie gets the chocolate factory. Edmund redeems himself. I like that. I like happy endings.

But, as you get older, you start seeing that sometimes stories *don't* have happy endings. Sometimes they even have sad endings. Of course, that makes for more interesting storytelling, because you don't know *what's* going to happen. But it's also kind of scary.

Anyway, the reason I'm bringing this up is because the more we looked for Gordy Johnson, the more I started realizing that this story might *not* have a happy ending.

We had started our search by simply Googling his name. But, it turns out, there are hundreds of Gordy Johnsons. Gordon Johnsons. Gordie Johnsons. There's a famous jazz musician named Gordy Johnson (which we theorized could explain the rumor the eye-shop man had heard about *our* Gordy Johnson). There are politician Gordon Johnsons. Construction worker Gordon Johnsons. Veterans. Lots of obituaries. The Internet doesn't distinguish between names of the living and names of the dead. And every time we clicked on one of those names, we would be relieved that it wasn't *our* Gordy Johnson. But sad that it was someone else's Gordy Johnson.

At first, Ximena didn't really join in the search. She would be doing her homework or texting Miles on one side of the bedroom while Summer and I huddled around my laptop, scrolling through page after page of dead ends. But one day, Ximena pulled her chair next to ours and started looking over our shoulders.

"Maybe you should try searching by image," she suggested.

Which we did. It was still a dead end. But after that, Ximena became as interested in finding out what happened to Gordy Johnson as we were.

How I Discovered
Something About Maya

Meanwhile, at school, everything was business as usual. We had our science fair. Remo and I got a B+ for our cell-anatomy diorama, which was more than I thought we would get considering I spent as little time on that project as possible. Ximena and Savanna built a sundial. The most interesting one was probably Auggie and Jack's, though. It was a working lamp that was powered by a potato. I figured Auggie probably did most of the work, since, let's face it, Jack's never been what one would call a "gifted student," but he was so happy to have gotten an A on it. He looked so cute!!! Like a little happy but somewhat clueless emoticon. ☺

And this was my emoticon when I saw him: ☺

By the end of February, the boy war had really escalated, though. Summer filled me in about what was going on, since she had the inside scoop on everything from Auggie and Jack's point of view. Apparently—and I was sworn to secrecy—Julian had started leaving really nasty yellow Post-it notes for Jack and Auggie in their lockers.

I felt so bad for them!

Maya felt bad for them, too. She had become obsessed with the boy war herself, though I wasn't sure why at first. It's not like she had ever made any attempts to be friends with Auggie! And she always treated Jack like a goofball. Like, back in the days when Ellie and I would point out how cute he looked in his Artful Dodger top hat, Maya would stick her fingers in her ears and cross her eyes, as if even the thought of him repulsed her. So I figured her interest in the war had to do with the fact that, quirky as she was, Maya had a good heart.

It was only one day at lunch, when I saw her hard at work on some kind of list, that I understood why she cared so much. In her notebook, where she designs her dot games, she had three rows of tiny Post-its with the names of all the boys in the grade. She was sorting them into columns: Jack's side; Julian's side; neutrals.

"I think it'll help Jack to know he's not alone in this war," she explained.

That's when I realized: *Maya has a little crush on Jack Will! Awww, that's so cute!*

"Sweet," I answered, not wanting to make her self-conscious. So I helped her organize the list. We disagreed about some of the neutrals. She ultimately gave in to me. Then she copied the list onto a piece of loose-leaf paper and folded it in half, then in quarters, then in eighths, then in sixteenths. "What are you going to do with it?"

"I don't know," she answered, pushing her glasses back up her nose. "I don't want it to get in the wrong hands."

"You want me to give it to Summer?"

"Yes."

So I gave the list to Summer to give to Jack and Auggie. I think Summer might have assumed that I had made the list myself, which I didn't correct because I *had* helped Maya work on the list, so I thought it was fine.

"How's the dance stuff going?" Maya asked me in her flat-voiced way that same day. I knew she was just trying to be polite, since she couldn't care less. But she was good that way. At least she made an effort to act interested.

"Crazy!!!" I answered, biting into my sandwich. "Mrs. Atanabi is absolutely insane!"

"Ha. Mrs. Mad-anabi," said Maya.

"Yeah," I said. "Good one."

"It's like you've been hibernating the whole month of February, though!" said Maya. "I've barely seen you. You never walk home with us after school."

I nodded. "I know. We've been practicing at lunch-time lately. But we'll be done soon enough. Just a few more weeks. The gala is on March fifteenth."

"Beware the ides of March," she said.

"Oh yeah! Right," I said, though I had absolutely no idea what she was talking about.

"So, want to see the sketches for my newest colossal dot game?"

"Sure," I answered, taking a deep breath.

She pulled out her notebook and launched into a detailed explanation of how she had stopped using grid patterns for her dots and was now using chalk art-style graphics to create murals, so that when the dots got filled in, they would "have a dynamic flow pattern." Or something like that. The truth is, I had trouble following what she was saying. The only part I heard for sure was when she said: "I haven't brought my new dot game to school yet because I want to make sure you're around to play it."

"Oh, sweet," I answered, scratching my head. I couldn't believe how bored I was at the moment.

She started saying something else about the dots, and I glanced over at Summer's table to distract myself. She, Jack, and Auggie were laughing. I could guarantee you one thing: they weren't talking about dots! There were times when I really wished I had the guts to just go and sit with them.

Then I looked over at the Savanna table. They were all laughing and having a good time, too. Savanna. Ellie. Gretchen. Ximena. All talking to the boys at the table across from them: Julian, Miles, Henry, Amos.

"Isn't she awful?" said Maya, following my gaze.

"Ellie?" I asked, because that's who I was looking at that exact moment.

"No. Ximena Chin."

I turned around and gave Maya a look. I knew she hated Ximena, but for some reason, the way she had said it, in this seething tone, just surprised me. "So, what is this thing you have against Ximena Chin?" I asked. "It's *Ellie* who ditched us, remember? It's *Savanna* who hasn't been nice to us."

"That's not true," Maya argued. "Savanna's always been nice to me. We used to have playdates all the time when we were in lower school."

I shook my head. "Yeah, but, Maya," I said, "playdates don't count. Half the time, our moms set those up. Now *we* get to choose who *we* want to hang out with. And Savanna is *choosing* not to hang out with us. Ellie is *choosing* not to hang out with us. Just like we're *choosing* not to hang out with some people. It's not that big a deal. But it's certainly not Ximena Chin's fault."

Maya peered over her glasses at the Savanna table. As I watched her, I realized she still looked exactly the way she did in kindergarten, when we would have tetherball games in the playground or go on fairy quests in the park at sunset.

In some ways, Maya hadn't grown up that much since then. Her face, her glasses, and her hair—they were almost identical to what they used to be. She was taller now, of course. But almost everything else remained unchanged. Especially her expressions. They were exactly the same.

"No, Ellie used to be nice to me," she answered very surely. "Just like Savanna was. I blame it all on Ximena Chin."

How February Made Us
Money, Too!

By the end of February, we'd made thirty-six dollars!

Mrs. Atanabi had been late to every single rehearsal.

Every.

Single.

One.

It got so that she would actually come to rehearsal with crisp dollar bills all ready in her hands to give us. She would literally show up, begin talking, hand us the money without even acknowledging it, and start the dance class! It was almost like it was the price of admission. What she paid to get through the door. So funny!

Then at one point halfway through the month, she herself suggested upping the amount of the penalty she would give us for being late from one dollar to five dollars. This, she assured us, would definitely keep her from being late in the future.

But of course that didn't work, either. And now,

instead of coming to rehearsal prepared with crisp one-dollar bills in her hand, she would come in with crisp five-dollar bills. Which she simply dropped on top of our backpacks by the door without saying a word. The price of admission.

Swoosh. Swoosh. Swoosh.

"God bless America."

Even Ximena said that now.

How Ximena Made a Discovery

Ascension **Transcends**
By Melissa Crotts, NYT *MuseTech*, **February 1978**

Ascension, in its world premiere at the Nelly Regina Theater, is the stunning debut by choreographer Petra Echevarri, recent graduate of Juilliard and winner of the Princess Grace Award. A mesmerizing reinterpretation of the dance fads of the '60s—as seen through the Kodachromic lens of the author's childhood in NYC's Barrio—this piece is a riveting and joyful homage to the scratchy, catchy, and soon-to-be-lost tracks of the decade. Chock-full of breathtaking leaps and innovative steps that belie Ms. Echevarri's own training in the classical style, the work takes one particular dance, the shingaling, and creates a visual narrative through which the rest of the work weaves.

"The reason I chose the shingaling as the centerpiece of this dance," explains Echevarri, "is because it's the only one of the dance fads of the time that actually evolved over the years to reflect the musical styles and genres of the musicians and dancers interpreting it. There are so many types of shingaling: Latin, soul,

R&B, funk, psychedelic, and rock and roll. It's the one dance that intersects every genre. The common thread.

"Growing up in the '60s, music was everything to me and my friends. I didn't have money for dance lessons. *American Bandstand* was my dance teacher. Those dance fads of the era were my training."

Echevarri didn't begin formal dance training until the age of twelve, but once she did, there was no looking back. "Once I got into Performing Arts, and then Juilliard," recalls Echevarri, "I knew I could do it. I could defy the odds. None of my neighborhood friends did. The 'hood is a tough place to leave."

When asked why she chose the shingaling as the main theme of her dance, Echevarri grows wistful. "A couple of years ago, about a month before graduating from Juilliard, I attended the funeral of a childhood friend—one of those girls who used to come to my house for *Bandstand*. I hadn't seen her for years, but I'd heard she was in a bad way, had gotten in with the wrong crowd. Anyway, her mother saw me at the funeral, and said her daughter had made a gift for me, a graduation present. I couldn't imagine what it was!"

Echevarri holds up a cassette tape. "This girl had made me a tape of every shingaling song from our childhood. Every single one. 'Chinatown' by Justi Barreto. 'Shingaling Shingaling' by Kako and His Orchestra. 'Sugar, Let's Shing-A-Ling' by Shirley Ellis. 'I've Got Just the Thing' by Lou Courtney. 'Shing-A-Ling Time, Baby!'

by the Liberty Belles. 'El Shingaling' by the Lat-Teens. 'Shing-A-Ling!' by Arthur Conley. 'Shing-A-Ling!' by Audrey Winters. 'Nobody but Me' by the Human Beinz. An incredible song list. I don't even know how she recorded some of them. But when I heard these songs, I knew I was going to create a dance woven around them."

The three dancers in the piece, all recent graduates of Juilliard themselves, bring a distinctive vocabulary to the montage, drawing viewers into an experience that is at once life-affirming and joyful, without any bubble-gum sentimentality. This lack of artifice owes as much to the rousing arrangement of songs, which blend seamlessly together, as it does to Echevarri's poignant narrative. Modern dance at its best.

How We Texted

Thursday 9:18 pm

Ximena Chin
Did you guys see the article I emailed you?
Charlotte Cody
O!M!G!!!! Is THAT really Mrs. Atanabi?
Ximena Chin
:) ;-O Crazy, right?
Charlotte Cody
R U sure? Who is Petra Echevarrrrarara?
Ximena Chin
It's her maiden name. That's her! Trust me. I was googling Gordy Johnson tonight and got bored and started googling Petra Atanabi.
Summer Dawson
I just read the article. Unbelievable! That's the dance WE'RE DOING!!!! Ascension!
Ximena Chin
I know! Amyaazzzinng!
Charlotte Cody
She looks so young and pretty in that photo.

Summer Dawson
Aww, that's so sweet, Ximena!
Ximena Chin
W@?????
Summer Dawson
That you were googling Gordy Johnson.
Ximena Chin
Yeah, well, now im curios too. I want to know what happened to him already.
Charlotte Cody
I shuldnt say this but My mom thinks that maybe he's—
Summer Dawson
Oh no!!! I think my mom thinkx so too.
Ximena Chin
Sorry guys. I sorta think maybe I agree . . . ?????
Charlotte Cody
RIP Gordy Johnson?????? 🙁
Summer Dawson
Nooooooo!!!!!
Charlotte Cody
I dont blieve it.
Summer Dawson
Me neither
Ximena Chin
K. 4get I said NEthing.
Summer Dawson
Said whaaaat?

Charlotte Cody
☺☺☺☺☺
Ximena Chin
    On completely unrelated note do yu guys want to sleep over my house 2moro night?
Charlotte Cody
    Yea! Let me ask my mom. BRB
Summer Dawson
    Sounds fun. Just us?
Ximena Chin
    Ya. COme @ 6?
Summer Dawson
    OK
Charlotte Cody
    My mom says fine so long as your parents home?
Ximena Chin
    Natch.
Charlotte Cody
    My parental unit who is at this moment violating my personal space and reading my text over my shoulder wants me to finish homework so I GTG. CU2moro! Gnight.
Summer Dawson
    Nighty night!
Ximena Chin
    Til 2moro! Cant wait! xo

How We Went to Ximena Chin's House

It was the first time we went to Ximena's house. Up until then, we'd always hung out at my house or Summer's apartment.

Ximena lived in one of those luxury high-rises on the other side of the park. It was a doorman building, very different from the apartments I was used to in North River Heights. Most of those are brownstones or small apartment buildings that are over a hundred years old. Ximena's apartment was ultra-modern. The elevator opened directly into the apartment.

"Hey!" said Ximena, waiting for us in the foyer.

"Hey!" we said.

"Wow, this is beautiful," said Summer, looking around as she dropped her sleeping bag in the hallway. "Should we take our shoes off?"

"Sure, thanks," said Ximena, taking our coats. "I can't believe it's snowing again."

I dropped my sleeping bag next to Summer's and pulled off my UGGs. A woman I'd never seen before came in from the living room.

"This is Luisa," said Ximena. "This is Summer, and that's Charlotte. Luisa's my babysitter."

"Hi," we both said.

Luisa smiled at us. "So nice meet you!" she said in halting English. And then said something in rapid-fire Spanish to Ximena, who answered by nodding and saying *gracias*.

"You speak *Spanish?*" I said, astonished. We were following Ximena over to the kitchen counter.

Ximena laughed. "You didn't know? *Ximena's* such a Spanish name. You want something to drink?"

"I thought it was Chinese!" I answered truthfully. "Water's great."

"Me, too," said Summer.

"My dad's Chinese," she explained, filling two glasses full of water from the refrigerator door. "My mom's Spanish. From Madrid. That's where I was born."

"Really?" I said. "That's so cool."

She set the cups of water in front of us while Luisa brought over a tray full of snacks.

"*¡Muchas gracias!*" Summer said to Luisa.

"*Muchas gracias,*" I repeated, in my terrible American accent.

"You guys are so cute," said Ximena, dipping a carrot stick into a little tub of hummus.

"So, did you grow up in Madrid?" I asked. Besides dancing, and horses, and *Les Mis*, the thing I love most in the world is traveling. Not that I had ever done any traveling—yet. So far we'd only gone to the Bahamas once, Florida, and Montreal—but my parents are always talking about taking us to Europe someday. And I plan on becoming a professional traveler after I'm done being a Broadway star.

"No, I didn't grow up there," answered Ximena. "I mean, I spend summers there—except for last summer, when I did the ballet intensive here in the city. But I didn't grow up there. My parents both work for the UN, so I kind of grew up all over the place." She took a bite of the carrot stick. *Crunch.* "Rome for two years. Then before that we lived in Brussels. We lived in Dubai for a year when I was about four, but I don't remember that at all."

"Wow," said Summer.

"That's so cool," I said.

Ximena tapped on the glass she was drinking from with her carrot stick. "It's okay," she said. "But it can be kind of hard, too. Moving around. I'm always the new kid in school."

"Oh yeah," Summer said sympathetically.

"I survived," Ximena answered sarcastically. "I'm not about to complain." She took another bite of her carrot stick.

"So, do you know other languages?" I asked.

She held up three and a half fingers as an answer, since her mouth was full. And then, after she swallowed, she elaborated: "English, because I always went to

American schools. Spanish. Italian. And a little bit of Mandarin from my grandmother."

"That's so cool!" I answered.

"You keep saying *that's so cool*," Ximena pointed out.

"That's so uncool," I answered, which made her laugh.

Luisa came over to Ximena and asked her something.

"Luisa wants to know what you guys would like for dinner," Ximena translated.

Summer and I looked at each other.

"Oh, anything is fine," Summer said very politely to Luisa. "Please don't go to any trouble."

Luisa raised her eyebrows and smiled as Ximena translated. Then she reached over and pinched Summer's cheek affectionately.

"*¡Qué muchachita hermosa!*" she said. And then she looked at me. "*Y ésta se parece a una muñequita.*"

Ximena laughed. "She says you're very pretty, Summer. And, Charlotte, you look like a little doll."

I looked at Luisa, who was smiling and nodding.

"Aww!" I said. "That's so nice!"

Then she walked away to start dinner for us.

"My parents will be home about 8 p.m.," Ximena said, waving for us to follow her.

She showed us the rest of the apartment, which looked like something out of a magazine. Everything was white. The sofa. The rug. There was even a white

312

ping-pong table in the living room! It made me a little nervous about being klutzy—which I have been known to be—and accidentally spilling something.

We made our way down the hall to Ximena's room, which was probably the biggest bedroom I've ever seen (that wasn't a master bedroom). My bedroom, which I shared with Beatrix, was probably one quarter the size of Ximena's bedroom.

Summer walked into the middle of the room and made a slow spin as she took it all in. "Okay, this room is actually as big as my entire living room and kitchen combined," she said.

"Oh wow," I said, walking over to the floor-to-ceiling windows. "You can see the Empire State Building from here!"

"This is, like, the most beautiful apartment I've ever seen!" said Summer, sitting down in Ximena's desk chair.

"Thanks," Ximena said, nodding and looking around. She seemed a little embarrassed. "Yeah, I mean, we've only been here since this summer so it doesn't quite feel like home to me yet, but—" She plopped down on the bed.

Summer pulled the rolling chair up to the giant bulletin board in back of Ximena's desk, which was completely covered with tiny photos and pictures and quotes and sayings.

"Oh look, a Mr. Browne precept!" she said, pointing to a cutout of Mr. Browne's September precept.

"He's, like, my favorite teacher ever," answered Ximena.

"Mine, too!" I said.

"What a cute picture of you and Savanna," Summer said.

I went over to see what she was pointing at. In between the dozens of little pictures of people from Ximena's life, most of whom we didn't recognize, were camera-booth-type photos of Ximena and Savanna—plus Ximena and Miles, Savanna and Henry, and Ellie and Amos. When I saw Ellie's picture up there, I have to admit, it was kind of strange for me. Like I saw her in a different light. She really did have this whole new life.

"I have to get a picture of *you* two for my wall," Ximena said.

"Oh, come on," said Summer, in her cute, disapproving fairy way as she pointed to a picture on the board. "Ximena!"

It took me a second to realize she hadn't said "Oh, come on" in response to what Ximena had just said.

"Oh, sorry," said Ximena, making a guilty face.

At first I didn't know what the problem was, since it was just our homeroom class picture. Then I realized that over Auggie's face was a tiny yellow Post-it with a drawing of a sad face.

Ximena pulled the Post-it off the picture. "It was just Savanna and those guys fooling around," she said apologetically.

314

"That's almost as bad as Julian's mom Photoshopping the picture," Summer said.

"It was from a long time ago. I forgot it was even there," said Ximena. I was so used to the dimple in her left cheek by now that I never confused when she was serious with when she was joking anymore. I would say her expression right now was definitely remorseful. "Look, the truth is, I think Auggie's amazing."

"But you never talk to him," said Summer.

"Just because I'm not comfortable around him doesn't mean I'm not amazed by him," explained Ximena.

At that moment, we heard a knock on the open door. Luisa was holding a little boy in her arms, who had obviously just woken up from a nap. He was probably about three or four years old and looked exactly like Ximena, except for the fact that it was very obvious he had Down's syndrome.

"¡Hola, Eduardito!" said Ximena, beaming. She held her arms out to her little brother, who Luisa deposited into her arms. "These are my friends. Mis amigas. This is Charlotte, and that's Summer. Say hi. Di hola." She took Eduardito's hand and waved it at us, and we waved back. Eduardito, who had still not completely woken up, looked at us sleepily while Ximena planted kisses all over his face.

How We Played Truth
or Dare

"The day I found out my dad died," Summer said.

The three of us were lying in our sleeping bags on the floor in Ximena's bedroom. The ceiling lights had been turned off, but the red chili Christmas lights that were strung all around the room gave the walls a pink glow in the dark. Our pajamas glowed pink. Our faces glowed pink. It was the perfect lighting for telling secrets and talking about things you would never talk about in the daylight. We were playing a Truth or Dare game, and the Truth card that Summer had drawn read: *What was the worst day of your life?*

My first instinct had been to put the card back and tell her to draw another one. But she didn't seem to mind answering it.

"I was in Mrs. Bob's class when my mom and grandma came to get me," she continued quietly. "I thought they were taking me to the dentist, since I'd lost a tooth that morning. But the second we got inside our car, my grandma started to cry. And then Mom told me that they'd just found out that Dad had been killed in action. *Daddy's in heaven now*, she said. And then we just all cried and cried in the car. Like, these huge, unstoppable tears." She was fidgeting with the zipper of her sleeping bag as she talked, not looking at us. "Anyway, that was the worst day."

Ximena shook her head. "I can't even imagine what that must be like," she said quietly.

"Me, neither," I said.

"It's kind of a blur now, actually," answered Summer, still pulling at the zipper. "Like, I honestly don't remember his funeral. At *all*. The only thing I remember about that day is this picture book about dinosaurs that I was reading. There was this one illustration of a meteor streaking across the sky over the heads of the triceratops. And I remember thinking my dad's death was like that. It's like the extinction of the dinosaurs. A meteor hits your heart and changes everything forever. But you're still here. You go on."

She finally got the zipper to unstick and pulled it up all the way to close her sleeping bag.

"But, anyway . . ." she said.

"I remember your dad," I said.

"Yeah?" she said, smiling.

"He was tall," I answered. "And he had a really deep voice."

Summer nodded happily.

"My mom told me all the moms thought he was *so* handsome," I said.

Summer opened her eyes wide. "Aww," she said.

We were quiet again for a few seconds. Summer started straightening up the card decks.

"Okay, so whose turn is it now?" she asked.

"I think it's mine," I answered, flicking the spinner.

It landed on Truth, so I pulled a card from the Truth deck.

"Oh, this one's so lame," I said, reading aloud. "'*What superpower would you like to have and why?*'"

"That's fun," said Summer.

"I'd want to fly, of course," I answered. "I could go anywhere I want. Zoom around the world. Go to all those places Ximena's lived in."

"Oh, I think I'd want to be invisible," said Ximena.

"I wouldn't," I answered. "Why? So I could hear what everyone says about me behind my back? And know that everyone thinks I'm such a phony?"

"Oh no!" laughed Ximena. "Not this again."

"I'm teasing, you know."

"I know!" she said. "But for the record, no one thinks you're a phony."

"Thank you."

"Just a faker."

"Ha!"

"But you *do* care too much about what people think of you," she said, somewhat seriously.

318

"I know," I answered, just as seriously.

"Okay, it's your turn, Ximena," said Summer.

Ximena flicked the spinner. It pointed to Truth. She picked up a card, read it to herself, then groaned.

"*If you could go out with any boy in your school, who would it be?*'" she read aloud. She covered her face with her hand.

"What?" I said. "Wouldn't it be Miles?"

Ximena started laughing and shook her head, embarrassed.

"Whoa!!!" Summer and I both said, pointing at her. "Who? Who? Who?"

Ximena was laughing. It was hard to see in the dim light, but I'm pretty sure she was blushing.

"If I tell you, you have to tell me *your* secret crushes!" she said.

"Not fair, not fair," I answered.

"Yes, fair!" she said.

"Fine!"

"Amos," she said, sighing.

"No way!" said Summer, her mouth open wide. "Does Ellie know?"

"Of course not," said Ximena. "It's just a crush. I wouldn't do anything about it. Besides, he's not into me at all. He really likes Ellie."

I thought about that. How just a few months ago, Ellie and I would talk about Jack. Having a "boyfriend" seemed like such a far-off thing back then.

Ximena looked at me. "I think I know who Charlotte's crush is," she said in a singsongy way.

I covered my face. "*Everybody* knows, thanks to Ellie," I said.

"What about you, Summer?" said Ximena, poking Summer's hand.

"Yeah, Summer, what about you?" I asked.

Summer was smiling, but she shook her head *no*.

"Come on!" said Ximena, pulling Summer's pinky. "There's got to be someone."

"Fine," she said. She hesitated. "Reid."

"Reid?" said Ximena. "Who's Reid?"

"He's in Mr. Browne's class with us!" I answered. "Very quiet? Draws sharks."

"He's not exactly popular," Summer said. "But he's really nice. And I think he's very cute."

"Ohhh!" said Ximena. "Of course I know who Reid is, duh. He's *totally* cute!"

"He *is*, right?" said Summer.

"You'd make a great couple," said Ximena.

"Maybe someday," answered Summer. "I don't want to be a couple *yet*."

"Is that why you didn't want to go out with Julian?" asked Ximena.

"I didn't want to go out with Julian because Julian's a jerk," Summer answered quickly.

"But you weren't really sick on Halloween, right?" said Ximena. "At Savanna's party?"

Summer shook her head. "I wasn't sick."

Ximena nodded. "I thought so."

"Okay, I have a question," I said to Ximena. "But it's not from the cards."

"Oh!" said Ximena, raising her eyebrows and smiling. "Okay."

I hesitated. "Okay. When you say you're 'going out' with Miles, what does that really mean? Like, what do you do?"

"Charlotte!" said Summer, smacking my arm with the back of her hand.

Ximena started laughing.

"No, I just mean—" I said.

"I know what you mean!" said Ximena, grabbing my fingers. "All it means is that Miles meets me at my locker after school every day. And he walks me to the bus stop sometimes. We hold hands."

"Have you ever kissed him?" I asked.

Ximena made a face, like she was sucking on a lemon. She wasn't wearing her contacts now. Just big tortoise-framed glasses, as well as a retainer she was supposed to wear at night. She didn't look at all like the Ximena Chin we were used to seeing in school. "Just once. At the Halloween party."

"Did you like it?" I asked.

"I don't know!" she answered, smiling. "It was a little like kissing your arm. Have you done that? Kiss your arms."

Summer and I obediently kissed our arms. And then we all started giggling.

"Oh, Jack!" I said, making slurpy noises while I kissed myself up and down my wrist.

"Oh, Reid!" said Summer, doing the same thing.

"Oh, Miles!" said Ximena, kissing her wrist. "I mean, Amos!"

We were cracking up.

"*Mija*," Ximena's mom said, knocking on the door. She poked her head in. "I don't want the baby to wake up. Can you keep it down a little?"

"Sorry, *mami*," said Ximena.

"Good night, girls," she said sweetly.

"Good night!" we whispered. "Sorry!"

"Should we go to sleep now?" I said softly.

"No, let's just be much quieter," said Ximena. "Come on, I think it's your turn now, Summer. Truth or Dare."

"I have another question that's not on the card, too," said Summer, pointing to Ximena. "For you."

"Uh-oh, you guys are ganging up on me!" laughed Ximena.

"We haven't done any Dares yet," I pointed out.

"Okay, this is the Dare," said Summer. "You have to sit at my lunch table on Monday, and you can't tell anyone why."

"Oh, come on!" said Ximena. "I can't just ditch my table without saying why."

"Exactly!" answered Summer. "So choose Truth."

"Fine," said Ximena. "So what's the Truth?"

Summer looked at her. "Okay, Truth. If Savanna, Ellie, and Gretchen hadn't gone skiing this weekend, would you still have asked Charlotte and me to a sleepover tonight?"

Ximena rolled her eyes. "Ohhh!" She puffed her cheeks out like a fish.

"You look like Mrs. Atanabi now," I pointed out.

"Come on, Truth or Dare," Summer pressured her.

"Okay, fine," Ximena said finally, hiding her face behind her hands. "It's true! I probably wouldn't have. Sorry." She peeked out at us from between her fingers. "I was *supposed* to go skiing with them this weekend, but then I didn't think it was worth my possibly twisting an ankle or something right before the dance, so I canceled at the last minute, and then I invited you guys over."

"Aha!" said Summer, poking Ximena in the shoulder. "I knew it. We were your plan B for this weekend."

I started poking her, too.

"I'm sorry!" said Ximena, laughing because we had started tickling her. "But it doesn't mean I don't want to hang out with you guys, too!"

"Have you had any other sleepovers in the last month?" Summer asked.

We were tickling her a lot at this point.

"Yes!" she giggled. "I'm sorry! I didn't invite you to those, either. I'm not good at mixing my friend groups! But I'll get better next year, I promise."

"Do you even *like* Savanna?" I said, giving her one last poke.

Ximena made a face that I realized was a perfect imitation of Savanna's *eww* expression.

Now Summer and I started laughing.

"Shh!" said Ximena, patting the air to remind us to keep quiet.

"Shh!" said Summer.

"Shh!" I said.

We all settled down.

"Okay, I have to admit," Ximena said quietly, "she's been *really* annoying ever since I started spending time with you guys rehearsing. She was so mad when she wasn't picked for the dance!"

"Probably mad that I got picked instead of her," said Summer.

"Actually, no, she was mad at Charlotte," Ximena answered, pointing her thumb at me.

"I knew it!" I said.

Ximena leaned her head on one shoulder. "She said—and this is *her* talking, not *me*—that you always get the good parts in shows at Beecher Prep because the teachers know you were in TV commercials when you were little. And that you try really hard to always be a teacher's pet."

"What. The. Heck?" I said, stupefied. "That is the craziest thing I've ever heard."

Ximena shrugged. "I'm just telling you what she told me and Ellie."

"But Ellie knows that's not true," I said.

"Trust me," answered Ximena. "Ellie never says anything to contradict Savanna."

"I don't get why she's always *hated* me," I said, shaking my head.

"Savanna doesn't hate you," Summer answered, reaching over to take Ximena's glasses off her face. "I think, if anything, she's probably always been a little jealous of you and Ellie being best friends."

"Really?" I said. "Why?"

Summer shrugged. She tried on Ximena's glasses. "Well, you know, you and Ellie tended to be kind of cliquey. I think Savanna probably felt a little left out."

This had never, *ever* occurred to me.

"I had no idea anyone felt that way," I said. "I mean, *seriously*, no idea. Are you sure? Did other people feel this way? Did *you?*"

Summer let the glasses fall to the tip of her nose. "Kind of. But I wasn't in any of your classes, so I didn't care. Savanna was in *all* your classes."

"Wow," I said, biting the inside of my cheek, which is a nervous habit I have.

"I wouldn't worry about it, though," said Summer, putting Ximena's glasses on my face now. "It doesn't matter anymore. You look really good in those."

"I don't want Savanna to hate me, though!" I said.

"Why do you care so much about what Savanna thinks?" asked Ximena.

"Don't *you* care what she thinks?" I asked. "Let's face it, you're different when you're around her, too."

"That's true," said Summer, taking the glasses off my face. She started cleaning them with her pajama top.

"You're much nicer when you're not with her," I said.

Ximena was twisting her hair with her finger. "Everyone's a little mean in middle school, don't you think?"

"No!" said Summer, putting the glasses back on Ximena's face.

"Not even a little?" Ximena answered, raising her right eyebrow.

"No," Summer repeated, adjusting the glasses so they were straight. "No one has to be mean. Ever." She leaned back to inspect the glasses.

"Well, that's what you think because you're a saint," teased Ximena.

"Oh my gosh, if you call me that one more time!" laughed Summer, tossing her pillow at Ximena.

"Summer Dawson, you did not just hit me with my favorite 800-fill-power European white goose-down pillow, did you?" said Ximena, standing up slowly. She picked up her own super-fluffy pillow and raised it in the air.

326

"Is that a challenge?" Summer asked, standing and holding her pillow up like a shield.

I stood up excitedly, holding my pillow in the air.

"Pillow fight!" I said, a little too loudly because I was excited.

"Shh!" Ximena said, holding her finger over her mouth to remind me to keep it down.

"Silent pillow fight!" I whispered loudly.

We spent one long second looking at one another, to see who would strike first, and then we just started going at it. Ximena brought her pillow down on Summer, Summer struck her from below, I made a long sideswipe at Ximena. Then Ximena came up and swung at me from the left, but Summer spun around and struck us both from above. Soon we were smacking each other with more than just pillows: the stuffed animals on Ximena's bed, towels, our rolled-up clothes. And despite our trying to be completely silent, or maybe *because* of it—since there's nothing funnier than trying not to laugh when you want to laugh—it was the single best pillow fight I've ever had in my entire life!

The thing that stopped it, or else it might have gone on too long, was the mysterious trumpet blast of a fart that came from one of us. It stopped the three of us in our tracks as we looked at each other, eyes open wide, and started laughing hysterically when no one took credit for it.

Anyway, two seconds later, Ximena's mom knocked

on the door again, still sounding patient but also obviously a little irritated. It was way past midnight.

We promised her we would go to sleep now and we wouldn't make any more noise.

We were out of breath from laughing so hard. My stomach actually hurt a little.

It took us a while to straighten out our sleeping bags and put the stuffed animals back where they belonged. We folded our clothes and returned the towels to the closet.

We smoothed out our pillows and lay down in our sleeping bags and zipped them up, and then we said good night to one another. I think I probably would have fallen asleep right away, but I got a case of the giggles, and then Summer and Ximena started giggling. We kept trying to shush one another by cupping our hands over each other's mouths.

Finally, once the giggles had passed and it got quiet again, Ximena started singing really softly in the dark. At first, I didn't even realize what she was singing, she was singing so quietly.

No-no, no, no-no, no-no-no-no.

Then Summer took up the song:

No, no-no, no, no, no-no, no-no, no-no.

Finally, I realized what they were singing, and sang:

No-no-no-no, no-no, no, no-no, no!

Then we all started whisper-singing together.

Nobody can do the shingaling

Like I do—
Nobody can do the skate
Like I do—
Nobody can do boogaloo
Like I do—

We were lying on our backs side by side as we sang, and made our arms and hands dance in sync above our heads. And we sang the whole song, from beginning to end, as quietly as if we were praying in church.

How Our Venn Diagrams Look

I know. I spend too much time thinking about this stuff. 😃

Charlotte

·not "popular"

·not considered
that pretty ☹

·cares
what other
kids think
about us

♥ Les Mis

"popular"

·has boyfriend

·not that nice
to everyone

Ximena

·wears
a bra

♥shingaling!

·loves dogs

·on honor
roll

·no boyfriend

·nice to
everyone

·no bra

·Super
pretty!

·does not care what
other kids think about her

·popular for real
(everyone ♥ her)

Summer

How We Never Talked About It

On Monday, there was no mention of the sleepover. It's like the three of us knew, instinctively, without having to say it out loud, that when we got back to school, everything would return to being business as usual. Ximena hanging out with the Savanna group. Summer hanging out with her tiny group. Me playing dots with Maya at my lunch table.

No one would have ever guessed that Summer, Ximena, and I had become good friends. Or that just a few days before, we were having silent pillow fights and sharing secrets under the pink glow of the red chili lights in Ximena's bedroom.

How I Failed to Prevent
a Social Catastrophe

The night before the gala, Mrs. Atanabi told us to take the day off and get some rest. She wanted us to make sure we had a nice healthy dinner and a good night's sleep. Then she gave us our costumes, which she had somehow managed to sew herself. We had already tried them on the week before, but I was so excited to come home and try mine on again, now that it had been fitted. The costume was inspired by this photo of the Liberty Belles:

THE LIBERTY BELLES
SHOUT RECORDING ARTISTS

MANAGEMENT
HORIZON PROMOTIONS, INC.

So that afternoon, I went home from school with Maya and Lina, the way I used to in the old days before I started hanging out with Summer and Ximena all the time.

It was one of the first nice days in March, when you finally get a hint of spring after the long, crazy cold winter. Lina had the brainstorm to stop at Carvel on our way home, which felt like a very "springtime" thing to do, so we walked in the opposite direction up Amesfort toward the park. As we were walking, I told them how I had heard that Savanna was telling people that the only reason I got a part in Mrs. Atanabi's dance show was because I had been in a TV commercial when I was little.

"No one believes that," Lina said sympathetically, kicking her soccer ball in front of her.

"That's awful!" said Maya, and it kind of made me happy that she got so mad about it. "I can't believe Savanna! She used to be so nice in lower school."

"Savanna was never really that nice to me," I answered.

"She *was* nice to me," Maya insisted, pushing her glasses up her nose. "Now she's evil. That whole group is evil."

I nodded. Then I shook my head. "Well, I don't know about *that*."

"And now they've turned Ellie against us," Maya said. "You know, Ellie barely even says hello to me anymore. Now she's evil, too."

I scratched my nose. Maya had a way of being very black-and-white about things. "I guess."

"I'm telling you, it's Ximena Chin's fault," Maya continued. "It's only because of her. If she hadn't started this year, everything would be the same as it was. She's the bad influence."

I knew that that was how Maya saw things. It was one of the reasons I never went into too much detail about the dance show I was in. She never really got that it was just me, Summer, and the dreaded *Ximena Chin*. And that was fine by me! I didn't want to have to defend my friendship with Ximena to Maya! I honestly don't think she would have understood.

"You know what I hate the most?" Maya said. "I hate that she's probably going to end up giving the fifth-grade commencement speech at graduation this year."

"Well, she does have the best grades of anyone," I answered, trying to sound as impartial as possible.

"I thought you had the best grades, Charlotte," Lina said to me.

"No, Ximena does," Maya interjected. She started counting off on her fingers. "Ximena. Charlotte. Simon. Me. And then either Auggie or Remo. Auggie's actually got better grades than Remo in math, but he didn't do that well in Spanish on his last few quizzes, and that's bringing his whole grade point average down."

Maya always knew what everyone else got on their tests. She kept tabs on homework assignments, essay scores. You name it, if it had a grade attached to it, Maya would ask you about it. And she had an amazing way of remembering all those details, too.

"It's crazy how you can remember everybody's grades," said Lina.

"It's a gift," answered Maya, not even meaning to be funny.

"Hey, did you tell Charlotte about the note?" Lina asked her.

"What note?" I said. Like I mentioned, I was a little out of the loop with these guys because I hadn't hung around them that much these last few weeks.

"Oh, nothing," said Maya.

"She wrote Ellie a note," said Lina.

Maya looked up at me and frowned. "Telling her how I feel," she added, peering at me over the rims of her glasses.

I immediately had a sinking feeling about this note.

"What did you write?" I asked.

She shrugged. "Just a note."

Lina nudged her. "Let her read it!"

"She's going to tell me not to give it to her!" Maya answered, biting the end of her long, curly hair.

"At least *show* it to me?" I said, now really curious. "Come on, Maya!"

We had stopped at the intersection of Amesfort and 222nd Street to wait for the light to change.

"Fine," Maya answered. "I'll show you." She started

digging into her coat pocket and pulled out a well-worn Uglydoll envelope with the word "Ellie" written on the outside in silver marker. "Okay. So, basically, I just wanted to let Ellie know how I feel about the way she's changed this year."

She passed the envelope to me, and then nodded for me to open it and read the note inside.

> *Dear Ellie,*
> *I'm writing as one of your oldest friends to tell you that you've really been acting different lately, and I hope you snap out of it. I don't blame you. I blame it on the evil Ximena Chin, who is negatively influencing you! First she twisted Savanna's brain, and now she's turning you into a pretty zombie just like she is. I hope you stop being friends with her and remember all the good times we used to have. Remember Mr. Browne's November precept: "Have no friends not equal to yourself!" Can we please be friends again?*
>
> > *Your former*
> > *really good friend,*
> > *Maya*

I folded the note up and put it back inside the envelope. She was looking at me expectantly.

"Is it stupid?" she asked me.

I handed the envelope back to her.

"No, it's not stupid," I answered. "But as your friend, I'm telling you that I don't think you should give it to her."

"I knew you would try to talk me out of it!" she said, annoyed and disappointed by my reaction.

"No, I'm not trying to talk you out of it!" I said. "You should give it to her if you *really* want to. I know you *mean* well, Maya."

"I'm not trying to *mean* well," she said angrily. "I'm just trying to be truthful!"

"I know," I said.

By now we had crossed the street and arrived at Carvel, only to see how super-busy it was inside. The line at the counter went all the way to the door, and every single table was full—mostly with Beecher Prep kids.

"Everyone had the same idea as we did," said Lina regretfully.

"It's too crowded," I said. "Let's forget it."

Maya gripped my arm. "Look, there's Ellie," she said.

I followed her gaze and saw Ellie sitting with Ximena, Savanna, and Gretchen—plus Miles, Henry, and Amos—at a table in front of the birthday-cake counter, which was all the way on the other side of the shop.

"Let's just go," I said, pulling Maya by the arm. Lina had already started kicking the ball down the block. But Maya stayed where she was.

"I'm going to give her my note," she said slowly, her expression very serious. She held the note I had just returned to her in her left hand, and now she waved it like a tiny flag.

"Oh no, you're not," I said quickly, pushing her hand down. "Not now at least."

"Why not?"

Lina came back toward us. "Wait, you want to give her the note *now*?" she said incredulously. "In front of *everybody*?"

"Yes!" Maya answered stubbornly.

"No," I said, closing my hand over the note. All I could think of is what a big fool she would make of herself if she did that. Ellie would open the note in front of everyone at her table, and they would get so mad at her for the things she said about Ximena and Savanna. Unforgivable things, really! But even worse, they would totally start laughing at her about this. "This is the kind of thing you would never live down, Maya," I cautioned. "You will absolutely regret it. Don't do this."

I could tell she was reconsidering. Her forehead was all scrunched up.

"You could give it to her some other time," I continued, tugging on her coat sleeve the way Summer sometimes tugged on mine when she was talking. "When she's alone. You could even send it to her in the mail, if you want. But do *not* do it now in front of everyone. I'm begging you. Believe me, Maya. That would be a social catastrophe."

338

I saw her rubbing her face. The thing with Maya is, she's never cared about popularity or social catastrophes. She's so good at keeping tabs on people's test scores and grades, but she doesn't have a clue how to read the social stuff. She gets the basics, of course—but in her black-and-white world, kids are either nice or evil. There's no in-between.

In some ways, that's always been one of the nicest things about her. She'll go up to anyone and just assume they're friends. Or she'll do something really nice for someone out of the blue, like giving Auggie Pullman an Uglydoll keychain, which she did just last week.

But in some ways, it's really bad because she has no defenses ready for when people *aren't* nice to her. She has no good comebacks. She just takes it all seriously. What's worse, though, is that she doesn't always get when people don't feel like talking to her. So she'll just keep chattering on or asking questions until the person walks away. It was Ellie who actually put it kind of perfectly a few months ago when we were griping about how annoying Maya could be sometimes:

"Maya makes it easy for people to be mean to her."

And now Maya was about to make it *really* easy for Ellie to be mean to her—in front of a whole bunch of ice-cream-eating kids! Because, despite my words, despite my basically begging her not to do this, Maya Markowitz walked into the store, wove her way in and out of the crowd of people waiting in line, and marched to the back table where Ellie and that whole group of mighty girls was sitting.

Lina and I watched from the sidewalk outside the Carvel. There was a floor-to-ceiling window in the storefront, which was the perfect place to see events unfold. For a second, it felt like I was looking at one of those nature videos on PBS. I could almost hear a man with a British accent narrating the action.

Observe what happens as the young gazelle, which has just strayed from its herd . . .

I watched Maya say something to Ellie, and how everyone at that table stopped talking and looked up at Maya.

. . . comes to the attention of the lions, who haven't eaten in several days.

I saw her hand the envelope to Ellie, who seemed a bit confused.

"I can't watch," said Lina, closing her eyes.

And now the lions, hungry for fresh meat, begin the hunt.

How I Stayed Neutral
—Again

Pretty much everything I predicted would happen happened as I predicted. After giving Ellie the note in front of everyone at the table, Maya turned around and started walking away. Ellie and the Savanna group exchanged laughing looks, and before Maya had even reached the next table, Savanna, Ximena, and Gretchen got out of their chairs to huddle around Ellie as she opened the envelope. I could see their faces clearly as they read the note. Ximena gasped at one point, while Savanna obviously thought it was hilarious.

Maya kept walking across the room toward the exit, looking at me and Lina as she walked. Believe it or not, she was smiling at us. I could tell she was actually very happy. From her point of view, she was getting something off her chest that had really been bothering her, and, since she didn't give a hoot what the popular group thought about her, she didn't see herself as having anything to lose. The truth is, Maya was beyond their being able to hurt her. It was only Ellie she was mad at because

Ellie had been her friend. But Maya really didn't care what those other girls thought about her, or that they might be laughing at her this very moment.

In a way, I have to admit: I admired Maya's bravery.

Having said that, I knew the last thing in the world I wanted right now was to be seen with her, so I started walking away from the window before she got back outside. I especially didn't want Ximena to see me there, waiting for Maya outside. I didn't want anyone to think I had anything to do with this kind of craziness.

Just like I had managed to stay neutral in a war among the boys, I wanted to stay neutral in what might have turned into a war among the girls.

How Ximena Reacted

Summer texted me later that afternoon. *Did u hear about what Maya did?*

Yes, I texted.

I'm with Ximena right now. We're at my place. She's really upset. Can you come over?

"Mom," I said, just as we were getting ready for dinner. "Can I go to Summer's house?"

Mom shook her head. "No."

"Please? It's kind of an emergency."

She looked at me. "What happened?"

"I can't explain now," I answered quickly, getting my coat. "Please, Mom? I'll be back soon, promise."

"Does it have to do with the dance number?" she asked.

"Kind of," I fibbed.

"Okay, text me when you get there. But I want you home by six-thirty."

Summer only lived four blocks away from me, so I was there within ten minutes. Summer's mom buzzed me in.

"Hi, Charlotte, they're in the back," she said when she opened the front door. She took my coat.

I made my way back to Summer's bedroom, where Ximena, just as Summer had texted, was crying on Summer's bed. Summer had a box of tissues in her hands and was consoling her.

They told me the whole story, which I pretended not to know too much about. Maya had handed Ellie a note in front of everybody, and the note was full of really "venomous" things about Ximena. That's how they described it to me.

"She called me *evil!*" said Ximena, wiping tears from her face. "I mean, what did I ever do to Maya? I don't even *know* her!"

"I was telling Ximena that Maya can be kind of socially awkward sometimes," said Summer, patting Ximena's back like a mom would.

"Socially awkward?" said Ximena. "That's not social awkwardness, that's just mean! Do you know what it's like to have everyone reading something *that* awful about you? They passed her note around the table, and everyone took turns reading it—even the boys. And everybody thought it was *hysterical*. Savanna practically peed her pants, she thought it was so funny. I pretended I thought it was funny, too! Ha-ha. Isn't it hilarious that somebody I barely know blames me for turning people into *zombies?*" She put air quotes on the word "zombies." Then she started crying again.

"It's awful, Ximena," I said, biting the inside of my cheek. "I'm so sorry she did that."

"I told her we would talk to Maya," Summer said to me.

I gave her a long look. "To do what?" I asked.

"To tell her how upsetting what she wrote was," Summer answered. "Since we're friends with Maya, I figured we could explain how it hurt Ximena's feelings."

"Maya's not going to care," I said quickly. "She won't get it, Ximena, believe me." How to explain to her? "Honestly, Ximena, I've known Maya for years, and in her mind, this wasn't about *you*. It's about Ellie. She's just mad that Ellie doesn't hang out with her anymore."

"Obviously. But that's not *my* fault!" said Ximena.

"I know that," I said, "but Maya *doesn't* know that, and she just wants to blame someone. She wants everything to go back to the way it was in lower school. And she figures it's your fault that things have changed."

"That's just idiotic!" Ximena said.

"I know!" I said. "It's like Savanna being mad at me for having been in a TV commercial once. It makes no sense."

"How do you know all this?" asked Ximena. "Did she tell you?"

"No!" I said.

"Did you know about the note beforehand?"

"No!" I said.

Summer rescued me. "So what did *Ellie* say when she read Maya's note?" she asked Ximena.

"Oh, she was so mad," answered Ximena. "She and Savanna want to go all out on Maya, post something supermean about her on Facebook or whatever. Then Miles drew this cartoon. They want to post it on Instagram."

She nodded for Summer to hand me a folded-up piece of loose-leaf paper, which I opened. On it was a crude drawing of a girl (who was obviously Maya) kissing a boy (who was obviously Auggie Pullman). Underneath it was written: "Freaks in love."

"Wait, why are they bringing Auggie into it?" Summer asked, incensed.

"I don't know," she said. "Miles was just trying to make me laugh. Everyone was laughing like it's all some kind of giant joke. But I don't think it's funny."

"I'm really sorry, Ximena," I said.

"Why does Maya hate me?" she asked sadly.

"You just have to put it out of your mind," I advised her. "And not take it personally. Remember you told me I have to stop caring so much what people think about me? You have to do the same thing. Forget what Maya thinks about you."

"I didn't ask to be part of Savanna's group when I started at Beecher Prep," said Ximena. "I didn't know who anyone was, or who was friends with who, or who was mad at who. Savanna was the first person who was nice to me, that's all."

346

"Well?" I answered, raising my chin and my shoulders. "That's not exactly true. I was nice to you."

Ximena looked surprised.

"I was nice to you," Summer added.

"What, now you guys are ganging up on me, too?" said Ximena.

"No, no way," said Summer. "Just trying to make you see it from Maya's point of view, that's all. She's not a mean girl, Ximena. Maya doesn't even really have a mean bone in her body. She's mad at Ellie, and Ellie has been kind of mean to *her* lately. That's it."

"Ellie hasn't really even been mean," I said. "She just ditched us for you guys. Which is fine. I don't care. I'm not Maya."

Ximena covered her face with her hands.

"Does everybody hate me?" she said, looking at us between her fingers.

"No!" we both answered.

"*We* certainly don't," said Summer, handing Ximena a box of Kleenex.

Ximena blew her nose. "I guess I haven't been *that* nice to her in general," she said quietly.

"Drawings like this don't help," said Summer, handing the sketch Miles had made back to Ximena.

Ximena took it and ripped it up into lots of little pieces.

"Just so you know," she said, "I would never have posted that. And I told Savanna and Ellie not to dare make any mean comments about Maya on Facebook or anything. I would never be a cyber-bully."

"I know," said Summer. She was about to say something else when there was a knock on the door.

Summer's mom popped her head in.

"Hey, guys," she said cautiously. "Is everything okay?"

"We're fine, Mom," said Summer. "Just some girl drama."

"Charlotte, your mom just called," Summer's mom said. "She says you promised you'd be home in ten minutes."

I looked at my phone. It was already 6:20 p.m.!

"Thanks," I said to Summer's mom. And then to Summer and Ximena: "I better go. Are you going to be okay, Ximena?"

She nodded. "Thanks for coming. Both of you, thanks for being so nice," she said. "I just really wanted to talk to someone about it, but I couldn't actually talk to Savanna and Ellie, you know?"

We nodded.

"I better go home, too," she said, standing up.

The three of us walked down the hallway to the front door, where Summer's mom looked like she was trying to organize the coats.

"Why the long faces, girls?" she asked cheerfully. "I would think you'd be jumping up and down for joy about the big day tomorrow! After all those rehearsals and all the hard work you've put into it. I can't wait to see you guys dancing!"

"Oh yeah," I answered, nodding. I looked at Summer and Ximena. "It *is* pretty exciting."

Summer and Ximena started smiling.

"Yeah," said Ximena.

"I'm actually kind of nervous," said Summer. "I've never danced in front of an audience before!"

"You just have to pretend they're not there," answered Ximena. You would never know that two minutes ago she'd been crying.

"That's awesome advice," said Summer's mom.

"That's what I said, too!" I chimed in.

"Are your parents going to be there, Ximena?" Summer's mom asked. "I look forward to meeting them at the banquet."

"Yeah," she answered politely, smiling with her dimple on full power now.

"All the parents are sitting at the same table," I said. "And Mrs. Atanabi and her husband."

"Oh good," said Summer's mom. "I'm looking forward to hanging out with everyone."

"Bye, Summer. Bye, Mrs. Dawson," said Ximena.

"Bye!" I said.

We walked down the stairs to the lobby together, Ximena and me, and then headed down the block toward Main Street, where she would make a left turn and I would make a right turn.

"You feeling better now?" I said as we stopped on the corner.

"Yeah," she answered, smiling. "Thanks, Charlotte. You've been a really good friend."

"Thanks. You, too."

"Nah." She shook her head, playing with the fringes of my scarf. She gave me a long look. "I know I could've been nicer to you sometimes, Charlotte." Then she hugged me. "Sorry."

I have to say, it felt really awesome hearing that from her.

"Cool beans," I said.

"See you tomorrow."

"Bye."

I walked past the restaurants along Amesfort Avenue, which were finally starting to get busy again now that the weather was becoming warmer. I couldn't stop thinking about what Ximena had just said. Yeah, she could've been nicer to me sometimes. Could I have been nicer to some people, too?

I stopped at the big intersection for the light. That's when I noticed the back of a man in an orange parka boarding a bus. With a black dog next to him. The dog was wearing a red bandanna.

"Gordy Johnson!" I called out, running after him as soon as the light changed.

He turned when he heard his name, but the doors of the bus closed behind him.

How Mrs. Atanabi
Wished Us Well

In the upper-floor studios of Carnegie Hall, which is where Mrs. Atanabi had us get ready for the show, there's a hallway with framed pictures and programs of some of the great dancers who've performed there over the years. As we walked down that hall on the way to change into our costumes, Mrs. Atanabi pointed to one of the photographs. It was a picture of the Duncan Dancers, Isadora Duncan's daughters, posing very theatrically in long white tunics. It was dated November 3, 1923.

"Look, they're just like the three of you!" she chirped happily. "Let me take a picture of you girls in front of it," she said, pulling out her phone and aiming it toward us.

The three of us instantly posed next to the picture, standing the same way the dancers were: me on the left, hands in the air facing right; Summer on the right, hands in the air facing left; and Ximena in the middle, arms spread out in front of her facing the camera.

Mrs. Atanabi snapped several shots, until she was content with one, and then the four of us—because Mrs. Atanabi was every bit as excited as we were tonight—giddily trotted to the back room to get into our costumes.

We weren't the only ones performing tonight. The Upper School Jazz Ensemble and the Upper School Chamber Choir were already there. We could hear the sounds of trumpets and saxophones and other instruments echoing through the hallways, and the choir doing warm-ups in a large room next to our dressing room.

Mrs. Atanabi helped us with our hair and makeup. It was so awesome how she transformed each of our hairstyles into big, round bouffants with curled, flicked-up ends, topped by a cloud of hair spray. Although we all had such different types of hair, Mrs. Atanabi somehow made us match perfectly!

We were going on last. It felt like such a long wait!

We held hands the whole time and tried to talk ourselves out of being completely panicked.

When it was finally time for us to go on, Mrs. Atanabi brought us downstairs to the back stage of the Stern Auditorium. We peeked through the curtains at the audience as the Upper School Chamber Choir finished its last song. There were so many people! You couldn't make out anyone's face, because it was so dark, but it was the biggest auditorium I had ever seen—with balconies and gilded arches and velvet walls!

Mrs. Atanabi had us take our positions behind the curtains: Ximena in the middle, me on the left, Summer on the right. Then she faced us.

"Girls, you've worked so hard," she whispered, her voice shaking with emotion. "I can't thank you enough for all the time you've put into making my piece come to life. Your energy, your enthusiasm—"

Her voice cracked. She wiped a tear away excitedly. If we hadn't read that article about her, we might not have understood why this was all so important to her. But we knew. We never told her we had found that article about her. That we knew about her childhood friend. We figured if she had wanted us to know, she would have told us. But knowing that little piece of her story somehow made the dance and everything leading up to it that much more special. Funny how all our stories kind of intertwine. Every person's story weaves in and out of someone else's story.

"I'm just so proud of you, girls!" she whispered, kissing us each on our forehead.

The audience was applauding the choir, which had just finished. As the singers streamed backstage through the wings, Mrs. Atanabi made her way around the front of the stage to wait for Mr. Tushman to introduce her, and we took our positions. We could hear Mrs. Atanabi introducing the number we were about to dance, and us.

"This is it, guys!" Ximena whispered to us as the curtain started to rise.

We waited for the music to start. Five. Six.

Five-six-seven-eight!

It's the shingaling, baby!

How We Danced

I wish I could describe every second of those eleven minutes on stage, every move, every jump. Every shimmy and twist. But of course I can't. All I can say is that the whole thing went ABSOLUTELY PERFECTLY. Not one missed cue or fumble. Basically, for eleven solid minutes, it felt like we were dancing ten feet above the rest of the world. It was the most thrilling, exciting, tiring, emotional, fun, awesome experience of my life, and as we ramped up to the big finish, stoplighting to *Well let me tell you nobody, nobody* before busting into Mrs. Atanabi's signature shingaling, which was a variation she invented, I could feel the energy of the entire audience as they clapped along to the song.

Nobody, nobody
Nobody, nobody
Nobody, nobody . . .

And then we were done. It was over. Out of breath, beaming from ear to ear. Thunderous applause.

The three of us bowed in sync, and then we took our

individual bows. The audience hooted and hollered.

Our parents were ready with flowers for us. And my mom handed me an extra bouquet, which we gave to Mrs. Atanabi when she came onstage with us to take a bow. I wished, for a second, that all the fifth graders who'd ever laughed behind Mrs. Atanabi's back could see her now, right this minute, as I was seeing her. In her beautiful gown, her bun perfectly made—she looked like a queen.

How We Spent the
Rest of the Night

A little later, after changing out of our costumes, we joined our parents for dinner in the banquet hall downstairs. As we wound our way through the round tables full of teachers, other parents, and a lot of grown-ups we didn't know, people congratulated us and complimented our dancing. I thought to myself, *This is what it feels like to be famous.* And I loved it.

Our parents were all sitting together at a table by the time we got there, along with Mrs. Atanabi and her husband. There was a little round of applause from them as we sat down, and then, basically, we spent the rest of the evening talking to each other non-stop, breaking down every second of the dance, where we'd been nervous about not making a particular kick, where we'd gotten a little dizzy coming out of a spin.

Before dinner was served, Dr. Jansen, the headmaster of the school, gave a short speech thanking everyone for coming to the benefit, and then asked Mrs. Atanabi, as well as the choir teacher and the jazz teacher, to stand up for another round of applause. Ximena, Summer, and I cheered as loud as we could. Then he talked about other things, like financial goals and fund-raising, and stuff that was so boring I couldn't wait for him to stop. Later, after we'd finished our salads, Mr. Tushman made a speech about the importance of supporting the arts at Beecher Prep so the school could continue to nurture the kind of "talent" they'd watched tonight. And this time he asked all the students who had performed tonight to stand up again for another round of applause. Around the room, the kids from the jazz ensemble and choir stood up with varying degrees of willingness and shyness. The three of us, though, weren't the least bit shy about standing up for another round of applause. What can I say?

Bring it on!

By the time coffee was being served, all the speeches were over, and people had started walking around and mingling. I saw one couple come over to our table, but I couldn't remember who they were until Summer jumped out of her seat to hug them. Then I knew. Auggie's parents. They kissed Summer's mom and then circled around to me and Ximena.

"You guys were so amazing," Auggie's mom said sweetly.

"Thank you so much," I answered, smiling.

"You must be so proud of them," Auggie's dad said to Mrs. Atanabi, who was next to Summer.

"I am!" Mrs. Atanabi said, beaming. "They worked so hard."

"Congrats again, girls," said Auggie's mom, giving my shoulder a little squeeze before making her way back to Summer's mom.

"Say hi to Auggie for me," I called out.

"We will."

"Wait, those were *Auggie's* parents?" said Ximena. "They look like movie stars."

"I know," I whispered back.

"What are you guys whispering about?" said Summer, coming between us.

"She didn't know they were Auggie's parents," I explained.

"Oh," said Summer. "His parents are *so* nice."

"It's really ironic," said Ximena. "They're so good-looking."

"Have you ever seen Auggie's big sister?" I said. "She's *super*-pretty. Like she could be a model. It's crazy."

"Wow," said Ximena. "I guess I thought, I don't know, that they'd all kind of look like Auggie."

"No," Summer said gently. "It's like with your brother. It's just how he was born."

Ximena nodded slowly.

I could tell, smart as she was, she'd never thought of it like that before.

How I Fell Asleep—Finally!

We didn't get home until pretty late that night. I was super-tired as I washed all the makeup off my face and got ready for bed. But then, I don't know why, I couldn't fall asleep. All the night's events kept crashing over me like soft waves. I felt the way you feel like when you're on a boat, rocking back and forth. My bed was floating in an ocean.

After about half an hour of tossing and turning, I picked my phone up from where it was charging on my nightstand.

Anyone up, I texted Summer and Ximena.

It was after midnight. I was sure they were asleep.

Just wanted u guys to know that I thnk ur the two most amazing people in the world and Im glad we got to b such good friends for a while. Ill always remembr this night. Its the shingaling, baby!

I put the phone back on the nightstand and karate-chopped my pillow to make it comfy. I closed my eyes, hoping sleep would come. Just as I felt myself finally drifting off, my phone buzzed.

It wasn't Ximena or Summer. Weirdly enough, it was Ellie.

Hey, Charly, Im sure ur sleeping but my parents just came home from the gala and said you guys were absolutely unbelievably incredible. Proud of you. Wish I coulda been there to see you dance. You deserve it. Lets try to hang out after school next week. Miss u.

It sounds stupid, but her text made me so happy, tears instantly welled up in my eyes.

Thnx so much, Ellie! I texted back. *Wish u could've been there too. Would love to hang next week. Miss U2. G'night.*

How Maya Was Surprised
and Surprised Us All

I woke up feeling so exhausted the next morning, Mom let me go to school late. I saw that both Ximena and Summer had texted me first thing in the morning.

Ximena Chin

I feel the same way, Charlotte. What a night!

Summer Dawson

I <3 U 2!

I didn't text them back because I knew they were in class. I missed the first three periods, and didn't see either of them until lunch. Summer, as usual, was sitting with Auggie and Jack. And Ximena, as usual, was at the Savanna table. For a fraction of a second, I was going to go over and say hello to Ximena, but the image of Maya standing in front of that same group of kids yesterday was still fresh in my head—and I didn't want to give Ximena even the sliver of a chance of disappointing me with anything but a really friendly hello.

So I waved to her and Summer as I walked over to my usual table, and sat down next to Maya. The girls at my table asked me how last night had gone—some of them had heard about it from their parents—but I spared them too many details because I knew they'd lose interest after thirty seconds. Which is exactly what happened.

Not that I could blame them, really.

The main thing on their minds—in fact, the *only* thing they wanted to talk about—was the note that Maya had given to Ellie yesterday in Carvel. That note, it turned out—which by now had been quoted or read aloud by half the grade—was Maya's first ticket to a kind of popularity she'd never experienced before. People were talking about her. Kids were pointing her out to curious sixth graders who had also heard about the note.

"I'm the queen of the underdogs today!" Maya herself said.

I could tell she felt triumphant. She liked the attention she was getting.

I had intended to tell her how hurt Ximena had been by her note, how it had made her cry. But, in a strange way, I also didn't want to rain on Maya's parade.

"Hey, you!" said Summer, nudging me so I could scoot over.

"Hey!" I said, surprised to see her there. I looked over at her table, but Auggie and Jack had already left.

"Hi, Summer," said Maya eagerly. "Did you hear about my note?"

Summer smiled. "Yes, I did!" she answered.

"Did you like it?" Maya asked.

I could tell Summer didn't want to hurt Maya's feelings, either, so she hesitated in answering.

"Where are Auggie and Jack?" I interjected.

"Working on some top-secret notes to leave in Julian's locker," she answered.

"A note like mine?" said Maya.

Summer shook her head. "I don't think so. Love notes from someone named Beulah."

"Who's Beulah?" I said.

Summer laughed. "It's too hard to explain."

I noticed that Ximena was looking at us from all the way across the cafeteria. I smiled at her. She smiled back. Then, to my surprise, she got up and walked over to our table.

Everybody at the table stopped talking as soon as they saw her standing there. Without even being asked, Megan and Rand scooted apart and Ximena sat down between them, directly opposite Maya, me, and Summer.

Maya was completely shocked. Her eyes were open wide, and she almost looked a little scared. I had no idea what would happen next.

Ximena clasped her hands in front of her, leaned forward, and looked straight at Maya.

"Maya," she said, "I just want to apologize if I've ever said or done anything to insult you. I never meant to, if that's the case. I actually think you're a really nice person and super-smart and interesting, and I really hope that we can be friends from now on."

Maya blinked, but she didn't say anything. Her mouth was literally hanging open.

"Anyway," said Ximena, now seeming a little shy, "I just wanted to tell you that."

"That's so nice of you, Ximena," said Summer, smiling.

Ximena looked at us with that winking expression of hers.

"It's the shingaling, baby!" she said, which made us both smile.

Then, as quickly as she'd sat down with us, she got up and walked back to her table. I looked out of the corner of my eye and saw Ellie and Savanna watching her. As soon as she sat down at her table, they came in close to hear what she had to say.

"That was so nice of her, wasn't it?" Summer said to Maya.

"I'm shocked," answered Maya, taking her glasses off to wipe them. "Totally shocked."

Summer gave me a little knowing look.

"Maya, whatever happened to that giant game of dots you were working on?" I said.

"Oh, I have it here!" she answered eagerly. "I told you I was waiting until you're around to play it. Why? You want to play it now?"

"Yeah!" I answered. "I do."

"Me, too," said Summer.

Maya gasped, grabbed her backpack, and pulled out a tube of paper that was folded in thirds and slightly bent at the top. We watched her unfold it and carefully unwind the sheet of paper, which took up the entire width and length of the lunch table. When it was completely stretched out, we all looked at it. Stunned.

There wasn't one square inch of the gigantic paper that wasn't covered in dots. Perfectly drawn, evenly spaced lines of dots. But not *just* dots. Beautiful grid patterns connected by swirls. Waves of lines that ended in spirals, or flowers, or sunbursts. It almost looked like tattoo art, the way blue ink can cover someone's arm so completely, you don't know where one tattoo starts and another ends.

It was the most unbelievably beautiful game of dots I've ever seen.

"Maya, this is incredible," I said slowly.

"Yeah!" she said happily. "I know!"

How Some Things Changed, and Some Things Didn't

That was the only time, and the last time, that Summer, Ximena, and I sat at a lunch table together. Or at any table, for that matter. We went back to our different groups. Ximena with Savanna. Summer and Auggie. Me and Maya.

And that, honestly, was fine with me.

Sure. Maybe there was part of me, the part that loves happy endings, that wished things had changed. Ximena and Ellie would suddenly switch tables and start sitting at my table, along with Summer. Maybe we'd start a new lunch table together, with Jack and Auggie, and Reid—and Amos!—at the table next to ours.

But the truth is, I knew things wouldn't change much. I knew it would be the way it had been after the sleepover. Like we had taken a secret trip together. A voyage that no one else knew about. And when we returned from our journey, we each went back to our own homes. Some friendships are like that. Maybe even the best friendships are like that. The connections are always there. They're just invisible to the eye.

Which is why Savanna would have no idea that Summer and I got to know her friend Ximena as well as we did. And why Maya wouldn't understand the effect her note had on me and Summer. Or why Auggie didn't know the first thing about *any* of this stuff that was going on. "He has his own stuff to worry about," Summer had told me once, when she explained why she had never even told Auggie she'd gotten picked to be in Mrs. Atanabi's dance. "He doesn't need to know about all this girl drama."

That's not to say there haven't been some changes that *have* happened.

As we entered our last few months of fifth grade, I definitely noticed that Ximena made more of an effort to branch out to other girls in our grade. And when she sees me in the hallway now, she always gives me a warm hello—regardless of whether she's with Savanna. Also, even though Ellie and Maya never patched things up, Ellie and I have hung out after school a couple of times. Not that it's like it used to be, of course. But it's something, and I'll take it.

Small steps, as Mrs. Atanabi would say. It starts with small steps.

And the truth is, even if Ximena, Savanna, and Ellie *did* suddenly invite me to sit at their table, I wouldn't go now. It just wouldn't seem right. First of all, I wouldn't want to get an angry note from Maya or have her bare her teeth at me across a room But mostly, it's because I realized something the day she unrolled her magnificent dot game across the lunch table: Maya's been my friend through thick and thin. My *friend* friend. All these years. In her clumsy, loyal, slightly annoying way. She's never judged me. She's always accepted me. And that group of girls at my lunch table, the ones I have nothing in common with? Well, guess what? We have a lunch table in common! And a ridiculously beautiful game of dots that we play over lunch, with the different-colored markers Maya's assigned to each and every one of us. Which we have to use or she gets really mad at us.

But that's just Maya. And that will never change.

How I Talked to
Mr. Tushman

The last day of school, Mr. Tushman's assistant, Mrs. Garcia, found me in seventh period and asked if I would come talk to Mr. Tushman right after school. Maya overheard her and started giggling.

"Ooh, ooh, Charlotte's in trouble," she sang.

We both knew that wasn't the case, though, and that it probably had to do with the awards they were giving out tomorrow. Everyone assumed that I would win the Beecher medal because I had organized the coat drive, and the medal usually went to the student who did the most community service.

I knocked on Mr. Tushman's door right after the last-period bell.

"Come in, Charlotte," he said enthusiastically, signaling for me to sit at the chair in front of his desk.

I always loved Mr. Tushman's office. He had all these fun puzzles on the edge of his desk, and artwork from kids over the years framed and hanging on the walls. I noticed immediately that he had Auggie's self-portrait as a duck displayed behind his desk.

And then suddenly I knew what this meeting was about.

"So, are you excited about tomorrow's graduation ceremony?" he asked, crossing his hands in front of him on the desk.

I nodded. "I can't believe fifth grade is almost over!" I answered, unable to restrain my happiness.

"It's hard to believe, isn't it?" he said. "Do you have plans for summer?"

"I'm going to dance camp."

"Oh, how fun!" he answered. "You three were so amazing at the benefit in March. Like professional dancers. Mrs. Atanabi was so impressed with how hard you worked, and how well you worked together."

"Yeah, it was so much fun," I said excitedly.

"That's great," he said, smiling. "I'm glad you've had a good year, Charlotte. You deserve it. You've been a joyful presence in these hallways, and I appreciate how you've always been nice to everyone. Don't think things like that go unnoticed."

"Thank you, Mr. Tushman."

"The reason I wanted to have a little word with you before tomorrow," he said, "and I'm hoping you can keep it between us, is that I know *you* know that among the many honors I give out tomorrow, one of them is the Beecher medal."

"You're giving it to Auggie," I blurted out. "Right?"

He looked surprised. "Why do you say that?" he asked.

"Everybody's assuming I'm getting it."

He looked at me carefully. Then he smiled.

"You are a very smart girl, Charlotte," he said gently.

"I'm fine with that, Mr. Tushman," I said.

"But I wanted to explain," he insisted. "Because, the truth of the matter is, had this been like any other ordinary year, *you* would probably be getting that medal, Charlotte. You deserve it—not only because of all the hard work you did on the coat drive, but because, like I just said before, you've been a really nice person to everyone. I still remember how, right from the start when I asked you to be Auggie's welcome buddy, you embraced that wholeheartedly and without equivocation."

Have I mentioned how much I love the fact that he uses big words and assumes we understand them?

"But, as you know," he said, "this year has been anything *except* ordinary. And when I was thinking about this award, thinking about what it represents, I realized that it can be about more than community service—not to devalue that at *all*."

"No, I know totally what you mean," I agreed.

"When I look at Auggie and all the challenges he has to face on a daily basis," he said, patting his heart, "I'm in awe of how he manages to simply show up every day. With a smile on his face. And I want him to have validation that this year was a triumph for him. That he's made an impact. I mean, the way the kids rallied around him after the horrible incident at the nature reserve? It was because of *him*. He inspired that kindness in them."

"I completely get what you mean," I said.

"And I want this award to *be* about kindness," he continued. "The kindness we put out in the world."

"Totally," I agreed.

He seemed genuinely delighted by my attitude. And a little relieved, I think.

"I'm so glad you understand, Charlotte!" he said. "I wanted to tell you beforehand, so you wouldn't be disappointed during the ceremony tomorrow, since, as you say, everyone's assuming you're getting it. But you won't tell anyone, right? I wouldn't want to ruin the surprise for Auggie or his family."

"Can I tell *my* parents?"

"Of course! Though I'm planning on giving them a call myself tonight to tell them just how proud I am of you at this very moment."

He got up and reached across the table to shake my hand, so I shook his hand.

"Thank you, Charlotte," he said.

"Thank you, Mr. Tushman."

"See you tomorrow."

"Bye." I started walking toward the door, but then this one thought popped into my head, like a fully formed idea. I had no clue where it came from.

"But the award *can* go to two people, right?" I asked.

He looked up. For a second, I thought I saw the tiniest bit of disappointment in his eyes. "It has, on a *few* occasions, gone to a couple of students who've done a community service project *together*," he answered, scratching his forehead. "But in the case of Auggie and you, I think, the reasons he would be getting it are so different from the reasons you would be—"

"No, I'm not talking about Auggie and me," I interrupted. "I think *Summer* should get that award."

"Summer?"

"She's been such an *amazing* friend to Auggie all year long," I explained. "And not because you *asked* her to be his welcome buddy, like with me and Jack. She just did it! It's like what you just said about kindness."

Mr. Tushman nodded, like he was really listening to what I was saying.

"I mean, I've been *nice* to Auggie," I said, "but Summer was *kind*. That's like nice to the tenth power or something. Do you know what I mean?"

"I know exactly what you mean," he answered, smiling.

I nodded. "Good."

"I really appreciate your telling me all this, Charlotte," he said. "You've given me much to think about."

"Awesome."

He was looking at me and nodding slowly, like he was debating something in his head. "Let me ask you something, though," he said, pausing as if he were trying to find the right words. "Do you think *Summer* would want a medal just for being friends with Auggie?"

The moment he said it, I knew exactly what he meant.

"Oh!" I said. "Wait a minute. You're right. She wouldn't."

For some reason, the image of Maya baring her teeth at the Savanna table across the room popped into my head.

Friends definitely aren't about the medals.

"But let me think about it tonight," he said, getting up.

"No, you're right," I answered. "It's good the way you had it."

"You sure?"

I nodded. "Thanks again, Mr. Tushman. See you tomorrow."

"See you tomorrow, Charlotte."

We shook hands again, but this time he took my hand in both of his own.

"Just so you know," he said. "Being nice is the first step toward being kind. It's a pretty awesome start. I'm supremely proud of you, Charlotte."

Maybe he knew it and maybe he didn't, but for someone like me, words like that are worth all the medals in the world.

How Ximena Rocked
Her Speech

Good morning, Dr. Jansen, Mr. Tushman, Dean Rubin, fellow students, faculty, teachers, and parents.

I'm honored to have been asked to give the commencement speech on behalf of the fifth grade this year. As I look around at all the happy faces, I feel so lucky to be here. As some of you know, this was my first year at Beecher Prep. I won't lie: I was a little nervous about coming here at first! I knew that some kids have been here since kindergarten, and I was afraid I wouldn't make friends. But it turns out that a lot of my classmates were also new to the school, like me. And even the kids who have been here a while, well, middle school is a brand-new ball game for everyone. It's definitely been a learning experience for all of us. With some bumps along the way. Some hits and misses. But it's been a wonderful ride.

Earlier this year, I was asked to perform in a dance choreographed by Mrs. Atanabi for the Beecher Prep Benefit. It was amazing for me. My fellow dancers and

I worked really hard to learn how to dance together as one. That takes a lot of time. And trust. Now, you may not know this about me, but as someone who's gone to a lot of different new schools over the years, trust hasn't always been easy for me to give people. But I really learned to trust these girls. I realized I could be myself with them. And I'll always be grateful for that.

I think what I'm most looking forward to next year, my fellow fifth graders, is building that trust with all of you. My hope is, as we start sixth grade, as we get older and wiser, that we all learn to trust each other enough so that we can truly be ourselves, and accept each other for who we *really* are.

Thank you.

How I Finally Introduced Myself

I had texted Summer and Ximena the day I saw Gordy
Johnson getting on an uptown bus, and we were all
thrilled to know he was alive and well. There was so
much else going on at the time, though, that we really
hadn't had the chance to talk about it too much. We got
excited, kept our eyes peeled to see if we'd spot him again
somewhere else in the neighborhood, but we never did.
He was gone. Again.

The next time I saw him wasn't until the beginning
of July. Suddenly he was there again, sitting in front of
the A&P supermarket awning, playing the same songs
on his accordion that he had always played, his black
Labrador lying down in front of him.

I watched him for a few minutes. I studied his open
eyes, remembering how they used to scare me. I watched
his fingers tapping the buttons on the accordion. It's
such a mysterious instrument to me. He was playing
"Those Were the Days." My favorite song.

I went up to him when he was finished.

"Hi," I said.

He smiled in my direction. "Hello."

"I'm glad you're back!" I said.

"Thank you, missy!" he said.

"Where did you go?"

"Oh well," he said, "I went to stay with my daughter down south for a spell. These New York City winters are getting tough on these old bones of mine."

"It was a cold winter, that's for sure," I said.

"That's for sure!"

"Your dog's name is Joni, right?"

"That's right."

"And your name is Gordy Johnson?"

He tilted his head. "Am I so famous that you know my name?" he asked, cackling.

"My friend Summer Dawson knows you," I answered.

He looked up, trying to think of who I might have been talking about.

"Her father was in the marines?" I explained. "He died a few years ago. Sergeant Dawson?"

"Sergeant Dawson!" he said. "Of course I remember him. Glorious man. Sad news. I remember that family well. You tell that little girl I say hello, okay? She was a sweet child."

"I will," I answered. "We actually tried to find you. Summer and I were worried about you when you weren't here anymore."

"Oh, honey," he said. "You don't needs to worry about me. I make my way around all right. I'm not homeless or anything. I got a place of my own uptown. I just like to have something to do with myself, to get out with Joni. I take the express bus in the morning right outside my building. Get out at the last stop. It's a nice ride. I come here out of habit, you know? Nice people here, like Sergeant Dawson was. I like to play for them. You like my music?"

"Yes!" I said.

"Well, that's why I'm out here playing, girl!" he said excitedly. "To brighten up people's days."

I nodded happily.

"Okay," I said. "Thank you, Mr. Johnson."

"You can call me Gordy."

"I'm Charlotte, by the way."

"Nice to meet you, Charlotte," he said.

He extended his hand. I shook it.

"I better go now," I said. "It was nice talking to you."

"Bye-bye, Charlotte."

"Bye-bye, Mr. Johnson."

I reached into my pocket, pulled out a dollar bill, and dropped it into his accordion case.

Swoosh.

"God bless America!" said Gordy Johnson.

About R. J. Palacio

R. J. Palacio lives in New York City with her husband, two sons, and two dogs. For more than twenty years, she was an editorial director, an art director, and a graphic designer, working on books for other people while waiting for the perfect time in her life to start writing her own novel. But one day several years ago, a chance encounter with an extraordinary child in front of an ice-cream store made R. J. realize that the perfect time to write that book had finally come. *Wonder* is her first novel. She did not design the cover, but she sure does love it.